KU-715-583

MARVIN 9T5

Dan Robinson is Cardiff born and bred. Working class. Stuck in the nineties, held fast by jungle and hardcore. MARVIN 9T5 is his first novel.

Twitter: @MARVIN_9T5

MARVIN9T5@gmail.com

Cardiff Libraries
www.cardiff.gov.uk/libraries

Llyfrgelloedd Caerdydd
www.caerdydd.gov.uk/llyfrgelloedd

CL

ACC. No: 02927087

MARVIN 9T5

Dan Robinson

Published in 2017 by FeedARead.com Publishing

Copyright © Dan Robinson

The author asserts their moral right under the Copyright, Designs and Patents Act, 1988, to be identified as the author of this work.

All Rights reserved. No part of this publication may be reproduced, copied, stored in a retrieval system, or transmitted, in any form or by any means, without the prior written consent of the copyright holder, nor be otherwise circulated in any form of binding or cover other than that in which it is published and without a similar condition being imposed on the subsequent purchaser.

A CIP catalogue record for this title is available from the British Library.

This novel is dedicated to the memory of

Louise Anne Pugh

1981–2003

These words are the only way I know how . . .

With love and gratitude to Alison.

Contents

Prologue
Spring 2018

Jackpot! The man's fingers tingle on the chrome door latch as he watches his fully laden family estate car disappear up the road in a cloud of grit and diesel fumes. What a fucking result! His wife and kids have barely begun their journey down to the sister-in-law's in Weymouth but in his mind they're already a million miles away. He paces the hallway, anxious hands fumbling for his mobile phone. Scrolls the list of contacts, unable to decide which of his less savoury associates to call first. Marcus is a good bet – bit of a wanker but always has decent coke connections, not to mention a gob and libido that's sure to get them both laid, provided nobody is too picky. And this weekend certainly isn't about being picky. This weekend is hit and run, smash and grab, a supermarket sweep of debauchery and the clock is ticking so let's get this show on the road!

Marcus is taking his sweet time to answer the phone, presumably septum deep in a mountain of Bolivia's finest. As the ringing drones on the man considers all the possibilities that lay before him. Freedom. Three whole days to shag, smoke and sniff anything not nailed down in the south Wales region. Time to find himself again, find the person he used to be, young, carefree, when everything made sense and nothing mattered, fun was everything and everything was fun . . .

At least that's how he remembers it . . . doesn't he?

. . . but what about . . . ?

. . . no, not that . . . something else, think about something else . . .

. . . concentrate on the present – fuck the past, dwelling is for fools . . . let's get wasted, live for the moment . . . right? Right!

He breathes an audible sigh of relief when a teeth-chattering Marcus finally answers, indifferently definite about the absolute certainty of them both getting utterly obliterated this weekend. No sooner have scant arrangements been made than the man is out of the door, jacket only half pulled on because for him utter obliteration simply can't come soon enough.

Part I : Breaking Out

Summer 1995

1

Guilty? I dun't feel guilty fuh fuck all, butt. Anyone who says I do is a stinking liar. Leh's geh tha straight yur an now. Mr Davies has gone an dropped the G-word right off the bat buh I was ready cos ih's par fuh the course when teachers an parents mix – they pin you down an slice you open wi surgical-grade guiltys or disappointeds or ashameds an expect you to spill yuh guts all over their desks. I fell for ih once, when I was much younger an I been suffering ever since so terribly sorry old Davey boy buh you wun be gehrin a peep out uh me today or ever again. Try asking someone who gives a fuck.

'Well don't you, Lee? Imagine how your father must feel, having to come down and sort out your mess.'

Ih's you who sent the letter home Einstein, noh me! I was more than happy on the knock every day. Logic dun work on teachers though, especially noh on shrivelled up, coconut-headed ones like dick-splash Davies.

'Shall we start with the truanting?' he goes, tilting his head an squeezing his lips to look like a big, grey-bearded fanny.

I tuck my arms an chin into my t-shirt cos one glimpse uh bare flesh an he'll be on me, sucking blood an brains an secrets till there's nothing left to tell. Ignore him is best, like a Pengarw park wasp, dun move a muscle while yuh lolly drips down yur arm an hopefully he'll take his questions elsewhere. I focus on the back uh one uh the blue plastic school chairs where big bubble letters scream out: MARVIN 9T4. Marvin's my nickname, if yuh wondering – wha people who knows me calls me. People like Mr Davies an Dad call me Lee.

'Why don't you feel able to come to school?'

Last year's version, ih is. I was in school much more back then, even if ih was mostly the detention room. Such a regular they ended up giving me my own time-out seat buh I MARVIN'd tha fucker an all. Much better at the bubble writing now mind, an the 9T5 joins up cooler than the 9T4. If Mr Davies makes me come back they'll be gehrin plenty uh this year's updates, leh me tell ew.

'Are there any specific problems you'd like to share?'

'Dodgy alarm clock,' I says at last, cos the daft doggy's begging for a bone.

'I'm sorry?'

'Alarm clock – batteries gone, deado.'

'But you haven't been to school once in seven weeks.'

'Heavy sleeper,' I shrug as the coconut-headed cunt wrestles wi the urge to belt me in front uh Dad. The old man saves him the bother, reaching over an smacking me one round the lughole fuh being a "chopsy little fucker". Mr Davies sortuh squirms a smile out buh there's no hiding the scurrying fear behind his eyes cos Dad's rocking an rolling all over the show, a loose cannon reeking uh booze an bad intentions, one clumsy comment away from T-minus zero. First time Mr Davies has met my father this is, cos he only goh the deputy head job recently. Certainly ain' the first time my dad's been down the school mind, noh by a long chalk an from the way Mr Davies is buttering the old fart up you can bet yuh bollocks he's yurd all abou his past visits.

'Now Lee, I realise you might find it difficult to talk about certain things but you really must understand that we're not the enemy here – we're on your side. We just need you to trust us – to open up.'

Thas my cue to disappear. I slide down my chair like I've slipped under in the bath an I dun stop till I'm halfway round the u-bend. Down yur Mr Davies' worn out words ain' nothing buh the rub of anchor chains on the bow – a drastic improvement I'm shewer every fucker will agree buh as usual people just cahn leave me be. Fast as I swim, Dad's trawler-net hands soon scoop me up off the bottom uh the ocean an dump me flapping an gasping on the sizzling grill.

'Lee, this is incredibly important,' Davies says, scratching his head. 'We're talking about your whole future here. Don't you–'

'–want me baby!' Scrambled his little coconut good an proper wi tha one – ih's just too easy wi some people.

'Excuse me?' he goes. 'What–'

'–is love? Baby dun hurt me! Loves ah one, I do!' I could play this game all day buh there's no need cos Davies has already cracked an now yur comes the true colours pouring out.

'Enough! Sit up straight for goodness sake. I've never in all my years teaching met such a rude, badly behaved pupil!'

Bad bad bad – you'll yur this one a loh if you stick around wi me buh wha poor old Mr dull-as-dogshit Davies an the rest cahn grasp is tha I ain' bad at all. I'm just fair. People treat me like dirt so I treat them like dirt. Teachers wun listen to me so I dun listen to them. The whole uh Pengarw looks down ihs nose at me, so I give the whole town the same treatment back. Fair's fair, anyone can see tha buh like I said – logic an teachers just dun't mix.

The Coconut Kid's finally twigged he's wasting his breath on me so turns his attentions to the old man, giving him all: 'I don't know how you cope, Mr Bray' an 'You must be so embarrassed, Mr Br–'

Dad cuts him off with a toxic blast uh Strongbow gas from the pit of his gut an I flash Davies a look like: *embarrass this fella? No chance.* Davies glosses ih, determined to find some common ground buh unfortunately for him ih's strictly private property wi my father an trespassers will be kneecapped. Leh's keep tha to ourselves fuh now though, yeah?

'I understand there's been some disruption to family life recently. It must be difficult, trying to raise children on your own . . . I am right in saying that Mrs Bray is no longer in the family home, aren't I?'

Uh oh, now yur gunuh geh ih dickhead, talking abou my mother who goh fuck all to do wi you, who you dun know fuck all abou. I'm itching fuh Dad to take a swing at the nosey prick buh once again the old man leaves me high an dry. Head in hands, he breaks down, straggly yellow hair falling to the desk between Golden Virginia fingers.

'At my wit's end I am, pal,' he goes, flecks uh white foam peppering his salty stubbled chin. 'Cow left us months ago, left me alone wi the two boys buh they're trouble, see? They're bad – takes after her they do . . .'

Talk abou a show up. My knuckles weld to the sides uh my chair as a stream uh gross, slimy words crawl out his mouth one after another like piss-soaked rats from a sewer pipe. I rock from side to side, pure rally car bombing through the lanes, handbraking round corners, wind so strong in my yurs I cahn yur these cunts an their lies cos they dun know everything, dun know tha Mam's been in touch buh I ain' telling, ain' showing um the letter thas barely left my pocket since I found ih laying on the doormat a few weeks ago. I recite the words as I throw my blue plastic Cosworth round a hairpin on two legs, know every line off by heart cos this is ih, my only hope uh making things right again, uh fixing everything I've ruined.

Davies seems to grow in confidence as the old man chews his yur off buh if he knew my father like I do he wouldn unclip his seatbelt just yeh. Davies being Davies though, he trundles on oblivious. 'Weren't you aware of Lee's truancy at all, Mr Bray? We sent several letters to your address, tried telephoning too but the line seems to have been disconnected.'

No shit – way Dad's been pissing ih up the wall we're lucky to have running fucking water, butt. The phone was one less problem to worry abou as far as I was concerned buh the letters, they kept coming. Managed to catch every one 'cept the last. When Mam's letter come through the door ih threw me for a loop an nothing else seemed to marrer. Stopped checking for a bih, took my eye off the ball an yur we are, like.

'I only goh one letter, an the phone was a nuisance so I ditched ih. The boy's always up at the crack uh dawn an out all day – how was I to know he wadn at school?'

'I see your point, but I wonder if you've noticed any changes in Lee's behaviour over the past few months?'

'Noh really – always been a little bastard, havn he?'

'Mr Bray, a number of staff members have noted a deterioration coinciding with the recent upheaval in home life. At times like these children need a strong support network – I really think Lee might benefit from having someone to talk to, wouldn't you agree?'

'Whas to talk abou?' Dad grunts, pulling out his pouch uh baccy and papers. 'If he's naughty he gehs a fucking hiding. Simple.'

'Well, with all due respect, perhaps . . .' Mr Davies trails off, double-taking the baccy pouch so horrified you'd think Dad was sat there wanking instead uh rolling a fag. 'Um, perhaps that approach hasn't been particularly effective up to this point.'

Knew ih, goh too big for his boots an now he's gun have to swallow the shit storm heading his way. Dad's fingers freeze on the fag he's rolling an Davies falters, realising too late tha he's overstepped the mark.

'Noh shewer I likes yuh tone, pal,' the old man growls in warning.

'I – I certainly mean no disrespect but we as a school have a duty of care to Lee, to ensure we take appropriate action before potential problems escalate. I'm sure you understand.'

'Yeah, I understand alright – crystal. This is a fucking stitch-up, in ih? Soften me up, geh me saying too much then send those social working bastards round to have a good nose in our lives again! Uh?' Dad's fizzing like a shook up three litre, quarter turn from blowing his top completely.

'I can assure you this is no "stitch-up" Mr Bray, we're simply concerned . . . there's no mention of Social Services at this point.' His posher-than-usual tone tells the whole world he's shitting ih, some uh the high notes he's hitting enough to make a choir boy wince.

'"At this point"? Fuck's ah s'posed to mean?'

'You must believe me, there's no conspiracy. This is purely about Lee's welfare–'

'Ih's yur own welfare you wanuh worry abou butt,' Dad goes, sending the crappy plastic chair skidding backwards as he springs to his feet. *Roll up, roll up! Smash the coconut, win a prize!!* Mr Davies is determined to poop the party mind, bounding across the class an scratching at the door like a dog with a duff bladder. I goh everything crossed fuh Dad to fuck this up so royally I never gohruh come back to school again buh as usual the old boy keeps his audience guessing with a sudden change of heart. He begs, pleads, pleeease pleeease dun tell the Social, they'll take the boys, he'll do summin stupid an Mr Davies wouldn wanuh puh the family through even more stress would he course he wouldn so leh's all sit down an sort this out like adults, yeah?

He walks a wobbly Davies back to his chair like a trainer carrying a boxer to his stool after a heavy round. I'm half-expecting him to whip out the water bottle, start flapping a towel or summin buh he just pats him down, straightens his tie an mumbles some bollocks abou buying him a pint if he ever sees him up the Leather Jug. As likely as me flying to the Moon next Thursday buh still.

Any hopes I had abou gehrin off light are fading fast cos Davies has pulled himself together an is now all business – no more social worker crap, he lays ih straight on the line. The local authority won't allow me to stay home. End of summer term's close. Make the next three weeks to geh um off our backs. Next year's my last in Pengarw High an early exits are far easier to negotiate when I hit sixteen. Sorted.

'Cahn ew just give him a tick everyday till the holidays? Who's to know?' Dad says, warming my heart with his touching show uh confidence.

'Hmm.' The cogs are turning an you just know Davies ud do ih like a shot if he thought he could geh away with ih. 'No, no, out of the question. And it would rather be avoiding the problem.'

Finally we geh ih from the horse's mouth. I'm a problem. Buh like I said, I'm nothing if noh fair. These fuckers see me as a problem buh ih cuts both ways. Will I come to school next week? We'll see. Mr Davies reliably informs us the next step is the courts fuh Dad, then social workers an reports an fucks knows wha else so ih's looking like I'm gun have to bite the bullet. Buh three whole weeks? Best noh hold yuh breath, thas all I'm saying.

2

Cold fresh air washes me clean as I dangle my legs off the mountainside like a kid on a seesaw. Pengarw is Toy Town from up yur, little Scalextric joyriders bombing round an round the estate while tracksuited ants scurry in an out uh their pebbledashed nests. I wadn hanging round back at the school, saw my chance an shot straight through Road Runner style. Left Wile E. an the Coconut Kid still mumbling half-arsed apologies to each other cos away from prying eyes ih woulduh been my turn for a battering an there'd be no sorrys afterwards neither. So fuh now I'm staying put, up where Dad an school are a million miles away an if I wish hard enough Monday morning might never come. I wun go home till long after sunset, till I'm shewer the old boy's conked out. Cahn take chances wi the likes of him.

No problem to stick round yur anyway – loves this place, I do. A big wasteground wonderland full uh fly-tipped freezers an burnt out cars where me an the foxes can kick back, safe from double-barrels an cracking phone cords. Dun tell the boardie man buh when I'm on the knock you'll always find me either yur or down in the abandoned lock-up garage round the back uh the shops. The lock-up's good fuh hiding away buh tonight I need space, I need air, a strong whistling wind to blow the maggots clean out uh my rotten head.

Mam.

My face prickles hot as Mr Davies' threat echoes in my mind – those social workers wi their questions an crisps an pop an my big flapping gob running like Linford Christie. Talking to them caused this whole mess in the first place – if I blab again Mam might never come back. Without thinking the letter's back in my hands an I'm unfolding ih ever so gentle, shielding ih from the wind as though the words might blow right off the zig-zag sellotaped paper. Every line's precious – the only contact since she left over six months ago an fucked if I'm lehrin go again. Ih's addressed to me an my brother Darren buh I hid ih from him like I hid ih from Dad cos the only thing those two couldn ruin is a piss up in a brewery an this is too important to risk. Nestled in the middle is an American penny she sent fuh good luck buh I'm still waiting fuh the thing to start working. Anytime yesterday ud be great.

My mate Buncy dun believe in luck – reckons there's this thing a load uh acid-tripping hippies invented in the sixties called karma tha basically means we all geh wha we deserve in life. S'pose he must be right cos I was one hell of a naughty fucker when I was younger an now I'm eating my just desserts. Dun go thinking I feel guilty though, right? I told you before, I dun feel guilty fuh fuck all, no marrer wha some teacher or counsellor or any other stupid cow says. Mam dun feel guilty fuh me does she? Never said so in her letter – just a load of old shit abou how great she's doing, living in some posh place in Cardiff called Cherrywood Close, probly some big mansion with a lake an tennis courts where she can be happy without us causing murder. I sent her a letter back saying how good I been, how much I've changed buh she cahn be tha bothered cos there's been no reply since.

I light up a fag an watch as the point uh the mountain opposite skags the falling sun, bursting a flood uh golden yolk out across the rocky skyline. Ih makes me feel pure small an pointless cos there's so many questions I'll never know the answer to an so many decisions I'll never know how to make. Restlessness gnaws buh night time's coming an thas when me an Pengarw comes alive. Most people think you cahn see so well in the dark buh if they went where I goes an seen wha I sees they'd know tha night time's when yur eyes are opened widest of all.

Right on cue a pair uh headlights cut through the murk sending me diving fuh cover behind a pile of old mattresses. Wha we goh yur then? Souped-up motor or banger tends to mean kids smoking spliffs buh this is a red Audi, proper swanky thing tha might spell jackpot: older bloke cheating on his wife. I scuttle from mattresses to fridge to wardrobe pure SAS commando, listening hard fuh heavy breathing or suspension springs creaking cos if yur extra careful you can geh a right eyeful – bouncing tits, arse, the loh. I'm abou to sneak up fuh a closer look when a girl's voice stops me dead.

'Origh, you wanted somewhere quiet to talk so start talking. An make ih quick, fuh fuck's sake.'

Hmm, noh looking like my night cos tha rough twang ain' exactly whispering sweet nothings, is ih? The accent's strange too, noh from round yur buh somehow familiar. I wonder if thas . . .

'Doan play me fuh a fool,' a bloke's voice cuts in, every bih as tense an spiteful as the girl's. 'You knows full well why I'm yur. Aimee. You been trynuh geh in touch.'

'So wha if I have – she's my little sister, in she? You *caa*hn keep us ap*aa*rt.'

See, there ih goes again, tha Cardiff twang. Ih's Becca, Becca Lewis I'm shewer. No one else talks like ah up yur. If only I could see past the bloke to the passenger seat, geh a good look of her face.

'I can an I fucking well will,' barks the fella, some Frank Butcher lookalike wi tinted glasses an a comb-over. Pure mackintosh man if ever I seen one. Why would Becca Lewis be in a car wi this weird old perv? 'Yur's money – three hundred quid. Take ih an stay away from all of us forever, right?'

'Fuck yuh money!' Becca scoffs. 'I'd be happy if I never seen you or my mother ever again buh you ain' keeping me away from my sister! Now you've said yuh piece so best you fucks off before Jason finds you an rips you a new arsehole.'

Jason's her boyfriend, Jason McKinley, Mucksy they all calls him – proper rough customer. You wan anything round yur, an I mean anything, you goes to Mucksy buh you berrer like hospital food if you cahn pay the going rate. Becca's the only girl who can give him as good as she gehs, sort uh woman who can break yur heart an yuh bollocks all in one look so dun go thinking just cos she's hard she ain' the lushest in Pengarw, hands down.

'Still knocking round wi tha druggy vermin, uh you?' Frank goes, less than phased. 'When you gunuh grow up, eh? Settle

15

down with a nice fella, start a family uh yur own? Might as well cos you ain' goh one with us no more – noh after yuh filthy lies.'

'Lies? You fucking scum, everyone knew you were guilty. Everyone!'

'Yuh mother didn seem to think so, did she? Was her idea if you wanuh know the truth, sending me up yur wi the money. She doan wan you an neither do Aimee so leave the girl alone.'

'Why's ah, keeping her all to yuhself is ih Derek? Gunuh start on her next eh, *Daddy*?'

'Doan be disgusting – Aimee's my daughter, my own flesh an blood. You cahn compare her to a filthy little whore who couldn wait to jump into bed with her own mother's boyfriend!'

If my chest swells any bigger I'll be able to float away from this nightmare cos ih's gohruh be a good five minutes since I last drew breath an the horror show ain' over yeh.

'I was thirteen yuh sick cunt – a child!'

'Who d'you think yuh kidding wi this sweet an innocent routine – no way was I yuh first, no fucking way.'

'Forgeh ih, I doan have to listen to this.' The passenger door clunk clicks an in a split second I see her lit up, tha thick fringe an heavy makeup unmistakeable. Quick as a flash the light goes out though cos sleazy Frank Butcher's leant over an pulled the door shut on her.

'Hey, hey, now take ih easy,' he goes, ice in his voice melting to slime so suddenly ih sends my stomach plunging, big-dipper style. 'Calm ih down, there's no need for all this. Leh's come to an understanding – we could still have summin, you an me.' Yo-yo sized goose pimples roll down my arms an I know I should call out buh the smack of his lips on her neck deafens me an I just cahn think straight. There's another lip-smack then a yelp as the wad uh money bursts in a paper cloud an Becca slams the door in his face. A stray fiver flutters to the ground from the driver's window an I dash out to grab ih, pure Wimbledon ball boy on crack. There's no mad chase after her like I'm expecting. Instead, Sleazy Frank watches as she disappears into the shadowy lane, slowly pulling a cigar from his pack, taking time to sniff ih up an down before lighting.

I'm reminded uh the old ironmasters my grampy used to tell me abou – rich, horrible bastards who come to the valleys an took wha they wanted wi no care fuh nobody else. This pure rage grips me an I scramble around for a rock cos I swear I'll take the fucker's head off yur an now buh while I'm searching the engine jolts to life again an the fat controller screams off in his terrifying mobile ironworks, glows uh red an orange scorching the night through a haze uh smoke an fumes, leaving me alone in this wasteland feeling more useless an empty than ever before.

3

Night-time is creeping up the mountainside inch by inch like damp up a bedroom wall. I reload my AK-47 an head into the breezeblock jungle, wary uh hatchback tanks an guerrilla squads in their standard issue desert boots an White Sox caps. Avoids these types like the plague usually buh tonight they're right in my firing line cos I'm flush courtesy uh Creepy Frank an my mission's clear. Rendezvous at the chippy on the high street, nobody moves, nobody gehs hurt, exchange cash fuh grub and stuff myself stupid in the back alley. Simple. Or maybe noh so simple cos yur comes a goon squad now, six helmets an a pit-bull scouting fuh the notorious Marvin Rambo, SAS commando extraordinaire. Roll fuh cover, pull the pin an lob a grenade over the hedge. 3 . . . 2 . . . 1 . . . BOOM! Off to a flyer, sovereigns an sweatpants everywhere. Three old biddies gehs ih next, gunned down as they totter home from their church group gangbang, bullet holes tracing their frumpy figures perfect against the wall. Time to go undercover, crawling through gardens, peeking through windows at fat families cwtched up on settees shouting quiz show answers at Roy Walker an Barrymore through mouthfuls uh junk food. Lucky fuckers.

Now I'm deep in the valley, grey pebbledash of our estate swapped fuh slate an stone from black an white times when the Rhondda was a place to come to noh a place to run from. Or so they tells you in school, buh you know my opinions on tha loh – large pinch uh salt, thas all I'm saying.

A noise has me ducking behind a parked car, breaking glass quickly followed by a raucous cheer which rattles the windows uh the Labour Club across the road.

'Out, yuh bloody idiot!' A sharp female voice chases the mumbling brown bear as ih shambles away, pausing every few steps to jet wash the pavement with an endless supply uh beery carrot stew. Gross as fuck buh nothing's gunuh puh me off my grub now I'm so close cos ih's been a good fortnight since I last et anything. There's one last detour I gohruh make though cos I've spotted tha Jesus-creeping shaggy doo right on wanker Gerard locking up the youth club. This one's personal – I'm thinking hands-on, maybe choke him out good an slow wi cheese wire while he fills his hippy corduroys to the brim. Teach the cunt fuh lording ih – had ih in fuh me from day one, old Gerard buh who wants uh go to a shitty little kids' youth club anyway? Truth be told I was glad he banned me. When he's safely round the corner I whip out my dick an give the doorway a proper dousing. Trynuh geh ih through the letterbox is a mistake mind cos tha spring action is vicious an I'm noh looking for a DIY sex change, thanks all the same. Fucking youth club, wha a joke. Little nippers running round playing pretend? I'm way too mature for all ah, butt. Telling ew.

Chippy HQ's in sight so I radio back to base an set up my sniper rifle, ready to pick off any stragglers if the queue's gehrin out of hand. Leh's geh the low down – couple uh old boys out early to beat the closing time rush, a lone fatty probs going up for his third tea uh the night, a dad wi two kids, girls – I stop dead, the sound uh Frank Butcher's lips smacking on Becca's neck corkscrewing my mind. All I can do is pray I yurd wrong cos if summin like ah can happen to the hardest girl in Pengarw then no one's safe an every fucker's a suspect. I leh the crosshair hover over the dad in the fish queue, finger poised on the trigger. One sign uh funny business an the cunt's head'll be coming clean off, trust me.

When a mother with a pushchair rolls up I geh this daft urge to shout out a warning abou the man inside buh stop myself, noh least because her hands are full enough wi the little rusk-muncher in the buggy. Poor cow's run ragged, bartering fuh silence wi chips, okay, *an* sausage in batter, yeah *an* Panda Cola if he's really good an dun mess round buh good luck wi tha love cos all the boy does is scream tha he never wanted

19

sausage in batter he wanted jumbo sausage an she berrer noh geh Panda Pop cos nothing less than proper Coke will do. He flings his little Taz of Taz-Mania teddy to the floor fuh the third time buh she's finally given up an joined the queue tha by now's almost out the door. If I wanuh eat tonight I berrer geh a move on so ih's hop, skip an jump over the road an straight up to the door.

He's still grizzling for his ted as I geh up close. Hell of a size to be sitting in a pushchair he is, 'specially one wi pink bows so I'm guessing he's just performed to sit in his little sister's. Selfish, stropping, pain in the arse – the boy's playing a dangerous game tha I know all too well. Thas why I cahn just walk on by, why I gohruh reach out an help cos if I'd had someone to warn me maybe I wouldn be in this mess right now. I crouch down to his level, shushing him pure gentle so he knows I'm no Frank Butcher. The crying stops instantly like a brick to a stereo. I ask his name buh those sweetie-encrusted lips stay tightly sealed. No problem, I tell him – he can be Chocolate Chops if thas the way he wants ih. He cracks half a smile buh he's still wary so I fetch his Tasmanian devil toy with a wiggly dance, keeping just out uh reach uh those grasping hands.

'Whas yuh teddy's name, Chocolate Chops?' I says.

'Taz.'

Now we're gehrin somewhere. 'Oh, hello, Taz,' I goes, shaking his furry little paw. 'He's cool, in he? Tell me summin, Chocolate Chops – is Taz a good teddy or a bad one?'

'Good,' the little tyke replies without missing a beat.

'I thought as much,' I goes, inspecting the wild-eyed Looney Tune in my hands. 'He looks a good un. Bet Taz is always good for his mam an dad, in he?'

'Dun be silly,' the kid laughs. 'Teddies dun have mams an dads! They comes from a shop, dun they!'

'Uh oh, yur a clever one you are, boy,' I goes, cos this little fucker ain' half as daft as I was at his age. 'Buh *you* goh a mam an dad, havn ew? You always good for yewer mam an dad?'

'Yeah, always.' At least he dun lie as good as me – those big blinkers ain' fooling no one.

'Glad to yur ih,' I goes. 'Being good's always best cos every time yuh nice Taz an all his friends leave yummy sweets under yuh pillow in the night, d'you know tha?'

'Nuh.'

'Well ih's true – you just cahn uv checked properly, thas all. Try ih when you wakes up in the morning, yeah?'

A slack-mouthed nod tells me I goh him where I needs him. Now ih's time to geh serious cos nipper or noh, the kid deserves to know. 'Noh all kids are good though, uh they Chocolate Chops? Some kids shout an lie an perform an never say nice things to their mams. You know wha happens then? Goblins. Goblins come an take her an she'll leave an never ever come back. I should know – they took my mam.'

His eyes stretch open, wide an watery as the Bristol Channel an I realise too late how far I've pushed.

'No no, dun cry, I'm only trynuh help you. Dun wan the goblins to take yuh mammy, do you?'

Thas ih, chance blown. Screaming? You never yurd screaming till you yurd this kid hit the high notes, trust me. 'Mammy! Mammy!' he's going, an she appears like Candyman, no time to run.

'Frigging hell's going on? Wha you done to my boy?'

I throw Taz of Taz-Mania to the floor buh she's already puh two an two together.

'You nicked ih! You nicked my boy's teddy!'

No I never, ih wadn like ah buh a mother on a mission's an unstoppable force an the more I try to explain the angrier she gehs. Now the dad wi the daughters comes out for a nose, an the old fellas, all ganging up to rub in the fact I've fucked everything up again buh no way am I hanging round to listen. I tells um right where to stick ih an I'm gone, back into the shadows where I'm on top, Marvin Rambo SAS commando calling the shots. I shoulduh known better, shoulduh learnt from last time. From now on ih's number one I'm looking after. Fuck everyone else. Guilty? I dun feel guilty fuh fuck all butt. Anyone who says I do is a stinking liar.

4

'Can ew fuck, Bunce!' I says, standing up on the swing an pumping my legs as hard as I can. I'm top uh the world yur, butt, flying high above the whole valley hundred miles an hour, noh a care in the world. Saps like Buncy havn goh the bottle I goh so they come out wi bullshit stories to make umselves look clever. Good job I'm noh shy when ih comes to setting the silly fucker straight.

'Serious, Marv,' he goes, trailing his clumsy feet back an forth in the dirt. 'Ih happened to a woman up Merthyr. Miss Holton told us in PSE class before.'

Right, time to knock ih on the head. My hands start to slip off the chains so I bail at the last minute an watch as the swing wraps round an round on the crossbar. Then I puhs my foot out to stop Buncy dead. 'Dun be so fucking dull,' I says, going right up to him. 'You cahn geh a girl pregnant off a blow job. Ih's impossible.'

'Thas wha you thinks. They showed us a video an everything.'

'When? I never seen no video.'

'Well you wouldn, would ew? Yuh never in fucking school, butt.'

'Listen, if they were showing films like ah in class I wouldn go on the knock ever again. Telling ew!'

'Maybe if you come uh school once in a while you wouldn have to ask such stupid questions. You *can* geh a girl pregnant off a blowie, buh only if she swallows, in ih?'

'Next you'll be saying you can give um a baby up the arse. Geh real.'

'No, no, see now yuh proving how thick you are. Fanny an mouth is inwards, like. Arse is outwards. Try to keep up, will ew?' The cheeky fucker shakes his head all slow an sorry an ih's lucky he's such a sap or he'd be gehrin a right smack in the gob. I've done ih before, plenty uh times. People knows noh to mess – most are too scared to hang round wi me these days buh I dun need no one anyway, never have. I only lehs Buncy tag along cos I feel sorry for him.

'You been sniffing too much uh this, butt,' I says, snatching the marker out of his hand an taking a good long huff.

'Give ih back!' Buncy's up off his swing buh I'm already over by the benches. He grabs my arm, making me mess up the 9T5.

'Fuck's sake, Bunce! Cahn wait two minutes, can ew?'

'Calm down, yuh name's everywhere anyway. *Marvin 9T5, Marvin 9T5*. Waste of ink, ih is.'

'Any better suggestions, clever clogs?'

'Watch.' He crouches down an gehs to work wi the pen. *Can ya tell what it is yet?* Ih's s'posed to be a woman spreading her legs buh the fanny looks like some weird Egyptian eye with all fuzzy hairs round ih, stuck on top of an arse. Buncy dun take kind to my laughing, mind. 'Wha would you know, Marv?' he goes. 'Never been near a girl in yuh whole life.'

Cheeky cunt. Cops on to his second cousin at some family party an ever since he been acting like he's fucking Casanova. Carry on an he'll be gehrin my trump card: the cat rumour. I lay tha one on him an ih's game over buh he's so thick he thinks I've forgoh.

'So c'mon. How far uv you gone with a girl, then?' He's smirking while he says ih, like I'm squirming or summin. As if. Keep pushing, Tiddles.

'Well I fucked yuh mother last night. Does she count?'

'Pff, wanker! Admit ih, you never been wi one. I bet you dun even know wha an orgasm is, do you?'

'Yes I do, course I do.' Bollocks, knew I shoulduh gone to more uh those PSE classes.

'Wha , then?'

'Ih's–' Shall I say ih? I'm gun have to say summin, in I? 'Ih's when you spunks yuh load.'

'EH-ERR!' he goes, like the buzzer off *Family Fortunes*. 'Our survey said: EH-ERR! When a bloke blows his load ih's called *cumming*. Only a woman can have an orgasm, an she goes like this–' He runs over to the little elephant thing on springs an starts to ride ih going: 'Ooh ooohh, oh yeah, OH YEAH, OH YEAH, OHHHH–'

'Shurrup, will ew? Yuh embarrassing,' I says, looking round to make shewer no one's yurd an fuck a duck if I dun see the Francis twins approaching with a bunch uh girls from school. A stone bounces off the railings next to me an I psych myself up, ready to take um on. Buncy clocks um an all an climbs off the kids' toy, his face all flat an grey.

'Alright ladies?' Carl Francis says through a hangman smile. I shake my arms an legs a bih to loosen um up an I'm abou to crack my knuckles when Craig comes rushing up after him, straight towards me like a runaway train. I'm ready for him though, side-stepping pure slick just at the last second.

'Calm down, Marv, yuh fucking mongo,' he goes, spazzing out. 'Goh terrible nerves, this boy, havn he Carl?'

The girls go over to the benches, chatting an giggling an all ah. Stacey Evans is with um, looking every inch a real woman with her crimped up hair an bright red lipstick. Lush ain' the word. Different class she is, butt. Too good fuh these silly little girls, an for a pair uh pricks like the Francis twins an all.

'So where've you been then?' Carl goes to me. 'Dun go to Pengarw High no more, is ih?'

'I'm back in tomorrow.' Thanks fuh reminding me, cunt face.

'We yurd you goh sent to a special place fuh remos,' says Craig. 'Jamie Rees seen you on the Sunshine Coach snogging the window!' The stupid blond bumfluff on his top lip wiggles up like a caterpillar till you can see all clumps uh yellow cheese stuff stuck in between his manky teeth. Carl's decking himself over his brother's wisecracks, sucking in deep breaths of air an hawing like a donkey, buh trying a bih too hard though, if you know wha I mean.

'Nah, serious now. D'you have a nice time on holiday or wha? '

Ih's bound to be a trap buh I gohruh ask: 'Wha holiday?'

'You know – yuh trip to Belsen.'

Now Carl's almost pissing himself. Ih's so obvious he's puhrin ih on, pure shameful. 'Wha d'you call Marvin with a pair uh Doc Martens on?' he huffs. 'A golf club!'

Yur we go, same old shit. Belsen case, Ethiopian, I've puh up wi those names ever since the juniors buh starving Hank Marvin's the one thas really stuck. I'm so used to ih these days ih dun bother me. Marvin's who I am.

'Fucking state uh the boy,' Craig goes on, poking a finger into my ribs. 'Six stone wet through. Abou time you puh some meat on those bones, in ih, Marv? We'll all have a whip round if yuh short uh grub.'

Ih's bollocks, them saying I'm too skint to afford food. Eats loads, I swear I do. Just naturally wiry, Bruce Lee style. Proved pricks like the Francis twins wrong tons uh times, pure raiding my mother's fridge when I was a nipper an sharing out the food with all the kids in the street. Till Dad wen loopy an made me knock on every door asking fuh the grub back buh the point's still proved in ih? How could I have dished out those goodies if we never had nothing in the kitchen? Exactly.

Craig's waiting for a reaction buh I just have a little chuckle under my breath cos the whole thing's hilarious to be honest. Craig dun seem to think so though.

'Wha you laughing at, yuh smelly gypo?' He steps forward, jamming a shoulder into my chest. My heart starts to thump where I'm losing my temper buh before I goh a chance to lay him out flat summin strange happens. Buncy speaks out.

'Leave us alone, eh boys? We havn done nothing to you, uv we?' His voice is doing a bih of a Mr Davies buh this is still a turn up fuh the books. Ih's usually me who's gohruh deal with um while he mooches in the background. Looking a bih sorry for himself now, mind.

'You can shut yuh mouth an all, creep. Whas the score wi you two, then? You queers or wha?'

There's more laughter from Carl an some uh the girls on the bench join in, too. 'Well, they'd have to be really. I mean, there's no way either uh the ugly cunts ud geh laid with anyone else, is there?'

'No, wait a minute now, Carl. Remember this is Bunce we're talking abou. He's definitely had some *pussy* before, havn he?'

The girls whisper together in a huddle, then there's a scream an they screw their faces up like we're the sickest pair uh perverts going. 'Oh my God, thas disgusting!' Gemma Price says an they all scream again. Carl starts meowing. I move a few steps away from Buncy cos the end uh the day there's no point us both gehrin tarred wi the same brush is there?

'RSPCA goh wanted posters out fuh this cunt,' Craig says an the laughs go up again. I join in a bih an all just to geh us on their good side buh Buncy gives me a look like I've kicked him in the nuts. Ih's done the trick though cos Craig seems to have lost interest, drifting over to the benches, purring as he goes. Next thing I know he's all over Zoe Asher, tonguing her face off, hands everywhere. Wha these girls see in him's a mystery to me, buh at least he havn managed to geh into Stacey Evans. Him an his brother been after her fuh years buh they'll never geh her. She's too good fuh this loh – you can tell the way she's sat, in amongst um buh still sortuh separate, gazing off in a world of her own.

All of a sudden Zoe breaks away, looks right at me an whispers in Craig's yur. Then he shouts over: 'Oi, Marvin, wha d'you wan, a fucking picture or summin?'

Making out I been caught perving buh the end uh the day ih's hard noh to notice two people humping each other in front uh you.

'Never seen anyone copping on before?' Zoe goes, showing off her train tracks as she laughs.

'Marvin gehs a stiffy when his mam kisses him goodnight,' Carl says. Then he hesitates for a minute before going: 'Well, he used to before she done a runner!'

My jaws snap together like a bear trap. I catch his eye an we're locked, staring each other out, skin over my knuckles pulled tight white. Buh ih's senseless starting while his brother's around in ih, so I give him a look tha says I'll catch him on his own an even though he dun show ih he deffo gehs the message. Then Stacey Evans stands to leave, pure bored wi the whole thing. The rest follow, Carl right behind like a lost puppy dog buh he'll never geh into her. Never.

'See you later girls,' Craig calls to us with a limp wrist wave. Noh as smart as he thinks though cos the ink must've still been wet on the bench an now he's walking away wi Buncy's fanny-eye printed on the arse of his tracksuit bottoms. Buncy nudge-nudges buh I blank him an storm off.

'Marvin, dun go gehrin upset over them,' he goes, catching hold uh my shoulder.

'My mother never done a runner,' I says, shrugging his hand away. 'She's always asking me to visit. I'm going there soon, as ih happens.' Ih's noh a complete lie, buh there again, ih's noh exactly true.

'How come you never talks abou her no more? Has summin happened – is tha why you been so arsey lately?'

To save me having to answer I crank up the mean an moody act, watching after the Francis boys an going: 'They're lucky I never smacked um . . . I swear I was this close to losing ih then.'

'Yeah, you always say tha.'

For a second I'm thinking uh starting cos I could definitely take Bunce. He seems to sense ih coming an goes: 'Ih's noh my fault you lehs um walk all over you – if you wants uh geh anywhere in life yuh gun have to stand up fuh yuhself eventually.'

Yur we go, found his bollocks fuh the first time in fifteen years an now he's dishing out life coaching advice? Shall I smack him one? Deep down I know ih's noh gunuh do any good though, so I just keep on walking like I goh somewhere to go.

Usually I spend the days wishing fuh nightfall buh as the sun drops this evening my stomach goes with ih, squishing my nervous guts to mush. Buncy's talking abou going home buh thas just another step closer to school in the morning an I'd rather do the hokey cokey on the A470 than face up to tha right now. We're passing by the Handies, which is like a training centre thing where the handicaps used to earn their dole money before Thatcher or Major or one uh them loh closed ih down. Suddenly I gehs a bright idea. Leh's do ih over!

27

I'm straight through a gap in the railings buh Buncy shuffles round outside, looking like he needs a good fart.

'Nor, ih's gehrin late, Marv. There's fuck all in there anyway, 'cept a load of old junk.'

'C'mon, ih'll be a laugh.'

'Buh we might geh caught.'

'So? Never bothered you before, uv ih?'

'Only I'm on my last warning at Club. Geh in trouble once more an I'm banned, Gerard said. Ih's the new rules, Marv . . .'

Him an his fairy youth club, ih's all you yurs off the cunt these days. 'Wha you still messing round there for Bunce? Tha place is fuh little wankers.'

'No, I know buh they goh this cool Storey Arms trip coming up though an I've already paid my deposit, see?'

'Ooh, Storey Arms, big wows! Gunuh play action heroes in the hills wi yuh bum chum Gerard? Pathetic. Gerard this, Gerard tha, who gives a fuck?' I make a move, nodding for him to hurry up.

'No fuck you Marv! I'm sick uh yuh moods an yuh bad attitude. I tries talking to you abou ih an you just gehs even nastier. Well you ain' dragging me down wi you – if you wun't face yuh problems there's nothing I can do to help, is there?'

'Problems? Nah, you goh ih wrong, Bunce. Only people who care abou stuff goh problems – I stopped giving a shit abou anything ages ago an I've never been better, yeah? If you cahn handle ih you can fuck right off, butt.'

'Fine, I will then!'

Bollocks – didn think tha one through, did I? 'No Bunce, please dun go butt. I'm sorry, alright? If I could explain what's wrong you'd be the first person I told. Serious. I just needs you to stay out a little bih longer – cahn go home yeh, butt. Done ih fuh you in the past, havn I?'

Goh him there cos Buncy's family was terrorised out uh the last place they lived an when he first moved to Pengarw he was right off the rails. Now he thinks he can turn goody two-shoes an leave me on my Tod? No chance. He knows he havn goh a leg to stand on so we're over the car park an pulling back one uh the loose window cages without another word. People uv been yur before. We done ih ages ago, buh the council's been out to board ih up again since. Now ih's only the gluies tha knocks around buh they ain' abou tonight, thank fuck. As soon as we geh inside we're off, booting office doors open an throwing stones at the last remaining window panes. I'm pure buzzing buh Buncy's acting a right sap, going on abou bare cables an broken glass, saying ih's too dangerous an ah.

'Now who's the pussy?' I says, grabbing a bunch uh electrical wires from the false ceiling an pretending to geh a shock.

'Yuh tapped in the head – I'm going.'

'Wait!' I spy this battered settee in the corner, covered wi dried-up glue bags.

'Nor,' he's going. 'Nor, Marv,' buh he cahn say nothing with his previous. Like tha warehouse down the Blackfields Estate last year. Tha was his idea, going on abou ih being a laugh an all ah – I couldn be arsed buh I never started whining like him. Made the papers an everything – three hundred grand's worth uh damage, they said. Said there was new technology to catch the culprits, buh they never goh us. We both knows how to keep our mouths shut, in ih? Technology dun mean fuck all, ih's grassing tha gehs people caught. Buncy might be a knob sometimes buh he sticks to the golden rule, same as me. He's staring at the floor now cos he knows he goh no place to talk. I just smile an spark up the flame.

5

There's no way I been asleep more than two seconds buh yur I am, eyes wide in the early morning murk, too knackered to move an too hot to stay still. I peel my face off the pillow an flop down on the cool side uh the quilt, steeling myself fuh a ten-mile trek over to the window. Maybe no point though cos the net curtain's already flapping like a chicken's chin an down in next door's yard I yur Bruno growling so clear he may as well be cwtched up next to me.

Thanks to tha mangy mutt I'm too twitchy to drift straight back off so there's only one thing fuh ih. I starts flicking through the girls from school in my mind like I'm shuffling a pack uh those dirty playing cards Buncy's father hides on top of his wardrobe. Pick a card, any card. I settle on Stacey Evans. Havn done her for ages an seeing her in the park brought ih all back. Red bra an paper-thin shirt she used to wear – wanked over tha for a month solid. Every fucker did, I reckon. Even Mr Burton used to eyeball her pure sly. My dick stiffens up as I set the scene in my mind. Burton's told her to geh out uh class fuh talking, buh ih's obvious he's only done ih cos he cahn handle having to look at her tits all day, knowing he goh no chance, like. So she legs ih, crying an upset an no one sticks up for her, noh even Carl Francis who's sitting there like a spare prick. I jumps up from the back uh the class and goes after her, calling Burton all the pervy old cunts under the sun right to his face. She's blubbing away in the locker room, moaning abou how no one helped her an when she finds out wha I done she's all over me. Next thing I know we're both pure going for ih in the store cupboard, copping each other while I'm feeling her fanny an she's rubbing my dick, except ih's me rubbing ih cos I goh my hand down my undies buh I'm half asleep now an I cahn quite tell whas real an whas noh.

I'm almost there buh this weird tang catches the back uh my throat an throws me off my stroke. I cahn place ih buh I've smelt ih before – sortuh like chemicals or smoke or . . . my eyes flick open. Smoke? Fire! The fucking house is on fire! Then a million tiny needles jab into my scalp an I realise ih's noh the house thas blazing. Ih's me! Round I go on the bed, slapping at my head pure spastic. I tumble to the floor an a figure looms up out the shadows. Now I know the score. The Handies. He's found out.

'Wake Dad up an I'll fucking kill ew.' Only a whisper buh ih rings in my yurs like a thunder clap. A rasping spark illuminates the shadow for the longest second, his face all orange an jagged like a Halloween pumpkin. He puffs hard on the fag a couple uh times to make shewer ih's burning then crouches down, waiting fuh me to speak. I know I gohruh choose my words careful yur buh I berrer say summin quick cos my brother dun tend to like being kept waiting.

'Darren, I never done nothing, I swear.' I shield the stubbly patch on my head to leh him know how good he goh me. Like thas gunuh stop him.

'Shut yewer mouth, yuh dirty little wanker. Been messing round wi Dad's guitar again, havn ew?'

Dad's guitar? Might be a trick so play ih cool an say fuck all's best, in ih?

'Dun't gimme the dumb routine! I took a right hiding cos uh you last night. Thinks thas funny, is ih?'

'Nuh . . .' The smell uh burnt hair still hangs in my nostrils, churning my stomach till my eyes water.

'So tell the truth then, yuh lying little shit!' He springs forward with his teeth gritted. 'One uh the strings was broke and he blamed me! Why would I wanuh touch his crappy old guitar? Everyone knows ih's you cahn keep yuh hands to yuhself in this house.'

'Buh I never wen near ih, honest I never. Probly done ih himself when he was drunk.' Darren ain' buying ih, though. Never believes me, even when I'm telling the truth.

'You wanuh pray Dad stays in tonight cos when I gehs you on yur own . . .' He dun need to finish the sentence. We all knows the drill.

Now he's said his piece I'm just furniture. I creep back on to my bed an stay there, watching for any sudden movements as he hunts for his work boots under piles uh junk. I need to check the damage in the bathroom mirror buh fucked if I'm moving a muscle while King Cunt's still on the loose. Finally he's out the door, dead leg an dirty look his parting gifts. Sneak previews uh whas in store later tonight buh he can keep dreaming if he thinks I'm hanging round for a beating. I'll camp out, run away – wha'ever. Noh bothered, butt.

As I tiptoe across the landing I'm thinking of all the different ways I could kill Darren so the coppers wouldn know ih was me who done ih. Maybe tell him there's a girl wants shagging up the woods then jump out an stove his head in with a rock. I'll say he goh a job in Scotland, send Dad a postcard of an oil rig or summin – then when he dun come home fuh Christmas we can just assume he fell into the sea one boozy night an thas tha. End uh story.

Eurgh! Cold puke squishes between my bare toes an ih's a miracle I dun spew myself. Gross! Who done ah, I wonder? Noh my father, thas fuh shewer – wouldn waste the booze. Most of his mates are the same way so they must be on an extra specially wild bender. Spells fireworks when they wake up, guaranteed buh I ain' planning on being around when ih happens. I quickly splash some water over my face an check the damage in the mirror. There's a scorched yellow patch on the top uh my head buh luckily ih's been ages since I last had my mop chopped an a bih uh scruffing covers the burnt spot over a treat. I think again abou bricking Darren up the woods buh knowing my luck I'd bottle ih an he'd batter me twice as bad. The cunt.

Back in the bedroom I whip off my undies an search around fuh some clean clothes. As usual, Ian Rush is giving me the creeps from the wall over Darren's bed, those piercing blue eyes cutting me open as he holds the Coca-Cola Cup aloft like the remains of his last victim. I turn my back to him so only the crinkly yellow page three girls can see me, then on goes undies, socks an last century's itchy black trousers. Fuck knows where my school shirts are, mind so I gohruh make do with a crumpled old *Knight Rider* t-shirt which has belonged to both me an Darren at certain points, an even my dad if I remember right. I flatten ih out best I can, throw ih over my head an jam my feet into my trainers.

Time's ticking on now cos I gohruh be at Hooley's shop in ten minutes. I hobble down the stairs like Long John Silver, balancing my weight between wall an banister cos a rampaging father's only ever a creaky floorboard away at this time uh morning. I catch sight uh the old bastard through a gap in the door, lying pure awkward on the settee like summin out uh *The Exorcist*, arms an legs twisted all over the place. Part uh me's shitting ih in case he wakes up buh I cahn help staying a while, laughing to myself cos one sock's dangling halfway off his foot as though trynuh make a run for ih. I wouldn blame ih, mind. You can smell those stenching feet from yur. When he farts an rolls over I realise I been pushing my luck an I'm out into the kitchen without a second to waste. There's fuck all in the cupboard bar a couple uh tins uh sweetcorn an a packet uh Smash so tha rumble in my stomach's gun have to wait till I gehs to Hooley's.

6

Ih's lush an cool inside Hooley's shop. The boards over the windows cut out most uh the sunlight buh there's still a few narrow rays slicing through the cracks like deadly laser beams. I duck an dodge my way through to the storeroom, careful noh to geh a hole melted right through me buh ih's only fucking abou, like. I'm noh a little kid.

As per usual the fat porker's in the way, wedged behind the counter cannibalising a bacon sarnie. Grease an brown sauce drip from between his fingers on to some poor unsuspecting punter's newspaper as he gives ih the once over. Robbing old skinflint. 'Hiyaa Mr Hooo-leey,' I shouts, launching him three foot in the air before he rocks back on his stool like one uh those old weeble-wobbles you find in charity shops. Look out fuh the rescue crews flying over any minute – we're talking 10.8 on the Richter, minimum.

'Never mind "hiya", yewer late. Again,' he goes like I just stirred his coffee wi my bare dick. In the background the radio crackles . . . *and now the news at seven-thirty* . . . buh ih seems Hooley's been struck with a sudden bout uh deafness.

Out in the storeroom I'm straight to work, folding an stuffing a stack uh papers into the bright orange sack on the sideboard. Even wi my back to him, I can feel Flash staring me out from his basket in the corner. Me an dogs never mix, buh I hate this one more than any other. I hate ih cos ih's a bully. Noh so much of a flash these days mind with his back legs all twisted up an knackered. Jaw still works alright though, so I'm always careful noh to geh too close.

Hooley's sandwich uv set my stomach off so now I'm on a mission, snatching a quick glance over my shoulder to make shewer he's busy shouting at the news report on the radio. I tense up in case they mention anything abou the fire last night buh ih's okay cos he's going on abou Tories an perverts or summin. Thas all you ever yurs from him – used to be Thatcher buh now ih's Major this an Major tha. Boring bollocks tha means nothing to me buh I usually try to keep him happy by nodding at the right times. Humouring wankers like Hooley is always wise – make um think yuh daft enough an you can geh away wi murder. My hand nips into a box uh Wispas an the bar's in between the papers at the bottom uh my bag before you can blink. Flash gives a low growl in the corner. Keep growling, yuh evil cripple cunt. You cahn stop me.

'D'you yur? I said the bastards wants shooting, dun they?'

'Er, yes Mr Hooley,' I says as two coconut snowballs join the Wispa. I'm going in fuh the third time when Flash barks so loud ih makes my bones ache.

'Flash, cut it out, ew fucking nuisance!'

My head's buried in the stack uh papers, waiting fuh the scrape uh Hooley's stool buh the lazy fat fucker dun move a muscle. Open invitation to stock up, tha is butt. I waves a pack uh cheese an onion under the dog's nose before chucking um in my bag an flipping him the middle finger. 'Right, I'm off now,' I says, making a beeline fuh the door. Hooley's goh other ideas, though.

'Oi oi oi, wait a minute now.' He picks at his teeth with his nails, looking me up an down like I'm a horse he's thinking uh buying. 'I found some more posters out the back on the weekend. I need you to put um up fuh me after school, alright?'

This is a pisstake. I'm only s'posed to be the morning paperboy buh this fucker thinks I'm on twenty-four hour emergency call out. 'I, er, I dun think I'll have the ti–'

He waves a fat sausage finger in my face. 'Well bloody well *make* time then, in it? Plenty of other boys who'll take on the round if yewer not willing to pull yuh weight.' He points up to the posters – tatty pictures uh Van Damme an Steven Seagal an all them loh from when he done video rentals. The rentals stopped years ago cos every fucker was ripping him off left, right and centre buh he kept the posters cos he reckons a bih uh razzamatazz keeps the youngsters coming in. Joker! The only people who comes in yur are the sad old fogeys who cahn drive down to the supermarket.

'While yuh yur you can geh up on tha freezer there an take down *Double Impact*.'

'Buh my round, Mr Hooley. I'll be late.'

'Nonsense, it wun't take ew a minute.'

I'm freaking out wha wi the crisps an chocolate on me, like so I climb up wi the sack still swinging round my neck.

'Now take that off, ew bloody daft sod!' He's trynuh pull at ih buh if I leh tha happen ih's a dead cert the nosey cunt'll puh his snout straight in. We're sortuh stuck, wrestling each other buh the weight uh the papers sends me off balance. I puh my foot on to one uh the shelves to steady myself, squashing a load uh Swiss rolls as I go. Hooley flips his lid.

'Get down from there, yuh fucking imbecile! Yuh wrecking the bloody place!'

I think uh Chubby Brown when he says, 'some cunt's beat us to it!' cos the place is a dive anyway. I swear, if a stranger walked in off the street they'd be in two minds whether to call the police an report a robbery. All the shelves are half empty an whas yur is thrown around any old how. An ih's noh only the posters thas out uh date, neither. Dun think Hooley's ever yurd of a best before label. He's still ranting as I leave fuh my round, buh ih's all *blah blah blah* to me now. As soon as I'm outside I rip the wrapper off one uh the snowballs an jam ih in my mouth whole. How d'you like ah, yuh moaning old fart? I've only taken a few steps up the road when I yur him calling me back.

Fuck.

I try to geh rid of ih, chewing round an round buh the marshmallow's foaming right up an leaking from the corners uh my mouth. I think abou legging ih buh he's already waddled out to the doorway, his face pure red an sticky.

'Oi, Lee.' He's calling me by my real name, which is always a bad sign. 'Mind now, yuh still down on the takings from last week, right? I wants the full lot yur, tomorrow morning – no excuses. This is yewer last warning.'

I nods like ih's no problem buh inside my guts are doing a right old jig cos we all know tha money's long gone.

7

There's no time to go back to the shop. This heat's dragged so heavy on my back I might as well have been lugging the sun round in my sack uh papers. Buh the truth is I been carrying summin far heavier an more deadly than the sun. School. Judgement day's yur an I been sent straight to Hell. Every step I take I'm fighting the urge to go on the knock, to fuck off up the mountain or hide out in the garage round the back uh the shops. Ih's a no-go, though. Fuck this up an I could lose everything. Thoughts uh my father in court make my feet move faster, I break into a sprint as though he's coming up behind wi the phone cord in hand an pretty soon the brutal angles uh Pengarw High carve up the skyline in front uh me. My stomach's set on spin-dry as I hurry to catch the last few blue uniforms trickling in through the gates, flapping trainer sole scuffing the kerb an sending me sprawling forward into the road Superman style. Any embarrassment's quickly erased by screeching rubber tyres cos out uh nowhere a car bumper's staring me full in the face. For a while all I yur is the blood roaring through my head buh when the world drifts back into focus there's other sounds – angry voices from inside the car.

'. . . jumped out in front uh me . . .'

'. . . eyes on the road . . .'

'. . . no, shut *your* fucking mouth!'

I decide to leave um to ih buh my legs are all over the shop like Mr Soft off the adverts an by the time I've made ih across the road ih's only the school railings keeping me upright. Two angry horn blasts sag my legs an sap any strength I had left.

'Watch where yuh going, yuh dopey prick!'

I turn, ready to chops the guy off buh the scowling face tha meets me seizes my motor mouth mid-insult. I recognise ih in an instant – everyone round yur do. Ih's Mucksy.

'Sorry, butt. Didn see you coming.' My voice is wavy an weak an I'm cringing inside at how sappy I sound, especially when I clock who's sat next to him. There's more angry words between the two of um then Becca leans over an calls to me.

'Marvin, you seen my cousin Scott today?' My stomach flips as those dark panda eyes fix me hard like she'll cut my throat if I dun give her the answer she's looking for. I'm noh shewer how to play this cos I just snipered her cousin by the park noh fifteen minutes ago buh do I really wanuh geh involved? Ih's no surprise Scott's mixed up wi this loh – dickheads like him an the Francis twins idolise the likes uh Mucksy buh Scott's a hard cunt in his own right. So do I grass on Scott or lie to Mucksy an Becca? Time's ticking.

'Noh a trick question – you seen him or wha? ' Mucksy barks. Wouldn wanuh be in Scott's shoes, leh me tell ew. Even I'm gun have to work hard to avoid a split lip cos there's violence seeping out uh this psycho's every pore. Thing is I'm still dazed from the near miss an 'Erm, noh shewer' is the best I can do.

Mucksy explodes, spit flying from his gob as he bangs his fists on the steering wheel. 'Dun't fuck me around, butt! Just dun't!'

'Give ih a rest, Jase, yeah? Gehrin funny with him ain' helping anything, is ih?'

'You shut yuh fucking mouth, right!' The strings in Mucksy's neck rise up like tent ropes. 'You hadn uh dished my shit out to every fucker in short trousers we wouldn be searching the streets like a pair uh twats at stupid o'clock in the morning, would we?'

I blurt out, 'Scott's already in school,' cos this scene goh echoes uh creepy Frank Butcher up on the mountain an I dun wan another one uh them on my conscience.

'Well why didn you say so? Do us a favour Marv, go an geh him, yeah? Ih's really important.'

Becca probly thinks I'm friends wi Scott cos I used to go over his house years ago – loads of us did. See, when she first moved up from Cardiff she lived wi Scott's mam an dad an we'd all mess around, going through her knicker drawer an ah when she wadn there. I stopped calling over in the end though cos . . . well, I couldn be bothered with um anymore.

'Well, okay buh I dun really speak to him much these days, Bec . . .'

'Listen,' Mucksy butts in. 'You can have tea parties in the woods for all I care – just geh in there an tell him to come out!'

The school bell rings in the distance, giving me the excuse I need to geh going. Mucksy ain' convinced though, revving the engine hard an snatching a fistful uh my t-shirt before I can geh away. Uh course I'm shitting ih, buh I knows how to deal wi wankers like this. Play ih dumb.

'Whas the marrer, butt?' I goes, pure soft an dopey. When he snarls an image uh Flash in this fucker's denim jacket springs to mind an I'm fighting noh to crack up wi nervous giggles.

'Summin funny, is ih? Leh's geh ih straight – Scott dun walk out those doors in ten minutes an next time I see you . . . I'll run you over. Right?' One look at those cracked eggshell eyes an I know he ain' joking.

As soon as he slackens his grip I'm gone, tearing towards the gates. Before I can stop myself I'm shouting: 'Druggie dickhead! I'll geh my brother to fuck you up!' The motor screams up the kerb an along the pavement, forcing me to scramble up the school railings wi inches to spare. He's straight out the car, yanking at my legs until I fall to the floor.

'Gunuh geh me fucked up, is ih? C'mon then, go an geh yuh big bad brother – I'll lay him out next to you.'

I feel a bih uh piss seeping into my undies as he scruffs me round, an I'm going: 'Nor, nor, please butt, I didn mean ih . . .' Fucking right I never meant ih – noh least cos Darren's only hard when ih comes to giving me stick. If he knew I goh him mixed up wi Mucksy he'd shit his pants. Luckily Becca comes to my rescue.

'Jason, leave him! Fucking leave him, yeah? He's only a kid.'

I dun give him a second chance, shooting through to the safety uh the gates while I still goh all my teeth.

'Ten minutes!' he calls, buh he can sit an spin.

I think abou chopsing again buh when I open my mouth all tha comes out is: 'Dun call me a kid! I'm noh a kid!'

8

Fuck's sake. Late on my first day back, an all cos uh tha knob head outside. Only thoughts uh Becca can sweeten the bitter taste in my mouth like sugar in black coffee an I take off down the corridor wi fresh energy, straight through the minefield uh soggy tissue paper outside the boys' toilets. Bih too keen, a direct hit sends my feet off in six different directions at once like Shakin' Stevens after a night on the White Lightning buh a miracle keeps me standing an I press on, praying no one's seen.

I hesitate at my classroom door, careful to suss the situation before taking the plunge into enemy territory. Fuck all's changed by the look uh things. Miss Richards' still clinging to her desk like ih's a sinking ship in a sea uh mischief. Climbing on tables, kicking, punching, pulling – even compared to me these kids are no-hopers. I mean, I'm noh exactly Brain uh Britain buh half of um can barely count to ten without using their fingers. Thing wi me is, I fell behind years ago, like an I never goh a chance to catch up. I'm talking juniors, yur. Was a right handful, see an back then if you were naughty the teachers leh you play wi toys while the other kids done their learning. When ih come to high school I was so far gone they slapped me straight in Richards' Remo's class, end uh story. Noh bothered really, cos you dun need school to geh by in this world, just gohruh keep on yuh toes an I shewer as fuck knows how to do tha.

'Okay everyone, settle down now,' Miss Richards says in her goody goody gumdrops voice.

No one takes a blind bih uh notice.

She flaps the register like a dying fly an repeats herself, a touch louder this time buh each an every drippy word tha leaves her mouth is instantly swallowed up by the racket.

'Please, I've had quite enough already!' Finally everyone drifts to their seats, worried she might peak too soon – this daft cow's goh hours uh torture to go yeh. She blows a strand uh hair from her face an glances over to the clock above the door at the exact moment I set foot in the class. 'Lee Bray! Goodness, are you, er, what are you . . . ?'

'Mr Davies sent a letter home,' I goes cos she obviously thought I was long gone. Maybe she never knew abou the court thing, or maybe she just expected me to ignore the letters like usual.

'Oh, right, of course. Well – hurry up and sit down.'

'Shoulduh stayed away – place smelt better,' Jason Ellis says under his breath as I pass by, an before I can stop myself I've kicked out at the goofy cunt.

'Lee!' Miss Richards squeaks.

See. No marrer wha happens in this place, ih's always my fault. I'm starting to lose ih already. No way am I gunuh be able to handle weeks uh this shit. As soon as my arse hits the seat she's on my case again.

'Feet!'

I whip um off the chair next to me, if only to geh her to shut tha whingeing trap, like.

'Really, this isn't good enough. And where's your uniform?'

Fuck me, this is already the longest day ever.

I catch sight uh Buncy on the way out of assembly, his head bobbing along like a lost balloon in a blue uniform sky. 'Buncy! Oi, Bunce!' Fucker must have Maris Pipers in his yurs cos he keep on walking, dun even look round. Couple uh well-placed elbows through the crowd an I've caught him up though. 'Alright Bunce?'

'Marvin . . .' Straight away I can tell he's having one of his girly mood swings.

'Well who was you expecting, Herman fucking Munster – course ih's Marvin!' I pause for a minute before testing the waters. 'So wha you up to? Have fun last night?'

'Place is gutted – fire engines were out all hours,' he mumbles, little charcoal eyes looking anywhere buh my direction. 'We should never uh gone there.'

'Calm down butt, ih's cool,' I goes. 'We done loads worse an there's never been no comebacks, uv there? So relax. Come on, you can choose what to do tonight – anything you like, okay? No funny business.'

'Err, cahn come out tonight, Marv . . . helping Janine wi summin.'

'Janine?' Buncy hates, an I mean *hates* his sister with a vengeance, wouldn give her the skin off his shit. I'm starting to geh a good old whiff uh the fishiest fucking rat tha ever crawled through a Pengarw sewer an boy does ih stink. Time to cut to the chase. 'Havn been opening yuh mouth uv you, Bunce?' He dun say nothing, just whines like a naughty dog. 'You stupid cunt! Of all people, *Janine?* Well if the coppers gehs involved ih'll be you going down butt, no worries. You goh previous fuh criminal damage up Mountain Ash – they'll throw the fucking book at you fuh this.'

'Buh you done the Handies . . .'

'Nah, Bunce, I was pushed into ih – you does this sort uh thing all the time, remember?' I'm talking a loh braver than I feel buh I gohruh make him think before he speaks.

'She wun say nothing, I swear–'

'Ha! The Rhondda's very own human Tanoy – no, course noh!'

'Buh she promised as long as . . . listen, I cahn hang round wi you no more, Marv.' He quickly scans the foyer before whispering: 'I shouldn even be talking to you now. If she catches us she'll grass fuh shewer.'

We're in deep shit yur buh there's gohruh be a way out, even with a fruit an nutcase like Janine. 'Wha uv you said exactly? Tell her the gluies started ih – we only wen there to puh the fire out, right?'

'She'll never believe ih.'

'Course she will! If we geh our story straight an stick to ih she'll have no choice. This is yuh sister we're talking abou, Bunce. Noh exactly Columbo, is she? Even if she have goh the haircut!'

Instead uh laughing he stiffens up, eyes wide at summin he's clocked over my shoulder.

43

'So you thinks I'm stew-ped do you, Lee?' She stands there, hands on hips, grotty virgin socks an a scraggy Alice band like some overgrown junior school spastic – everything abou her screams "freak". Honest to God, anyone buh her an we might have a chance. 'Janine – you goh ih wrong abou last night. We–'

'Save yewer breath. Adam's told me everything.' She pushes her way in between me an the sheepish-looking Buncy, who's more than happy to shrink into the background. 'I'm noh having you bullying my brother, right? If I find out you been bothering him again, I'll tell the police everything.'

I'm gobsmacked yur. Every fucker an their granny picks on me, an now *I'm* being painted as the bully? 'Buncy, tell her,' I goes. 'Tell her ih wadn like ah, butt.'

He says fuck all – wun even look at me.

'Bunce . . .'

The bell fuh first lesson sparks a stampede an Janine takes the opportunity to whisk Buncy away without another word. 'I'm sorry, I'm sorry,' I call after um cos there's like a delay while my brain struggles to process whas actually happened. Then ih clicks. Why the fuck am I saying sorry? Tha cunt nearly killed people down the Blackfields an I never said a word! Now he wants to turn over a new leaf by selling me down the river? No chance! There's like a slow-motion *noooo!* from Janine as I fly through the corridor, target locked. Buncy splats the wall like soggy lettuce buh my heart's going an I cahn geh a proper connection, punches bouncing off him soft as raindrops. I'm shouting: 'You done ih too! Yewer no better!' buh I might only be thinking ih cos everything's happening so fast. The surge uh the crowd catches me off guard an Buncy snatches his chance to turn the tables. As soon as I hit the floor cheap shots pepper in from all angles. I kick out buh my trainer flies off an I yur a girl's voice, Stacey Evans I think, going: 'Urgh, ih touched my bag!' A rib shot takes my breath away an a whack to the nose unleashes streams uh vinegar tears.

Now Buncy's goh his elbow wedged in my throat an he's shouting: 'Stop ih, Lee! Stop ih!' buh he can go an geh fucked for all I care. My strength's deserted me, his BO an Lynx an gravy fumes rushing my head like a full tin uh gas an when the pressure releases an I float to my feet I reckon I've blacked out completely. The crowd scatters like a herd uh BBC 2 antelopes an realisation sets in as I clock the tracksuited lion in their midst. Mr Austin clears the stragglers with his PE whistle then lines me an Bunce up against the wall.

'Stand up straight, the pair of you!' he roars, marching up an down like Heil Hitler. 'What on Earth do you think you're playing at? You will *not* carry on in here like a couple of backstreet hooligans, is that clear? Both of you, Mr Davies' office this instant!'

Buncy scoots off sharpish buh I stick around, dabbing at my bloody nose to leh Austin know exactly who's at fault. No way am I taking the blame fuh this one.

'Well, what's the problem?' He takes a long look at me an shakes his head. 'You should be ashamed – straight back from suspension an look at the state of you already. You're a hopeless case, Lee. Get yourself cleaned up, for goodness' sake.'

'Buh Sir, ih wadn my – I mean, I didn . . .' I wadn suspended, I was mitching buh ih's pissing in the wind trynuh explain anything to this arsehole so I just goes: 'I need to find my shoe, Sir.'

He sighs an turns away.

The steady *drip drip drip* of a dodgy cistern matches the thick red drops beat for beat as they plunge from my nose to the basin. I splash my face wi warm water an gently probe fuh breakages buh my whole body's completely numb except this dull ache throbbing deep inside my chest. As I emerge from the toilets Mam's letter's back in my hands, her lucky American penny tingling my fingertips cos ih's all so clear to me now. This way will never work – if I wants Mam back I gohruh go direct. My feet begin to move faster, certainty pushing each footstep onward an suddenly I'm legging ih through the corridors towards the fire exit, past sulking Buncy outside the Deputy Head's office, past Mr Austin, past my doubts, worries, confusion an out into the bright sunlight without once looking back.

9

I'm noh bottling ih if thas wha you think. Dad's shewer to spot me if I go straight home to pack so laying low at my mitching lock-up till pub opening is the sensible option. Just need summin to pass the time, to stop these legs from fidgeting cos I can do this, I know I can. I trace my finger along the address line, lips moving as I re-read the words: *24 Cherrywood Close, 24 Cherrywood Close, 24* . . . How big is Cardiff really? Someone must know my mother's street – I'll ask every single person in the city if necessary cos I'm noh bottling ih, right?

My nerves jangle like hillbilly's banjo when a car pulls up outside. There's shouting an slamming an through a rusty hole in the shutter I see the same battered motor Mucksy an Becca were in earlier, driver-side door wide open, engine still running. Best sit tight cos the last thing I needs is a repeat uh this morning's performance buh they seem to have their plates full with each other right now.

'Geh yuh hands off me, yeah? I'm sick uh taking yuh crap, Jase.' Becca tries to sidestep him first left then right buh he buffers her back each time in some demented game uh Pong.

'Nah, nah – you ain' going nowhere till we gehs tha gear back off yuh cousin.'

'There's nothing else we can do fuh now – we'll catch up with him after school, yeah? Chill out.'

'Chill out? There's a schoolboy running round with an ounce uh my purest shit thanks to you an I should chill out? Mucksy punches the air inches from Becca's face. 'Lucky I dun knock yuh teeth out, yuh mouthy slag!'

Becca fires a vicious bullet uh gob to the ground at Mucksy's feet before storming off in the opposite direction.

'Yeah, thas right,' he's calling after her. 'Fuck off back to yuh step-daddy. Bet you wun't spit for him though, will ew?'

You can yur every single grain uh gravel explode under her heels as she turns an launches herself at Mucksy. At first ih looks like she might actually do ih, knocking him back against the car with animal rage buh in a couple uh seconds he's wrestled her down on to the bonnet, two wrists pinned by one hand. Now his fingers are clamped around her throat an she's gurgling an squealing an trynuh claw at his face. I'm shaking like a shitting dog buh fucked if I'm going out there. He'll kill me. I pace the garage floor, frantic thoughts fluttering round my head like moths in a jar, creepy Frank Butcher an the way Becca rescued me from Mucksy an the reason Mam left . . . ih's as though I'm watching myself from a distance, climbing through the gap in the wall wi no idea how to handle the situation in front uh me. Fighting the fucker ain' gunuh end well, an pleading probly wun do much good either buh as I close in these words seem to fall from my mouth without trying: 'Help! Please, you gohruh help – the coppers are after me!'

Mucksy stares aghast as though I've crawled out uh the nearest manhole covered in shit. 'Police?' he goes. 'Wha d'you bring um this way for?'

I'm just a spectator, no wiser than him as to wha I'll say next. 'Quick, leh me hide in yuh car!' I pull open the passenger door an go to climb in, waiting fuh the cunt to twig buh he takes the bait, kicking the door shut out my hands.

'No chance, kid. Find somewhere else to hide, I goh warrants out. C'mon,' he calls to Becca. 'Leh's go.'

She spits again, feet firmly planted in position.

'Geh in the fucking car, now!' You can see why he's so edgy – any copper worth their salt ud give him a pull wi those wild eyes an thick lines uh blood streaming down his face. Forty-two carat headcase, certified. Becca dun flinch mind an thankfully he's noh in the mood to force the issue, wheel spinning off into the distance without another word.

Wi Mucksy gone the backstreet falls silent bar fuh the steady hum uh the fan behind the chip shop an the thump uh my racing heart. Becca's leant up against the wall, frowning at

47

her fingernails in a world of her own. I wanuh say summin buh every last scrap uh bottle's evaporated in the morning sun. Ah, fuck ih, I'm out uh yur.

'So where's the police, then?'

I turn to face her buh her eyes dun leave her fingertips. 'Dunno . . . they were there a minute ago—'

'He'd batter you if he thought he was being fucked around. You know tha, doan you?'

'So?'

'Ain' you scared of him? Everyone else round yur is.'

'I ain' scared uh nobody.'

She breaks a pained smile like I'm some Downy trynuh do long division. 'Little hard man, yeah?'

'Noh really . . . ih wadn right, wha he was doing, thas all.'

If she's grateful, she ain' showing ih. 'Goh any fags?' she says, throwing herself down on the kerb in a huff.

'One left. We'll go halves.' I sit down next to her an spark a flame, secretly lingering wi vain hopes uh melting through the wall uh ice surrounding her.

Silence.

'I told yuh cousin you wanted to see him.' Bullshitting's always the best option in a pinch.

'Did you?' she goes, all the enthusiasm of a fatty at a salad bar.

'Yeah . . . he was cool abou ih, like. Tidy boy, Scott is.'

'Come off ih, Marv. He's a nasty little prick. Think I doan know they used to bully you?'

'Nor,' I squirm. 'They never, noh really. Messing round, thas all ih was.'

'If you say so.'

I cahn be fucked arguing cos we both know the score.

'The valleys is one giant cess pit,' she says. 'Wish I never moved up yuh – Cardiff's calling, back wi the old crew, living life instead uh wasting my time wi tha arsehole an his cronies. Geh some money together, then maybe London, abroad, fuck knows. Anywhere buh yur . . .'

She's pure rambling, talking more to herself than me buh I listen close all the same, checking her out every so often from the corner uh my eye. Belly flexing, crop top rising, thick fringe swishing – look up lush in the dictionary an you'll find a picture uh Becca staring back at you. My eyes skim up to her tits, then to her neck where deep red welts rise up against white skin. Bih too blatant mind, she trails off mid-sentence having clocked my game.

'Wha you looking at?'

'Nothing,' I goes, crawling up my own arse.

'No, go on, tell me wha yuh staring at.'

If anyone's staring ih's her, eyes burning through the side uh my head.

'Ih's just . . . there's marks on yuh neck. From Mucksy, like . . . did he hurt you?'

'No, he never fucking hurt me, origh? Whas ih goh to do wi you, anyway?'

'Nor, nor, I never meant – I was only asking, in ih?'

'Well doan ask, okay? Mind yur own business – an where's tha half a fag?' She plucks ih out my fingers, takes one drag an splutters wi disgust. 'Orr my God! Fuck you smoking menthols for?'

'Dunno – all I could geh.' She goh me feeling a prize plonker yur so I try to save the day wi summin Buncy once told me. 'They're better fuh you anyway cos they dun give you cancer like normal fags.'

'What?' she goes, creasing up. 'Who told you tha, yuh silly sod?'

Shoulduh known better than to listen to Bunce buh ih's too late to back out now. 'Ih's true, I seen ih on the telly. They done experiments on old fogeys in cages . . . or was ih monkeys?' Yuring her laugh is pure relief, noh just cos I goh myself out of a fix buh also cos her mood seems to be genuinely lifting.

'Anyway,' she says, 'brass cheek to talk abou anyone else's appearance. Seen yuhself lately? Must've been dragged through every hedge from yur to Merthyr.'

'Trouble in school,' I goes cos she's waiting for an explanation.

'Fighting? Who with – Scott? Those Francis pratts?'

'Nor, my friend, like. Or at least he used to be.'

'Teachers send you home? Suspended?'

49

'Walked out. Noh going back, either.'

'Gun have to go back sooner or later, mate. We all gohruh face our demons.'

'Planning on doing a runner yuhself, in you?' I goes, a bih too sharp fuh my own good. Luckily, she swallows the urge to strangle me.

'Well, origh clever clogs, buh where you gunuh go? Wha you gunuh do?'

'Stay wi my mam. She lives down in Cardiff . . . somewhere.'

'Wha d'you mean, "somewhere"?' She curls her lip an I notice one of her side teeth is chipped almost in half. Wadn like ah when she lived wi Scott, I'm shewer of ih.

'Er, she's moved lately – to a bigger house, pure massive. Six bedrooms, Artex walls, patio doors, the loh.'

'Cool.' She's drifting again, barely listening.

'Yeah, buh the thing is, I havn visited her since she moved an I'm noh exactly shewer . . . I goh an address, like . . .'

She looks blank.

'Wha I mean is . . . well, yewer from Cardiff, in you?'

'Barry, actually.' She's back to staring at her nails.

'Yeah, buh you knows Cardiff.'

'Whas yuh point?' Then the penny drops. 'Nah, nah, find yuhself another sucker, Marv. Goh way too many headaches uh my own right now.'

'I dun wanuh go wi you or nothing,' I lie. 'Thought you could have a look at the address, thas all.'

'Geh an A to Z,' she goes from inside her portable igloo.

'Buh I'm shit wi maps,' I whine, mouth buried in the crook uh my arm fuh maximum effect. 'Dun worry, I shouldn uv asked.'

Ha! Worked a treat!

'Origh, doan stress hard case.' Her gentle hand on my shoulder knocks the breath from my lungs. 'C'mon, leh's see tha address then.' She squints when I pass her the letter, cracked tooth showing loud an proud. Definitely wadn there before. 'Who the fuck wrote this, Joey Deacon?'

No idea who Joey Deacon is buh I know she's taking the piss. My face cahn show though cos she carries on regardless.

'Hmm, noh much to go on, no area or postcode, just a street name. I do remember there was a Cherrywood summin in Adamsdown. Woan find many mansions round there, mind.'

'Close to the prison? She said in the letter ih's close to the prison.'

'Well, yeah, I s'pose, buh yuh gun have to ask someone else. I cahn give you directions, ih's been too long.'

'Buh . . . you'd know ih on foot though, wouldn you?'

She fixes me with a dark brown stare like I'm this far from gehrin a slap buh ih dun stop me pushing. 'I wun't be no hassle – show me the street, thas all I'm asking.' Even wi my full desperado routine she's a tough nut to crack.

'Fuck off, Marv! Jesus! Yuh like a stray dog,' she says buh there's an unmistakable softening in those hard eyes. 'You should be in school. How would ih make me look, taking a fourteen-year-old down to the city? They goh names fuh people like ah, you know.'

'I'm fifteen,' I goes, pissed off she thought I was so young. 'Only a few years younger than you.'

'A fucking lifetime, kid,' she says in a way tha makes me feel closer to five than fifteen years old. Summin tells me creepy Frank Butcher ain' far from both our minds right now. We hit a quiet patch an I'm worried I've lost her buh finally she screws her mouth to the side an says: 'So wha you gunuh do fuh me?'

'Give you tha half a fag, didn I?'

'Pff, tried to poison me with a fucking menthol!'

'An I told Scott you were looking for him.' I'm tempted to mention the thing wi Mucksy buh I dun wanuh set her off nasty again.

'Nah, I reckon you can do better than tha. Tell you wha , help me out with a little favour an I'll show you where yuh mum lives. Deal?'

A certain tone in her voice tells me this is definitely a bad idea buh when uv I ever leh tha stop me before?

*   *   *

51

Me an my big mouth. Coulduh took my chances, made my own way down to Cardiff buh no, Gob Almighty ends up casing the house uh Pengarw's most notorious crook, his hell-bent ex-girlfriend in tow. We take cover in the bushes round the side, my mind racing a mile a minute while Becca tries to figure a way in. She's slating Mucksy from his hole to his pole, talking abou payback, how no one gehs away wi taking the piss out of her buh all I can focus on is those wide eyes shining secret an sexy in the leafy murk.

'You listening?' she snaps like elastic on my knicker-line daydream cos those leggings might as well be painted on.

'Yeah, course.'

'Go on then, geh moving,' she says pointing up to the bathroom window.

'Nor, Becca, I cahn . . .'

'C'mon, I know you done creepers before. Geh in an open up the back door – simple.' She strokes my arm an whispers: 'Please, Marv, I thought I could trust you.'

'You *can* trust me, honest. Buh Mucksy–'

'Fuck Mucksy!' she goes, jaw locked tight as her grip on my arm. 'Thought you wern scared uh no one. Great! Another bullshitter in my life, making promises he cahn keep!' She goh me feeling a right scumbag. I did promise, after all.

'I ain' bullshitting, just worried I might noh fit through the gap.'

Like an Etch-a-Sketch, one quick head shake wipes the harsh lines an tension from her features. The blank canvas gazing back at me goes, 'course you'll fit – noh exactly Hulk Hogan are you?'

There's no answer to tha so I'm up on the outhouse roof, shuffling along the ledge pure Milk Tray Man style. Fuh some reason people goh me marked as this mad criminal, burgling an robbing all over the show buh the truth is, apart from a few old warehouses I've only ever done garden sheds an garages. This is a step beyond. Sweat rolls as my hands fumble on the latch cos Mucksy's gunuh show up any minute now. Bet you a tenner.

'Whas taking so long?'

She ain' helping matters buh I think better uh telling her so.

'Oi! Hurry up, yeah? Yuh taking ages.'

Fuck's sake! My fingers slip an the window goes crashing into the metal frame. I barely goh time to throw myself flat on the outhouse roof before the neighbour's back door swings open. My heart pounds against the concrete fuh summin close to an hour till finally the nosey bastards go back inside. Part uh me hopes the window'll jam an we can give ih up an shoot through buh you should know my luck by now. Second try, ih slides smoothly open an I seem to be fitting through the gap no probs as well. Noh so fast, halfway in my belt catches on the window frame an I'm stuck, hovering inches from the stinking toilet below. Panic sets in cos someone's bound to notice a random pair uh legs waving round outside buh thas the least uh my worries when a sickening *riiip* plunges me face-first towards the shit-stained bowl. Curtain rings, shampoos, razors all rain down, each thing I puh back tidy bringing three more tumbling to the floor. Fought enough losing battles fuh one morning so I abandon ship an make my way downstairs to Becca.

Never expected open arms buh a bih uh gratitude wouldn uv gone amiss. Instead I'm shoved to the side as she bee-lines fuh the front room where stacks uh car radios an video recorders clutter the floor. Before I can stop myself I goes: 'Whoa! How'd Mucksy afford all this gear?'

She's disgusted enough to stop ransacking for a moment buh I never meant ih like ah. I know ih's dodgy, I'm noh stupid. She ain' in the mood fuh explanations, mind.

'Make yuhself useful, Marv. Grab some stuff, smash the place up – just do summin, yeah?'

I awkwardly kick an empty can buh ih feels forced so I end up standing there like a spare prick as she goes to town, flipping the settee an checking the lining underneath.

'Wha you looking for?'

'Money.'

'There's a fifty p by yur!' I swoop to pick ih up buh she snatches ih out my hand an throws ih across the room.

'Fifty fucking p! You taking the piss?' She rushes out to the kitchen an comes back in a minute later, still flustered. Th's yur somewhere,' she's going, 'ih gohruh be.' Now she's over to the gas fire, pulling the grate off while muttering curses, hopefully at Mucksy, maybe at me.

'Wha was ah? Dope?' I ask, spying the shiny brown block she's bundled into her pocket.

'Payback,' she says. 'If I cahn find no money this is the next best thing.'

'Th's massive! I never seen a lump tha big.'

'Thas cos yur a fucking joker.'

I laugh, trynuh catch a smile off her buh there's nothing coming back. She must feel bad though cos a moment later she tuts an says: 'Hey, doan cry, tough guy. I was only messing! Now, listen. We berrer geh out uh yur.'

Dun have to tell me twice. I'm gone.

'Hold on,' she goes, 'noh too clever fuh both of us to leave at once, is ih?'

'Well, no, buh—'

'So I need you to wait around for ten minutes, yeah?' Before I can argue she adds: 'You been wicked today, Marv. I knew you had more balls than the rest uh the dickheads round yuh.'

I play ih cool buh inside I'm buzzing. 'So wha time we leaving fuh Cardiff?'

Probly confused with everything happening so fast, she looks stunned for a moment. 'Er, tell you wha ,' she says as she pulling the door shut on me, 'I'll meet you down the train station in an hour. Goh a couple uh things to sort out first.'

The door clicks shut an I'm alone with a million racing thoughts, noh one uh which can even begin to make sense uh the maddest, most mental, fucked up morning ever.

10

Ten minutes, my arse – I'm out uh yur pronto buh noh before taking a quick scout fuh loot, cos I did the graft at the end uh the day. I dip three bottles from the stack uh Smirkenoff Genuine Vodka crates in the corner an scoop um up in my shirt, waddling towards the front door an freedom. Yeah, right. Like anything's ever tha simple in my world. Guess who's stomping up the garden path, jaw set heavy an determined like he's sucking on two giant gobstoppers? My limbs freeze solid as the keys jangle in the lock then reality kicks in an I'm gone, hurdling the overturned settee an skidding across the kitchen lino to the back yard. The bottles slip an burst *tsh tsh tsh* buh none uh tha matters, only one thing's important now. Escape.

Somehow there's enough strength in my wet spaghetti arms to lift me over the garden wall an straight down onto next door's prickly hedge. I'm skewered like a cocktail sausage, mouth open wide to scream buh the sound comes from somewhere back in Mucksy's house. Obviously delighted with our little makeover. No time to waste, I'm ducking washing lines an jumping trikes before he's goh a chance to express his gratitude in person, like.

When I finally emerge on to a street I find I'm only a few blocks from my house. Everything'll be sorted as long as Dad's still out fuh the count, buh the sound uh Saxon blasting on the stereo as I approach puhs paid to tha idea. The lounge curtain's flapping through the open window like a monstrous pink tongue, my father's cracked voice slavering out the words to "Never Surrender" from behind ih. He stumbles round the room, singing into the bottle between swigs uh cider. Thinks he's Ozzy Osbourne, the cunt do. Says heavy metal was his only true love an I s'pose he's right, bar fuh the booze uh course. Thas always the real number one with him, although his guitar an record collection have survived all the hard times when almost everything noh nailed down goh pawned or sold. Lashed up, he'll sometimes go on abou the band he started with his mates in high school. Thing is, Darren was born when Dad was sixteen an I wadn far behind, so while Valhalla wen round the country, playing the pubs an clubs Daddy Dear found himself stuck in the valleys with a couple uh screaming brats. They ended up gehrin a replacement guitarist an even goh a single in the charts, or so he says. You can see why he gehs wound up buh ih's noh our fault the silly fucker had kids so young, is ih?

So ih seems the old man's decided to relive his glory days at half ten on a Monday morning. I could wait fuh the pub to open buh there's no guarantee he'll be going, an time's tight if I'm gunuh meet Becca down the station. One thing's fuh shewer, the party'll be short-lived if he catches sight uh me buh there's a silver lining in the racket, so loud I might actually be able to geh in an out undetected as long as the record keeps playing an the cider bottle stays half full. Berrer geh a move on then.

Bruno the dog's giving Dad a run for his money as I sneak round the back, howling away an noh sounding much worse either, in all fairness. The pile uh dirty dishes in the kitchen sink rattles an bounces under the booming bass an you dun need to be Mystic Meg to foresee ructions wi the neighbours later today. Shame I'm noh gunuh be yur to witness ih.

Halfway up the stairs the record runs out an I freeze in the highest stakes version uh musical statues ever. He comes out for a piss now an ih's game over buh after a couple uh seconds another tune starts up, leaving me to silently thank my lucky stars. Maybe Mam's American penny is finally starting to geh ihs arse in gear.

I dive straight into the pile uh clothes on our bedroom floor, hoping to separate a few noh-too-bads from the millions uh completely-boggings laying there. Laundry ain' exactly high on my father's to-do list an I'm hardly swamped wi the latest gear anyway. After filling my rucksack with a couple uh bihs I take a minute to look around the room; at the tatty posters, the two knackered beds we'd hide under as kids when Dad was going loopy, the big old wardrobe Darren used to lock me in till I'd scream in the dark. Never could push my way out. However hard I struggled, however much I grew the cunt was always too strong. Well noh this time – I'll kick the doors off the fucking hinges cos I'm breaking out an nothing can stop me. No more sitting round waiting for a miracle – if I wants the good times wi Mam again I gohruh take responsibility, go down to Cardiff an fix wha I've broken.

Back to business, I shift my bed away from the wall as gentle as I can. The crusty *Razzle* wi Jo Guest falls out from under the mattress buh I push ih aside, noh interested fuh perhaps the first time in my life. My goal's a little wooden box under the floorboards, abou the only place in this whole house thas truly mine. There's a few quid left from the paper-round takings, enough for a one-way ticket an thas all I need.

I'm so preoccupied I dun realise how quiet the house uv gone. Noh at first anyway, an by the time I've clocked summin's noh right ih's too late. He stands there in the doorway, rollie between his lips, fingers twitching at his waist like a Wild West gunslinger.

'Wha you doing home?' The words churn like gravel in a cement mixer.

'Dad!' Think fast, think fast. 'I – I goh sent home fuh my uniform. Forgoh to my school shirt, see?'

'Dun't treat me like a fucking fool, boy! Come in yur wi yuh clothes stretched an yuh nose swollen thinking you can feed me a pack uh lies.'

'No, I swear ih wadn like ah! A kid at school started on me . . . I never wanted no trouble, honest to God.'

'Course you did, Lee. Course you wanted trouble cos that's all ew fucking are, in it! Huh? Answer me! You an yuh brother, the pair uh you. A fucking curse!' The cunt's ready to strike, coiled up tight like a boa constrictor. 'Cahn help ewself, can ew? You'll end up bringing those nosey bastards round yur again wi their files an their questions. Tha wha you want?'

'No,' I whines, pure laying on the sappy voice, all the while checking for an escape route. If I can just give him the slip one last time then he can stick his social workers an his hidings an his piss-head friends fuh good.

'You better hope they *do* take you away this time cos yuh life wun't be worth living wi me!' Suddenly his bloodshot eyes drop down to my waist. 'Wha you goh there? Wha you hiding behind yuh back, yuh little shit?'

'Nothing,' I goes cos he can fuck right off if he thinks he's pissing my ticket to freedom up the wall.

'Well, if ih's nothing, leh me see then!' He lurches across the room, so arseholed I swerve him pretty easy buh I've gone an snookered myself by stepping into a corner. 'Dun't piss me around! Gimme wha you got!' He's so close now I can smell the sour cider an shit mix on his breath, almost feel the scraggly yellow stubble on my cheek. Another snatch at my hand an fifteen years' worth uh rage finally erupts.

'No! Fuck you! I'm noh giving you nothing, I hope you die!'

His face goes blank for a minute, like I've told a clever joke an he cahn quite figure out the punchline. Before he gehs the chance to click I make a break fuh the door buh the old bastard's surprisingly agile now he's really angry, his faggy fingers catching hold uh my rucksack an bungeeing me backwards. At the last minute I slide my arms out uh the straps, leaving him to roll round on the floor like a paraplegic break dancer while I bomb down those rickety stairs making all the noise I likes.

I'm a good few streets away before stopping to catch my breath. Yur I am, hanging over the railings, gasping for air when ih hits me. I've spent all morning – no, all my life, running an hiding, from the boardie man, police, bullies, dogs, an where's ih goh me? Well, from now on I'm facing my problems head on. Just as soon as I gehs to Cardiff.

A train rolls into the station as I round the corner buh there's no panic cos Becca's noh due for another forty minutes. Time to find a little cubby an sit tight. I tramp over the footbridge as the automatic doors hiss open. Down on to the platform as the last few passengers board. Up alongside the train as the doors slide shut. Then I see her. Even from the back I can tell instantly – ih's Becca. I bang on the window, heartbeat keeping pace wi the engines as they ramp up fuh departure cos she's lost in a world of her own on the far side uh the carriage. The ticket guy arsing round with his whistle at the back uh the train's my only hope. He huffs an puffs when I call out buh lehs me slip on without a word. A brief wave uh relief's steadily replaced by outrage as I move through the aisles, seething at the thought uh gehrin ditched after everything I done for her. She goh some explaining to do. I plonk myself down in the seat opposite ready to tell her straight.

'Marvin! Marvin, thank God yur okay! I didn think you were gunuh make ih!' she rabbits as soon as she clocks me. Fast talk an wide eyes are dead giveaways. Bang to rights, butt. 'I tried to warn you buh there was no time – ih's Mucksy. He knows.'

Hang on, best geh tha foot out my gob cos I've jumped the gun yur, doubting her when ih's so obvious she couldn stick around wi tha maniac on the loose. 'Sorry, Bec, I never thought – he nearly caught me too . . .'

'We're well rid uh the cunt now, Marv. Come on, doan look so sulky. Everything's gunuh be origh.' A smile tha brings the sun out from behind the clouds convinces me she ain' bullshitting. There's no way.

She dun speak much for a while, just stares out the window with her lips puckered, probly stressing abou everything thas happened. Me though, I cahn shurrup.

'So whas ih like down Cardiff then?'

She screws up her face. 'Thought you used to visit yuh mother all the time? You tell me.'

Walked into tha one, didn I?

'Er, yeah – buh she lived on the outskirts, like. I'm talking abou the city centre.'

'Right, yeah.'

Phew. She bought ih. 'Only, my friend at school reckons there's these knife gangs tha jumps in yuh car at the traffic lights an forces you to drive um round an if you says no they puhs you in hospital an everything.'

'Behave, Marv, ih's noh the Bronx. Just another shithole like Pengarw or Merthyr or anywhere else, only bigger, thas all.'

Pure cringe – thas the last time I listen to Buncy! Becca's back to pouting at the window so I take the hint an quieten down. Fucked if I know her game. Acts like my best buddy one minute an wants uh strangle me the next. There's one uh those dinky bookie's pens on the table so I gives the cracked table-top the old MARVIN 9T5 treatment, thinking abou wha Dad used to say after Mam left. *Women ain't fuh figuring out, they're fuh sorting out! Thas where I wen wrong!* Even if I wanted to, I goh abou as much chance uh sorting Becca out as I have Nigel Benn.

I sink back in the seat, the rattling tracks below launching wave after wave of fireworks through my feet to explode in my stomach in a shower uh sparks an light. Another train shoots past in the opposite direction, rows of unknown faces flying by, could be anyone, could do anything. Like me. Soon the mountains an the river melt away an ih's all warehouses an office blocks an traffic. As we wind into the station there's only one thought clear in my mind. I'm never, ever going back.

11

Off the train an smack bang into the wildest rugby scrum this side uh the Arms Park, business suits versus tracksuits an me as the ball. A fat old tramp over on the bench acts as referee, deep in debate wi the big set uh platform weighing scales who I guess must be his linesman. Everyone's a fruit an nutcase, butt! Tha singing chocolate bar was obviously a regular down Queen Street station. The noises, the smells, ih's all too much an to make matters worse I've lost sight uh Becca. I barge through the crowd in a panic, accidently knocking into this biscuit-munching toddler being dragged along by his mam. He watches the biscuit roll away, those wide watery eyes reminding me so much uh little Chocolate Chops from back in Pengarw tha saving his treat suddenly becomes the most important thing in the world to me. I dive between the forest uh legs, broken hearted as this scar-faced seagull swoops before me an busts the biscuit to crumbs in his ugly beak. Plan B, check pockets fuh change – if I can just buy him another before he starts to blub . . . too late. One preoccupied yank from his mother an he's gone forever, devoured by the crowd out in the big wide world.

Dwelling's a luxury I cahn afford right now cos I've just seen Becca disappear down the steps an fucked if I'm losing her again. When I catch up in the tunnel below her welcome's Baltic.

'Hurry up, if yuh coming,' she goes over the echoes of a thousand lonely feet. 'Told you, I havn goh time to babysit.'

Grumpy cow wadn so arsey when I was risking life an limb to help her, was she? 'Well, maybe if you didn keep trynuh ditch me . . .'

She must feel bad cos she takes me to the side, her tone much sweeter. 'Listen, Marv, doan take ih personal, yeah? There's a loh on my mind right now buh I said I'd show you the address an I will, okay?'

See, sometimes all ih takes is a quiet word. Now she couldn be nicer, even leaning in for a surprise hug an buh as usual wi Becca there's more than meets the eye, the real surprise coming in the form uh Mucksy's cold, hard lump uh dope pressed flat into my hand. I protest, uh course, buh wha good's tha ever done me? She folds my fingers round the block an pushes ih towards my chest, whispering: 'Puh ih in yuh pocket,' before scooting off towards the exit. I'm still scratching my head as three big figures loom up ahead, tit helmets silhouetted against the bright daylight outside. Finally the penny drops.

I tell her there's no way – if they catch me ih'll be prison fuh shewer. They'll think I'm a drug dealer. She dun wanuh yur ih though, jamming me up against the wall with a pure deadly glint in her eye.

'Doan even think uh testing me, kid. Make a scene now an we're both gehrin done. Keep calm an you'll be fine – yur too young to geh pulled.'

So wha am I gunuh do? I'm tempted to throw the thing on the floor an move on. If she wants ih tha bad, she can geh ih herself. Buh there again, piss her off now she'll never show me to Mam's. Right, yur goes. My chest is snare-tight cos tha one copper's goh me marked, I'm shewer. He's itching to stop me – oh shit, this is ih . . .

A blast uh warm air from the street washes pure sparkling relief over me cos I only fucking made ih, butt. Scot-free! Now to catch Becca, who's shooting daggers at me from a nook under the nearby railway bridge.

'See, you need to listen to me more often,' she says, casually leaning up against the grimy stone work. 'Told you there was no danger of a pull.'

'Well, they never pulled you either.'

'Yeah, buh they might've.'

I frown, trynuh figure out if she's goh a point. Maybe she's right – maybe I'm being unreasonable abou the whole thing.

'Anyway, enough uh yuh cheek,' she goes, scanning fuh witnesses. 'C'mon, hand the weed ov–' I follow her gaze out to the street where two uniforms are passing by. Traffic wardens. No danger. We relax again only for a cloud uh pigeons to burst from the girders at the rumble of an overhead train. The pair of us jump out our skins an ih's quickly decided tha we need to keep moving. She leads me away from prying square-eyed office blocks, round the sleeping snake of a prison wall into old terraced streets like the one Buncy lives in back home. Just another shithole, only bigger. True, 'cept down yur they goh all Pakistani ladies in multicoloured dresses to go wi the usual biddies in curlers. Becca's doing her power walk routine again an by the time we reach Cherrywood Close I'm boiled in the bag.

'Well, there ih is.' She points to the dead end full uh newer houses an flats. 'Mummy's penthouse must be in there somewhere.'

Suddenly I'd give anything to be tucked away in my lock-up, far from unfaced demons, shoulders ten ton lighter buh thas rose-tint talk an I bet Becca would agree if she wadn halfway down the road, hair an hips coolly swinging out uh my life forever. Now ih's just me an the annoying voice in my head saying run on home. Even knowing my filthy mouth you'd be shocked by my choice uh words fuh tha little fella.

Focusing on the house numbers is easier said than done when there's rivers uh sweat stinging yuh eyeballs buh I wipe an plough, wipe an plough: 4 . . . 6 . . . 8 . . . number 10's starting early if the blasting sounds uh UB40 are anything to go by buh the pair uh doorstep zombies in his 'n' hers tracksuits an matching cans uh Tennents dun exactly look in the party mood. I avoid their stares an keep counting: 12 . . . 14 . . . 16 . . . Number 24 is huddled away in a corner, pokey little porch thing jammed between two others. The bottom half uh the door's boarded up an there's stacks uh black bags piled high in the garden. Cahn be the right address, shewerly. Only one way to find out.

Three separate knocks an still no signs uh life. I press my face against the bubbled glass, springing back as a black shadow looms in the passage beyond. The horror show dun end there though, door creaking open to reveal a pair uh sunken eyes peering through folds uh leathery skin.

All I can do is choke out, 'Mam' cos every last rehearsed line has gone an deserted me. Ih's noh just the situation, ih's the state of her . . . horrible. Might sound stupid buh I'd assumed escaping her problems ud make her a new person. Was half expecting to find her jogging round pure bright an bushy like Challenge fucking Anneka buh instead I'm face to face with a freaky bag uh bones in a grey Minnie Mouse sweatshirt. She opens her mouth wide, an for a second my heart leaps cos she's laughing! After all my stressing, she's actually glad to see me! The feeling soon fades as she reels back against the wall, sliding down, fingers burrowing scalp between knots of hair. Now I see the laugh is really a silent scream, buh maybe noh so silent cos like thunder after lightning she's wailing like a fucking stray cat.

I step into the hallway, checking behind for any street spectators. The two tracksuits uv fucked off so I close the door, hook my arms under hers an take her through into the front room where she collapses on to the settee, whining: 'No, no, no, you shouldn be yur – you shouldn uh come.'

The assault uh chip grease an stale smoke an unacceptable words sends the room swirling like a tombola drum. My sweaty palms clench the doorframe as I mumble: 'Buh yuh letter . . . I thought–'

'No! I shouldn uh sent ih! Wadn thinking straight, was I? Oh my God, I cahn handle this, my fucking head's going.' She sparks up a trembling Superking, coughing so hollow there might actually be one uh them spray can shakers rattling round inside her chest.

So many times I've played through this moment in my head – childish, really – imagining we'd both hug an leh ih all out like the families on daytime chat shows or wha have ew. Buh yur I am, doing nothing buh the spare-prick shuffle, struggling even to look at her. I wanuh say summin, to reach out buh I cahn seem to find the right moment, the right words.

'I sent you a letter back, Mam . . . didn you geh ih?'

'Terry took care of ih fuh me,' she croaks into the crook of her knees. 'He dun't wan me upset no more, see?'

64

'Oh yeah, who's Terry then?' Didn mention this fucker in the letter, did she?

Those sunken eyes flash through the straggles uh hair. 'Terry's a good man. Looks after me,' she says like I've accused the cunt uh fiddling kids or summin. 'An he goh a job. He's decent – noh like yuh father.'

'So – so thas ih? Wern you ever gunuh come back an see us?'

'Cahn you understand I gohruh geh myself sorted first, Lee? Cahn ew gimme a chance to geh my head together? You an yuh brother, always starting summin – knew I couldn take no more buh you had to keep pushing. Any wonder I'm like I am?' She springs up off the settee an I shrink back, braced fuh the blows.

'I'm better now,' I plead from inside my peek-a-boo boxing stance. 'Thas wha I came to tell you – ih's okay to come home cos I dun cause trouble no more. Noh once since you left, I swear.' The expected battering never comes cos she's dashed straight past me an instead assaulted the bottle on the counter, splashing pissy scotch into a grubby glass an sloshing ih back once, twice, three times an alchy. Her fuzzy breaths start to even out an when she finally speaks again her voice is much calmer.

'Listen love, I will be back to see you one day buh I'm just noh ready right now. My counsellor says I shouldn take steps I'm noh prepared for, see? Rush ih an I could end up back to square one.' Then she clears her voice like a little kid speaking in front uh the class: 'The healing pro-cess must be an organic development free from outside interference.'

'So thas wha I am? An interference?' The words squeak past the grenade wedged in my throat.

A bang at the door breaks the awkward silence an bounces Mam's eyes round her head like two watery grey marbles. 'Who the hell's ah?' she says, like I'm s'posed to know. 'Maybe ih's Terry, forgoh his keys.' The knocking gehs louder, an ih's funny how shook up she is considering this bloke's meant to be Prince Charming's hunkier brother. 'Yuh gun have to go, Lee–'

Now the door's gehrin pounded.

'Shit. Wait yur a minute, I'll take him out the kitchen. Then you slip away, okay? I'll write to you again . . . when I'm better.'

I slide behind the lounge door an puh my yur to the crack, just as eager as Mam noh to meet this Terry character.

'Who, love?' her voice rasps in the passage. 'No . . . no one yur by tha name . . .'

I breathe a bih easier cos ih's obviously noh Terry.

'I'm telling ew, I dun't know no Martin! . . . yeah . . . huh? Well why didn ew say so?'

The door clicks shut an my jaw drops open as Mam ushers a flustered-looking Becca through into the lounge. Ten minutes ago I was snivelling at the thought uh never seeing her again buh now I just wan rid cos the house is a mess an Mam's such a state an ih's all pure mortifying to be honest.

'Didn tell me you brought company, Lee. Wha d'you leave the poor girl outside for, all this time?'

I ignore her an turn to Becca. 'Alright? Whas going on?'

'I need to talk to you,' she says with a death-ray glare.

'Uh?'

'In *private*. Outside.'

Sooner the better, far as I'm concerned before Mam can really start embarrassing me. Oops, too late.

'Dun't mind me, bebs – you can say *aanything* in front uh me! I've yur'd ih all,' Mam cuts in, throwing her head back an laughing like a bar room slut. Fucking state of ih. Havn changed one bih. When ih came to serious talk she fell to pieces buh now there's a drink in her hand an someone new to impress an ih's party time again.

'So's there summin going on yur, or wha? My little boy all grown up, eh? Done well fuh yuhself there, Lee.' She gives us a big slow wink an laughs tha slutty laugh again an I'm pure shaking, I hate her so much.

'How abou a cheeky drink then?' She jiggles the bottle at Becca.

'We're going.' I barge past her to the door, literally sick to my stomach of her voice.

'Alright bebs, I know you understands.' Then she turns to Becca an breathes in her face: 'He understands – he's a good boy, he is.'

66

Her words chase me down the garden path like a swarm uh clueless gnats: 'I'll write to you Lee, when everything's better. Maybe Terry can take us out in the car. You can bring yuh girlfriend . . .'

I walk faster, break into a sprint, desperate to escape her mindless droning. At the end uh the street I stop dead. Hang on, I been short-changed – come all this way to make things right. Where's my second chance? I run back towards the house ready to kick the door through an beat ih out uh the selfish old slag. Barely even manage ten steps before my eyes are too blurry to continue so I collapse to the kerb wi my head in my hands.

'Marvin.'

My aching concrete jaw wun respond.

'Marv, you still goh the ganja.'

Fucking hell, wha a right old sucker I really am.

'You are, goh wha you wanted. Now fuck off an leave me alone, will ew?' I fling the lump uh dope at her, expecting a mouthful in return buh instead she parks her arse next to me an gives my knee a gentle shove.

'Didn quite go to plan, eh?'

'Leave me alone, alright?'

'Stop feeling sorry fuh yuhself. Ih's annoying. Yuh noh the only one wi problems, you know.'

I push my head further between my knees so she cahn see my tear-streaked face.

'Yuh mum's a right mess, in she?'

'So, she's still my mother!'

'Doan marrer who she is, if she ain' doing you no good then forgeh her. In this life you can only rely on one person. Everyone else'll fuck you around in the end. Did you really expect anything else from her?'

'I dunno . . . maybe. Needs my fucking head read, dun I?'

'Nah, you just gohruh learn the hard way, same as most of us. Now listen, how you gunuh geh home? Goh train fare?' She jangles her pockets fuh some spare coins.

'I dun wan no train fare. I'm noh going back.'

'Doan be daft, wha else you gunuh do? Hardly even know where you are.'

We both know wha I want. I leh my puffy pink eyes do the talking, expecting the palm-off buh instead gehrin a flexing finger in my face. 'Okay, leh's geh ih straight yur an now. I doan owe you fuck all. You tag along wi me, ih's strictly on my terms. Any clinginess, I'm gone. Any better offers, I'm gone. Anytime I feel like, I'm gone. Right?

'Right.' She dun notice my beaming smile, too busy shaking her head like she's lost a tenner an found a fag end.

'An try to keep quiet, yeah? Doan need you embarrassing me in front uh my mates.'

'Yeah, yeah, course.' Cheeky cow – way she goes on, you'd think I was a right plonker.

'So come on, leh's geh moving.'

I trot after her, sniffing up loose slugs uh snot as I go.

'Orr yeah, I goh a bone to pick wi you – wha exactly you been telling yuh mother abou me?'

'Nothing!'

'Doan play daft – all tha girlfriend talk. Where'd she geh an idea like ah from?'

'I never said anything! Honest!' I laugh an another snot bubble blows out my nose, right in front of her this time although thankfully she glosses ih.

'Well if you say so,' she says with a sideways smirk tha makes me laugh even harder.

'I swear on my life! She must've just puh two an two together.'

'Yeah, an come up wi' minus twelve!'

'Oi, whas ah s'posed to mean?'

'Be real, Marv. You an me? Tha wadn whisky she was drinking, ih was fucking turps!'

We both crack up again buh there's a strut in my step now, pure Travolta walking down the street loving the jealous stares from every fella we pass by cos the end uh the day, there's no harm in pretending, is there? Who's to know?

Autumn 2018

The man shuffles impatiently on the threadbare carpet of the crematorium foyer, doing his best to ignore the six or seven other walking wounded strewn about the place. He doesn't recognise any of them, but then, why would he? His mother had been a stranger for the last twenty-three years, virtually disowning him after his disastrous trip to Cardiff all that time ago. Frail seams of their relationship consistently torn apart by his clumsiness and naivety . . . no, not now, for fuck's sake. These things should stay where they belong, in a past best forgotten. Just pay his respects and leave, that was the plan. No sentimental indulgence, no trips down memory lane – or back-alley, as the case may be.

It's a relief when the chapel doors finally swing open and the mourners can begin to file in, moving with the dishevelled resignation of the lapsed alcoholic returning to explain himself after a three-day bender. Judging by the state of some of them, the comparison's dangerously apt. He shudders and makes to follow, instinctively checking over his shoulder for Karen's reassuring smile before remembering that he and his wife are no longer together. Then shuddering again as he remembers why.

A hand falls on his shoulder with all the tenderness of a garden rake and he turns to see two people he recognises, although for some inexplicable reason hadn't anticipated finding here. Their faces have aged for sure, but it's as though the father and brother he used to know are just millimetres below the surface, ravages of alcohol and time mere cosmetic applications, make-up to be casually wiped away on a whim. A few strained pleasantries are exchanged, every word dusted with enough frost to send a chill over this mild September morning. He doesn't know them and they don't know him anymore. After getting out he never went back home and what little connection they might once have had was now long gone.

They take their seats and listen as the piece-work minister bumbles his way through a half-arsed excuse for a eulogy. After skirting around the drinking and general themes of failure and defeat there's not a great deal left to say, so perhaps the minister's job and knock effort isn't too bad considering. The man isn't really listening anyway, busy travelling through space and time to a childhood home where he felt safe, tucked up in bed with his mother reading comic strips in the newspaper and laughing, cuddling . . .

He blinks and he's in some cliquey working men's club, buffeted against the bar by the surge of bodies desperate to drown sorrows and senses. His father slurs in his ear, something about getting his boys a drink but the old man's ninety proof breath suggests he's had more than enough already. One becomes four becomes eight and the scene descends into a series of blurred snapshots, his father's the only distinguishable voice in an ocean of sound, louder and more obnoxious with each swig of the jar. The man squints to focus on the drunken old fool who's enjoying himself so much he's near ready to whip out his guitar and have a right rousing sing-along. Sickening. Still going strong after all those years of self-abuse, sitting there laughing and drinking and breathing like he owns the whole fucking world. Suddenly the man is gripped with a raging sense of injustice. It's this old cunt who should be in the oven, not Mam, who'd only been driven to drink by Dad and Darren and . . . That's right. Forget those two wasters – if he wants someone to blame there's no need to look further than the nearest mirror. Sparks of impotent anger ignite the gallon of Stella in his belly. Fists clench, ready to lash out at whoever wants it, the first person to speak. A random nominates himself by catching the man's eye for a second too long but just as he's about to leave his seat someone budges down next to him, a heavily made-up girl in her early twenties, attractive and young enough to be out of his league but bearing an overpowering whiff of desperation that makes him feel right at home. She introduces herself as so and so's niece and he nods and smiles as much as his numb facial muscles will allow.

He says something unintelligible even to himself which seems to make her laugh and the way her dark panda eyes sparkle under her thick fringe stirs some indefinable emotion deep inside him. More drinks go round and more fags go round and the hand she initially used to give him a comforting pat on the knee seems to have taken up permanent residence. He knows which way this is going. No strings, no baggage, no relationship to destroy, no feelings to hurt. Around the back of the club they stumble in the cool night air, her just as needy as him. This is safe, this is easy. This what he wants.

Part II : Coming Up

12

'H – hello? Hello! What is, pliz?'

Becca crouches to meet the shifty eyes peering from the letterbox. 'I'm looking for a friend uh mine – Jamo, er, I mean Saul, Saul James. He lives in 46A.'

'Er, is not now 46A.'

'Huh? D'you mean he's moved away?'

'Da.'

'Where to?'

'Uhh, it 46B'

'Wha , he's in 46B? Can you geh him fuh me then?'

'Da, 46B.' The eyes flick from Becca to me an back again. 'Da.'

'So wha you waiting for . . . ?'

'Uhh – da.'

'What the fuck is he on abou?' Becca hisses to me before straightening herself out an going back for another shot. 'Listen, mate. I . . . am . . . looking . . . for . . . my . . . friend. He . . . used . . . to . . . live . . . here.'

The empty eyes blink.

'Tall guy,' she goes, holding a hand above her.

Another blink.

'Er, short hair.' She swishes her hands on top of her head.

No reaction.

'Dark, he is – you know, black.' She waves around her face.

'No, no! No more. Pliz, must go.' The flap snaps shut. Becca bangs the door an the voice comes muffled from inside: 'Pliz, no trouble. Must go.' Then there's silence.

'Argh, fuck ih!' She throws herself back, stamping her heel against the wall.

'I think he might uh been foreign.' The warranted look uh disgust spurs me into a spot uh damage limitation. 'Wha I mean is, maybe he was from a war zone – traumatised in the head, like. Seemed weird, didn he?'

'Probly expecting immigration to kick the door through any minih.' She blows a twist uh hair off her face. 'Bollocks! Goh no phone numbers wi me or nothing – shoulduh known this'd happen.'

'Noh stuck already are we? Thought you had loads uh mates down yur.'

'How abou shutting yuh trap, Marv?' Best take the advice an remain acquainted wi my two front teeth, I reckon. Even if I wanted to speak this shrill accusing voice has beaten me to ih.

'–You're looking for the half-caste fella.'

Clocked her type straight away – nosey old hag wi dentures like tombstones, noh a good word to say abou no one.

'So wha if we are?' Becca growls in warning, noh one to geh chopsed off at the best uh times, old biddy or noh.

'Just don't you go thinking people round yur are stupid. I said, I might be getting on in years but you can't pull the wool over my eyes. Different faces in and out every day, bastard music all hours – not one of them with a job, mind. Bloody disgusting, mun!'

'Listen love, save ih fuh Neighbourhood Watch, yeah? I'm just trynuh find my friend.'

'That's right, your "friend". Like I said, we know what's going on alright. You've all got that same look about you.'

Subconsciously my hands uv slipped down to my cock an balls, cupping them from the evil biddy's x-ray gaze.

'Oh! Doan be so fucking rude! We havn done nothing to you so geh back on yuh perch an shut ih!' As Becca takes a step forward this yapping streak uh brown shoots across the road an stops a yard in front of us, skirting from left to right like a demented leprechaun squaring up for a fight. Obviously the hag's sidekick – the little Yorkshire terrier's still trynuh geh at us as she scoops ih up into her arms like some freaky parody uh Rod Hull an Emu, her frizzy hair an big teeth completing the look to a T.

76

'Bloody state of you! Disgraceful! Out of yuh minds on all sorts!' she goes, tutting at my nervous giggles. 'Come on Harry, I know you don't like these bad 'uns. Can smell them a mile off, cahn you, boy?'

Halfway into her house she turns back with a funny glint in her eye. 'I'm surprised you come yur this time of day, mind. Your "friend" never shows his face till late afternoon. Thought you would've known that.'

*   *   *

We find a park a few streets away an decide to smoke on our next move, spurning the char-grilled, piss-stained benches in favour of a shaded patch uh grass under a tree. I watch closely as Becca skins up, fingers an tongue working the Rizlas pure effortless. Sometimes me an Buncy nicks bihs uh dope from my brother's stash buh neither of us can roll proper an ih's usually a struggle just to geh a few puffs. Noh Becca though. She knows the score.

'Reckon ih's worth trying back there in an hour or so?' I ask the mysterious figure barely visible through the thick blue haze.

'Dunno,' she says. 'Wouldn trust tha old cow as far as I could chuck her. Talking like Jamo's moved out one minih then only popped to the shops the next. Probly how the bitter old bag gehs her kicks, trynuh mess wi people who still goh life left in um.' She blows out a long stream uh smoke with a gentle sigh.

Secretly, I'm hoping this Jamo guy has moved away cos two's company an judging by the crowd she hangs round with back home he's bound to be trouble. Half-caste an all – Dad's always told me to watch out fuh the blacks cos they cahn be trusted. Reckons they're noh like us. Says the same abou people from Cardiff mind, buh there ain' many of either up the valleys so fuck knows how he become such an expert. Still, best to keep on my toes until I know wha I'm gehrin into. Time to test the waters. 'So whas he like, this Jamo?'

'He's cool.'

'Known him long?'

'Er, yeah, we go back years.'

So far, so good.

'Where to did you meet him, like?'

Spoke too soon – down crash the shutters again.

'I just knows him, origh? Nosey little fucker, in you?'

'S – sorry, I never meant to be funny . . .' There's a danger too many questions'll send us right back to square one buh thankfully she waves the gathering storm clouds away with a flick of her wrist.

'Look, all you needs to know is he's safe as fuck. If we ever manage to geh hold of him you'll see wha I mean.'

I ain' convinced, buh smile along anyway. 'Wha if we dun't, though? Where else can we go?'

'If we don't, we don't. Ih's no stress, I knows people. Mostly dickheads, like, buh I'll find somewhere to go. There's a few guys I could drop in on over Ely if ih comes to ih.'

Fucking hell, this just gehs worse. Bread riots an gang beatings – seen enough news reports on tha place to noh wanuh feature in the next, thanks all the same. 'Well maybe we should try back at the flat first, then?' I say, the idea uh Jamo turning up suddenly growing on me. 'No point rushing over to Ely, is there?'

She nods slowly, full red lips kissing the luckiest roach in the whole wide world. 'Well, wha'ever happens I need to offload this draw pretty quick. Noh wise to be walking the streets wi this much shit on me.'

'How much is there, d'you reckon?'

'Five or six ounces, easy,' she says, passing me the spliff an examining the goods in her bag. 'Ih's a ninebar when ih's whole buh a good chunk's missing, see.'

I lean in closer, pure wide eyes cos this is big-time amounts yur. Looking at the shiny brown block with ihs rounded edges I finally understand why they calls ih soapbar. Buncy always said ih was rhyming slang. You know, bar uh soap: dope. Thank fuck I never blurted tha pearl uh wisdom out. Dun wan her thinking I'm daft, do I? I try to sound knowledgeable by saying: 'Must be worth hundreds, all in seven-fifties, like.'

'Selling small pieces ud take forever – I'm looking for someone to take the loh.'

'Tha why yuh so desperate to find this Jamo?'

'I'm noh desperate to find no one,' she says fixing me wi dark brown disdain. 'Jamo's a good mate uh mine. Funny as fuck, friendly, cool. You goh nothing to worry abou so chill, yeah? They're different people down yur. Remember tha.'

From wha Dad's told me, how could I forgeh? Anyway, she dun have to draw me a picture cos the situation's crystal clear from where I'm sitting. Fancies the cunt, dun she? Probly done all sorts with him, years back. Will again, soon as my back's turned – bet you any money. I start pulling stubborn clumps uh grass out the ground, ripping an tearing when they dun come up as easy as I wanted. She ain' slow to cotton on.

'Digging fuh spuds, are you? Fuck's sake, you look like you just won first prize in a little dick competition! Saying my weed's crap, huh?' I turn away in a sulk as she playfully snatches at the spliff. 'Orr yeah, I geh ih, a ganja hog!' She pokes me in the side an I giggle then choke on the smoke. When I go for another puff she clamps my nipple between her thumb an finger so tight I shout an drop the spliff. 'One – nil! One – nil!'

Everything's cool between us now, cosy dope buzz making ih impossible to maintain the sulk. I lie back on the grass an close my eyes, the warm sun wrapped around me like a lush snug quilt . . .

*   *   *

'Urgh! Geh away yuh dirty bastard!'

Eyes snap open red alert, Becca stood over me swinging her bag by the strap like tha Highlander swings his sword on Hooley's videos. The source uh the panic's plain to see, a rampant ownerless Doberman bounding round us wi bad intentions. Fear uh gehrin savaged soon turns to embarrassment though cos this hound is ready for a different type uh action if you know wha I mean. Fortunately for us his attention's diverted by a dainty little poodle across the way an he sets off at a pace, tongue an todger hanging out to dry.

Becca capitalises on my grogginess, seizing the opportunity to build a solid head start while the full gravity uh the situation's yet to dawn on my smoke-addled mind. When the cock-teasing poodle gives ih the slip through a gap in the fence reality finally hits home. The randy fucker's out fuh some loving, choice now coming down to either me or Becca, who's halfway to the gate already. I break into a sprint an gain ground fast buh she's wise, zig-zagging to block my route when I go fuh the overtake. Stamina fails me as the dope in my system regroups an I know my heavy clunky legs wun carry me much further. Somehow we manage to cross the finish line an slam the iron gate shut, collapsing in fits uh giggles at how close we came to death by dog dick.

All the way back to Jamo's I'm twitchy, listening out fuh any signs uh panting coming up behind cos tha Doberman was like a thing possessed. Nothing there though. Must be paranoia off the dope. Becca's her usual sympathetic self, growling out the side of her mouth an snapping at the back uh my neck with her fingers.

'Seen the way he was looking at you, Marv. Reckon yuh luck's in there.'

'Uh? Shurrup!'

'Telling you now, kid, you woan be sitting for a month after he's had his way!' She grabs my arse an I jump four foot in the air, shocked cos no girl's ever touched me like ah before, though I'd never admit ih. I wonder if I should do ih back to her – thas how flirting works, in ih? No chance though cos we round the corner just in time to see two heavies wi clipboards banging on Jamo's door.

'Crafty old cow,' says Becca, holding me back.

'Who are they?'

'Well they ain' selling double glazing, whoever they are. Could be bailiffs . . . or maybe the council – no one we wanuh geh mixed up with, thas fuh sure.'

'D'you reckon tha old woman grassed on us?'

'Course she fucking did. Probly thinks we goh some info on Jamo. Look, look, there she goes now.'

The sour biddy walks across to the men, talking an pointing while they stand there nodding mean an moody. I'm only half paying attention though cos the paranoia's coming on strong again, panting behind me sounding louder than ever, hot breath on my neck realer than any stoned daydream . . . holy fuck, ih's behind me! Ih's escaped! 'Becca! Becca!' I tug her sleeve an she spins round, same look uh horror etched on her face, buh as usual wi Becca there's an ace up her sleeve.

'C'mon boy, c'mon!' She whistles an clicks, coaxing the dog towards the mother's meeting going on between biddy an baddies. As soon as the Doberman gehs a whiff uh little Harry ih goes mental, squashing a surprised yelp out the Yorkshire terrier with a big body slam straight out uh WrestleMania. The lady screams an flings herself into the fray buh the big dog bowls her over ten-pin style, way too powerful an horny to control. As she flaps around ih only goes an mounts her leg, humping away like a sex offender on day release. She ends up laying there groaning out for her little Harry, too knackered to fight the beast off. The two clipboards tiptoe over, fleeing wi their skirts around their arses when the Doberman growls in warning. Me an Becca are literally holding each other up cos this is the funniest thing I've ever seen, hands down. Serves um right though. Thought they were messing wi some stupid kids buh no one fucks wi Becca – she's always five steps ahead. Thas just one uh the million reasons I love her.

13

So this is the legendary Chippy Lane, an oasis in the parched summer streets uh Cardiff, Godsend fuh the gutsy an the ganja-baked. Mark me down fuh both. Hooley's manky snowballs might as well uv been a decade ago as I giant-step over empty chip wrappers pure man on a mission, slow-mo Olympics music looping in my yurs.

'Summin funny, spaz?' Becca says cos I've started sniggering under my breath. No time to answer though, wha wi the hot counter almost in touching distance, glinting solid silver in the sunlight. I snigger again.

Becca's taking forever, arguing the toss over prices an freshness buh I'm far too stoned an hungry to geh involved. Leant up against the wall outside I tear strips off the newspaper wrapper, shovelling in steaming chips like they're going out uh fashion. I'm halfway through the bag when I realise someone's watching me. A little short-arse standing across the street, maybe a year or two older than me, baseball cap perched high on top of his head like Brian Harvey out of East 17. When I catch his eye ih's the green light he's been waiting for.

'S'appening, brah?'

I swear, if Mother Teresa had a Cardiff accent her Lord's Prayer would sound like an invitation for a car park punch-up. Just summin abou tha cockshewer twang makes even the friendliest of um sound like they wants a scrap buh there's no mistaking this kid's intentions. Pure aggro, trust me. My jaw grinds to a halt as he saunters over, pops one uh my chips in his gob an promptly spits the hot chunks down at my feet. 'Urgh! Minging they are, B!'

I check over my shoulder buh Becca's horns are still firmly locked wi the poor sucker's behind the counter.

'Oh, wha you ignoring me for?'

Tha old chestnut. Seems the pricks in Cardiff are just as unimaginative as the pricks back home. 'Wadn ignoring you, butt . . .'

'Butt? Fucking *butt*? Best geh yuhself back up the valleys, kid. Sheepshaggers ain' welcome in my town, righ?'

'Ih's noh yewer town, anyone can come yur,' I say, instantly cursing my smart gob fuh the hundredth time today.

'Doan back chat me, sheepshagger cos I'll drop you on yur arse.'

'No, I never meant—'

'Fifty p, then!'

'Uh?'

'Gimme fifty pence an I woan hit you.'

'Spent all my money in there,' I goes, nodding back to the shop. Becca's still miles away. Fuck's sake.

'Yuh lying.'

'I'm noh.'

'Best you ain' fucking lying!' He puffs his chest out like a big budgie, relishing his upper hand.

'Honest to God, I havn goh nothing!'

'Origh, prove ih. Jump on the spot.'

'Wha? '

'You yurd, jump up an down, sheepshagger. Any coins rattle an yuh fucking teeth will too, righ?'

Cahn be serious, shewerly. I give a half-hearted hop buh ih ain' cutting the mustard.

'Do ih properly or I'll check yuh pockets myself an take everything you goh.'

I tense up, suddenly remembering my lucky penny. He cahn take tha, ih's all I goh left of . . .

'Oh! Fuck's going on out yur then?'

Never uv I been so glad to yur another person's voice. Straight away Brian Harvey loses his bottle. True, mind, Becca has tha effect on a loh uh clever cunts.

'Fucking pussy!' he says, sucking his teeth as he's backing away. 'Needs a girl to fight yuh battles fuh you?'

'Oh, hold on – you owes my friend an apology.'

'Yeah, yeah, wha'ever,' he goes, noh once breaking my gaze to glance in Becca's direction.

'Origh then, keep walking little boy.'

He takes her advice, looking back over his shoulder every few steps till he thinks he's far enough away. Then he says ih. 'Stupid slag.' There's a moment uh silence which seems to hang in the air for an eternity before Becca's bag uh chips explodes on the back of his head like a feather pillow, knocking his hat into the gutter. He picks a few chips out of his collar an examines um pure dumbstruck, pea-brain unable to register the fact tha he's just been Becca'd.

'I – I was only messing . . .' he stutters, wiping the gunk off his hat.

'Call me tha again an I'll puh you through the fucking wall.' Her eyes glaze an you can see by the way the kid's swaying he dun know how to handle her – laughably turns to me fuh help buh he wun geh no joy, wouldn tell him even if I knew.

'Whoa, whoa, ease up, yeah? Whas the problem?' Two blokes emerge from a shop across the street, a big bruiser complete wi bulldog jowls an a tall, dark, skinny one with his cap pulled down low over his eyes. Dodgy as fuck, the pair of um.

'Ih was her, boys. Started on me fuh nothing, she did.' With cronies in tow, Brian Harvey's miraculously found his bollocks again, now staring at Becca the way he was staring at me.

'Call trynuh rob someone "nothing"?' Becca fumes, blanking the two newcomers in favour uh the prey in her sights.

'I never tried robbing no one. Messing round, thas all. Wadn I, kid?'

'Well, was he?' the dark skinny one asks me, buh Becca nips ih right in the bud.

'Oh! Doan geh involved, yeah? This is fuck all to do with anyone else.'

'Damn, wha is ih wi you? Always picking on the little boys. Too scared to mess with a real man, huh?' skinny says, voice cracking up as though he's fighting to hold back a laugh.

84

'In yuh dreams yuh fucking cree – Jamo! No way, Jamo!' Becca screams an throws herself at him while me, Brian Harvey an the bruiser stand round scratching our heads. 'Jamo! Orr my God, I been looking everywhere fuh you!'

'Becca, love, long time no see! Whas the latest, man?' Jamo wraps his arms around her, big gap-toothed grin plastered over his face an I geh tha familiar twist in my guts cos Stevie Wonder could see whas going on yur. Very fucking cosy. She's loving ih too, eyes pure half-moons wi delight. Never looked at me like ah, uv she? I'll be gehrin ditched pretty soon, guaranteed.

'Listen, to be honest I was hoping I could stay at yours a few nights, Jam. Tried to find you over Roath buh things goh a bih mad, like. Take ih yuh noh living there anymore.'

'Pff, forgeh abou tha place,' he goes, looking uncomfortable. Then he adds, 'Never told no one nothing, did you?'

'Course I never. You'll piss when I tells you wha we goh up to, though. So whas happening, is ih safe to crash wi you, or wha? I'll make ih worth yuh while.'

I hope she's talking abou the dope buh the way they're giggling an gazing at each other I'm noh so shewer.

'Offer I cahn refuse, in ih?' he goes, making her squeal by squeezing his arms even tighter.

'Noh like ah, yuh dirty get! You fucking wish! No, I goh some business.'

'Sounds interesting. Listen, you can come back to my place if you really wanoo. I lives up Llanedeyrn now.'

'Yeah?'

'Yeah . . . wi Charmaine.'

Becca's mouth drops into a perfect O. 'Raz! Yuh wi Charmaine now?'

'Been together over a year,' Jamo goes, almost apologising. 'Buh doan go worrying abou ancient history. Water under the bridge, in ih? She'll be chuffed to see you.'

Becca screws her mouth up to the side, unconvinced. 'Hope yuh right, mate.'

'I'm always right.' Then he turns to East 17's finest. 'So wha was the noise before I showed up, anyway? Russy, you been causing trouble again?'

'Nasty piece uh work, he is,' Becca says, spitting the foul words out her mouth. 'Cahn believe you hang round wi someone like him, Jam.'

'Whas ih gohruh do wi you?' Russy goes an Becca flares up again, warrior queen ready for battle. Jamo nips ih in the bud though.

'Do us all a favour an disappear, yeah Russ? We're gehrin tired uh yuh bullshit to be honest, man.'

'So yuh gunuh take her word over mine? Fuck's sake! How am I gunuh geh home now?'

'Shoulduh thought abou tha before you started coming a cunt, in ih?' Jamo walks off an we all follow, leaving Russy to stare after us. 'C'mon guys, I think a little celebration's in order. Fuck me, of all the people to bump into. Baby Becca, like we used to call you! Member? Ha ha!'

'Yeah, thanks for reminding me,' she says, feigning embarrassment. 'How we gehrin to Llanedeyrn, anyway? Doan tell me you still goh tha clapped out old Lada.'

'Ih wadn a Lada yuh cheeky bitch!'

'Ih was a fucking death trap, wha'ever ih was.'

'Well ih doan marrer cos I goh an XR3 now. Tha to yuh liking, yuh Highness?'

'Hyng, doan lie, Jam – ih ain' an XR3, ih's a normal Escort with a spoiler stuck on!' The bruiser's first words come as a surprise, pure high an wavy like a chewed-up cassette tape. Close up, he dun look such a hard cunt either, more the big dopey type. Gohruh be a few sandwiches short of a picnic to be wearing tha thick old Spliffy coat in this sweltering heat.

'Cheers fuh tha – some fucking friend you are!' Jamo says. 'This is Wonk Eye, by the way. No prizes fuh guessing how he come by tha name.'

I try noh to stare buh ih's true the guy have goh one hell of a knock eye – noh so much lazy as bone fucking idle, butt!

'Hyng, I was only saying.' Wonk Eye pokes his fat bottom lip out like a sulky kid buh I dun think he's all tha hurt really.

'So who's this little fella, then?' Jamo nods towards me.

Becca jumps in to spare my tongue-tied blushes. 'This is Marvin. Wanted a mish to Cardiff, so I leh him tag along.'

'Ha, nice one, Marv!' Jamo flashes tha big grin again, an I cahn help buh return ih cos ih's like a bug, pure contagious. 'Stick with us spar, we'll look after you. Have a proper scream. An doan worry abou tha dickhead back there – Cardiff people ain' all like him.'

Straight away he goh me feeling easier buh as we walk to the car I cahn help checking over my shoulder. He's there, like I knew he would be, tha evil little Russy kid, staring at me with a face so twisted an angry you can bet yuh life ih ain' the last I've seen of ih.

14

We're over on two wheels as the car screeches to a stop outside the flats, Wonk Eye hurtling across the back seat an landing on my lap like a sixteen-stone babe in arms. Until he decides to unpeel my face from the window there's no choice buh to check out the vast pebbledashed sprawl they call Llanedeyrn. First impressions ain' great. Grey council boxes, high an low, same as our estate in Pengarw. Becca's words ring true again – same shithole, just bigger, thas all. Rougher, too? Everywhere's rougher when yuh from out uh town buh judging by the ten or twelve kids crawling all over a burnt-out Cavalier like ants on a giant ice-lolly, I'd say this place could give Pengarw a run for ihs money easy.

Yur comes trouble – boss ant leads his troops off the bonnet, swarming us to a standstill as soon as we leave the car.

'Goh a spare fag?'

'No such thing as a spare fag, yuh little ragamuffin. Otherwise they'd start selling packs of eleven, wouldn't they?' Jamo gehs the boy in a headlock an scruffs him round buh ih's play-stuff, noh the serious rumble I'm expecting.

'Doan be rude, Jam,' the kid goes, straightening himself out. 'You knows we always keeps a look out round yur.'

'Keep a look out? Cause fucking murder, more like.' He tosses a fag to the kid an a thousand little hands scramble to catch ih. 'Orr yeah, an fuh the last time: stop sticking spuds up car exhausts. Every cunt's been moaning abou you loh.'

'Never done yours though, did we?'

'Noh the point – doan shit on yuh own doorstep, in ih? You gohruh do stuff like ah, do ih to the rich fuckers over Cyncoed, origh?'

There's a laugh from the gang, an I must be honest, ih is impressive how Jamo handles these little shits.

'Serious though, you should know better. Next time ih'll be a word in yuh brother's ear, an you knows wha'll happen then.'

'Noh bothered. Goh locked up this morning.'

Fuh the first time since ih came, the grin's gone from Jamo's face. 'Yuh joking me! Wha for?'

'Only driving offences – had warrants out fuh time. Mother's going scatty up the house, breh. Believe!'

'Driving offences,' Jamo repeats to himself, no longer interested in small talk. 'Laters, yeah. I need to see Charmaine.' The crowd parts like the Red Sea an we follow Jamo through to the flats, me giving the gang my hardest stare as I go. 'Best you waits a minih,' Jamo says when we geh to the second floor landing, his infectious enthusiasm draining more an more with each step. Even the reassuring grin he flashes a grim-faced Becca's lacks the sparkle of before. There's history yur, guaranteed. He disappears into the flat wi Wonk Eye an pretty soon a voice tha ud shame the mouthiest docker comes floating out into the passage.

'. . . *the fuck you been, useless cunt . . . leaving me to deal wi . . .*'

A door slams an there's a crash like a load uh plates uv hit the deck. This Charmaine's no shrinking violet, leh me tell ew.

'*Char, Char love, I'll geh ih sorted . . . someone yur to see you . . .*' Jamo's saying, still cool despite the racket going on.

'*Who? Who wants to fucking see me?*'

Oh shit. Freight train footsteps rumble towards us buh I'm trapped, pure rabbit in the headlights, then WHAM! The door flies open an I'm face to face wi this bristling bleach-blonde pineapple staring wi murderous intent, though thankfully noh at me.

'Wha the fuck you doing yuh?'

Wadn expecting red carpet buh this is summin else. She stands, hands on hips, presumably waiting fuh a serious answer. I'm surprised she ain' chewing on a big wodge uh bubblegum – she's just tha sort, if you know wha I mean.

'Forgeh ih, I knew this was a bad idea.' Becca throws her hands up an makes to walk away.

'Hang on! You ain' going nowhere – noh without giving me an explanation.'

'Ih's been years, Char. I thought you might be pleased to see me.'

Charmaine sortuh chokes out a laugh. 'Pleased? After wha you done! Gavin nearly topped himself cos uh you! An you skanked all his money – mine too, remember?'

'Course I remember. Thas why I'm yur – to make up for everything. I never meant fuh things to end so bad wi yuh brother buh . . . you knows how messed up I was back then.'

'Ih's no excuse.'

'I know, I know ih's no excuse, an I'm sorry.'

'Easy to say, in ih? Buh how do I know you ain' gunuh start yuh shit again?'

'Charmaine, you were my best friend. Still are, like, even if you cahn stand the sight uh me no more. Listen, ih's fair enough if you doan wan me in the house buh I still wanuh pay the money back. Serious, now.'

Fuck me, I'm waiting fuh the ground to open up. Talk abou a spare prick.

'You might find ih hard. Gavin joined the army after you left. They sent him to Belfast a few months ago.' Charmaine gives Becca a look like ih's her fault this fucker's been shipped to a war zone. Maybe ih is, for all I know.

'Raz, I never thought . . . w – well maybe you can pass ih on to him fuh me, yeah? Goh his details, havn you?'

'Gimme the money, then,' Charmaine goes, holding out her hand.

'Well, thas another thing I wanted to talk to you abou. See, I havn goh ih yeh, bu–'

'Surprise, surprise! Becca's backing out on a promise!'

Becca drops her head, pure defeated. 'Cahn handle this no more, Char. Just wan ih back like we used to be. Please, gimme one more chance. I swear I woan leh you down again.'

A tired smile creeps into the corners uh Charmaine's mouth as she steps aside. The pair of um disappear without a word leaving me to choose between dying uh loneliness or inviting myself in. Loneliness ud take too long so in I go, poking my head into the front room in time to see the two girls shut themselves into the kitchen. So now ih's just me an the four walls. Place is a bih battered, to be fair. Noh tha I can talk, buh the wallpaper an dado rail stop in the middle uh the room, like whoever was decorating goh bored halfway through. There's a million multi-coloured paint spots on the floor tiles to match the million previous tenants. Council might as well puh a revolving door in an save every fucker the hassle uh gehrin keys cut. One little step into the room an Jamo an Wonk Eye burst through another door like a couple uh Jeremy Beadles. I flap as though I been caught snooping buh Jamo puhs me straight.

'Oh, Marv, doan just stand there, spar. Grab a chair. You'll be waiting a long time fuh those ignorant women to take care uh you!' He flashes tha grin at me again an suddenly I'm right at home. I settle on the end uh the settee, Wonk Eye next to me mouth breathing in his thick coat an cap. The jury's still out on this one, could be a proper psycho. Way he's staring ain' doing a loh to ease my suspicions.

'Fancy him or summin, d'you Wonk? Stop gawping at the poor man!'

I'm buzzing at being called a man an having a bigger man jump to my defence buh the wonky donkey ain' giving up tha easy. 'Hyng, gunuh tell us yuh name then, mate?'

Jesus, tha voice. There'll be a reel uh cassette tape spilling out his gob any minute now. Eyeball's doing overtime an all, swinging like a hypnotist's watch, goh me dizzy trynuh keep up.

'His name's Marvin, Wonk, you've already been told. Fuck's sake!'

'Is ih?'

'Yeah, yeah,' I say, trying an failing to concentrate on anything other than his roving rollerball.

'Hyng, where to you from, then? Noh Cardiff, are you?'

'Give him a round of applause, fu-cking hell,' Jamo goes, hands over his face.

'Hyng, hyng, I was only asking, Saul.'

'Nor,' I goes, feeling a cunt now cos I dun wanuh be rude, just cahn quite figure him out. 'I'm from Pengarw. Up the valleys, like.'

'Orr, cool. I wen on holiday to the valleys, once.'

Is he taking the piss?

'Yeah, Porthcawl, ih was. Trecco Bay. D'you live by there?'

I'm stumped, shewer the boy's on a wind up buh his expression's telling no tales. The eye pings again. Jamo groans. I look over towards the kitchen, door miraculously swinging open as I pray fuh Becca to re-appear.

'Everything sorted wi you pair, then?'

The two girls share a look. 'Yep.'

'Well doan sound too enthusiastic, will you?'

'Yes Saul, everything's great, thank you ever so much for asking.' Charmaine fires out each word with a separate head judder, pile uh peroxide curls dancing down from the pink bobble smack bang at the top of her head. A chopsy one, no doubt.

'See wha I gohruh puh up with?' Jamo says, winking at me. I smile back. Wrong move.

'Find summin funny, is ih?' Charmaine snaps. 'Who d'you think you are, taking the piss out uh me in my own flat?'

'Uh?' The room's shrunk to the size of a phone box, only occupants me an her.

'Mouthy fucker, are you? Smart cunt?'

Usually yeah, buh a jungle cat called Charmaine's well an truly goh my tongue today.

'Yurd you wants uh stay for a while.'

'Well, long as you dun mind, like,' I say, hilarious words considering her attitude so far.

'I woan mind as long as you knows how to behave yuhself. If Becca says yur origh, then I'll go along with ih. Fuh now.' She narrows her eyes as if to say, *I'm watching you.* I just play dead till she's tired uh mauling me.

'In case you didn realise, Marv, thas Charmaine's way uh saying welcome to Cardiff!' Jamo saves my bacon again by breaking the awkward silence. 'Now love, if yuh quite finished wi the Gestapo routine we goh some serious shit to sort out. When did Mikey call over?'

'Couple uh hours ago – tamping he was. Wants his money. Today.'

Jamo breathes out hard, gappy teeth whistling. 'Fuck's sake!'

'So you picked up off Mathers like you was s'posed to? Yuh gun have to shift ih pretty quick to geh Mikey's cash.'

'Noh happening, love. His little brother's outside – told me Mathers goh locked up this morning.' If Jamo sinks any further into his armchair he'll disappear.

'Origh go an see Taffy Gonzalez then,' Charmaine says through pinched-up lips.

'Orr, come on Char, noh Taffy. Biggest merchant going. All he's ever goh is tha bunk squidgy black – more chance uh gehrin block up off an ounce of Oxo.'

'Well you gohruh geh the money somehow, Jam,' she shrieks. 'I'm noh having tha lunatic calling over again.'

'Mikey ain' tha bad.'

'Noh tha bad! Noh tha fucking bad? He smashed Gerald Mooney's toes with a hammer fuh thirty quid! Thirty fucking quid!' She's really freaking now, pineapple bouncing left to right as she paces the floor.

'Thas a bullshit story,' says Jamo without much conviction.

Becca cuts in quick before Charmaine's goh a chance to swing fuh someone. 'Er, I might be able to help you out, as ih goes. Remember I said I had some business? Check this.' She lays the bar on the coffee table an sits back, pure lapping up the stunned faces. Jamo's eyes bulge at the big block uh dope, then over at Becca, then Charmaine an back to the dope.

'Fuck me, there's more than half a ninebar there! Where'd you geh hold uh tha?'

'You should know better than to ask, Jam. D'you wanuh do some business or wha? '

'Fucking right, how much for an ounce? Ih'll have to be tick, though. You knows the score, we're brassic.'

'Nah, nah.' Becca shakes her head. 'Listen, I'll puh ih straight: I wants cash quick . . . wanuh clear my debts wi you loh an all. So if you can bang ih out, I'll give you a cut. How much d'you reckon we'll geh fuh the loh?'

Now Jamo's strictly business, clearing a space on the table while shouting orders at every cunt like a sergeant major. 'Love, go an puh the cooker on, an geh me the knife an scales.

Wonk, pass me the paper an pen off the window sill, man.' He starts scribbling some stuff down on the pad. 'Okay, there's six ounces there, at least. If I knock um out in 'teenths an half-a-quarters we'll be looking at over seven hundred quid.'

Becca wades in wi the kibosh. 'Nuh, too long. I told you, ih needs to be quick.

'Noh being funny Bec, buh people round yur doan buy in ounces. Might be able to move a few halves like, buh ih's mostly small pieces.'

She twists her mouth up at the side, clearly thinking uh trying her luck elsewhere. Jamo seems to sense ih coming, quickly adding: 'You'll be surprised how fast ih sells – been dry round yuh lately so every fucker's clamming for a decent draw. An anyway, whas the big rush? First time we seen you fuh years an you wants uh go shooting off straight away? Stick around, we'll have a bubble like old times. Wha d'you say?' The famous grin's back with a vengeance an I gohruh be honest, I'm hoping she'll say yeah myself.

'Okay, okay, deal! Fuck me, ih's impossible to argue when yuh like this. Now we gunuh geh a little celebration going or am destined to die uh thirst?'

'Wonk Eye, make yuhself useful an geh some cans. Use the electric money in the kitchen cupboard. Anyone else gunuh chip–'

BANG BANG BANG!!

Everyone freezes.

'Who the fuck is tha?'

BANG BANG BANG BANG!!

'Sounds like police! Shit!'

The whole flat erupts in a mad scramble. Becca snatches the soapbar up an stuffs ih down the side uh the settee. Jamo stretches out an arm an clears the shit off the coffee table in one fell swoop. I jump up out my seat, spin around in a circle an sit back down. The intercom starts to buzz. My heart starts to pound.

'JAMO! JAMO, OPEN THE FOCKING DOOR!'

'Hang on, was tha Shifty?'

'JAMO! C'MON YUH CUNT, OPEN THE DOOR!'

94

Jamo creeps over to the window. 'An ih is – ih's Shifty. Wonk Eye, leh him in, quick!'

Footsteps clatter the concrete staircase, front door blown open by the force uh the jibbering hurricane tearing across the room, pure Taz of Taz-Mania, destroying everything in ihs path. The madman twists, turns, swan dives over the settee then sprawls on the floor giggling as the heap uh plastic packets he lost in the dismount rain down around him. One lands in my lap – a pack uh pink hair rollers, sort old ladies wear.

'Whas going on, Shift?' Jamo goes after picking his jaw up off the floor.

'Shushhh!' this Shifty practically shouts with his finger to his lips like some cracked-out librarian. He crawls to the window on his hands an knees, pokes his head over the sill an ducks back before he's even had a chance to see anything. Second time round he plucks up enough courage to have a proper check an once he's satisfied the coast is clear, turns to the row of expectant faces. 'Hwahahaa, s'appenin' guys! Looks like you seen a ghost or summin.'

'Nah, just a giant bellend trynuh give his mates heart attacks, thas all.'

'Orr, sorry guy, sorry. Safe, yeah, nice one. Never meant to freak you or nothing. Been on a mad raise I have, Jam!' Shifty flicks his wrist an snaps his fingers together. 'Check ih out!'

'Hair curlers? Fuh real?'

'Yes, guy! Some silly focker left a van wide open round by the Maelfa. You knows the score – you snooze, you lose, breh! Pretty lively for a little bloke, though. Come after me like Linford, guy, I swear down dead!'

I watch with amazement as this maniac leaps an bounds, gathering up his curlers an spitting out words like machine gun fire, more cartoon character than a real person. Must be summin in the water down yur – every one of um's chicken oriental, butt!

'Still managed to geh away wi the goods though,' he goes, pure chuffed with his pile uh loot.

'Shift, they're fucking hair curlers, mate.'

'Yeah, and?'

'*Yeah and*, wha you gunuh do with um? Who's gunuh wanuh buy curlers?'

Shifty's face drops for a second, as though this small matter never crossed his mind. Then he snaps his fingers together again, party back on track. 'Listen guy, when the old dolls down the bingo gehs a load uh these they'll be chucking their pensions at me.'

'Taking money off old ladies now, Shift? A new low, even fuh you', Charmaine chips in.

'Nor, nor . . . well, yeah, why noh? Only gunuh geh ripped off by them bingo hall crooks, yeah? Yeah! Might as well geh some quality merchandise fuh their cash. I'll be doing um a favour. Come to think of ih, why doan you try a nice new hair-do?' He vaults the coffee table an accosts Charmaine with a curler.

She swerves him, squealing: 'Urgh, geh off yuh daft twat!'

'Go on darlin', you'll look a million pesetas. Lahvley jubbly!'

'Yeah, Del Boy's abou your dap,' says a wary Charmaine. 'My hair's curly as fuck anyway – try her over there, you goh no chance wi me.'

For the first time since he crash landed, Shifty seems to realise there's new people in the room. His eyes light up at Becca, tha familiar knot in my stomach tightening like a noose when he slides up next to her an slips an arm round her waist.

'Orr yeah, so who's this little cutie pie then?'

The surge uh relief when she gives him the cold shoulder's like six spliffs at once. There's enough competition from Jamo without anyone else muscling in.

'Origh love,' Shifty whispers loud enough fuh people in Hong Kong to yur. 'I was gunuh charge top dollar to tha miserable cow over there buh I'll do you a special offer, in ih? Buy one an geh a free gift, know wha I mean?' He raises his eyebrows an nods towards his trousers.

'Pff, you can keep yuh little magg-i to yuhself,' Becca goes.

I'm gutted when Shifty rocks wi laughter like ih's the best answer he coulduh yurd. 'Magg-i! Yuh cheeky bitch, I goh too much for a little girl like you to handle!' He turns to

Charmaine. 'Who's this, yuh friend is ih? Proper feisty one, yeah? Yeah! I like ih!'

Jamo pulls the plug: 'Eyes back in yuh head a minih, Shift. We were in the middle uh some business before you crashed the party. So whas happening, Bec?'

The bar reappears an Shifty's eyes stalk fuh the second time in as many minutes. 'G'waan! Wha a nugget! Definitely sticking wi you loh tonight – someone tick me a seven-fifty, ih's time to geh block up!'

15

'Okay, so I wanuh know,' Jamo goes, shoving another ice cold can uh Carling into my hand. 'Whas the real situation between you an Becca?'

A long swig uh my drink only buys so much time buh luckily Shifty chooses tha exact moment to dive-bomb the settee, sending beer up my nose an down my chin. While I'm busy milking the choking fit Becca's busy dashing my dreams with a cold dose uh reality.

'Eurgh, fuck off Saul – wha d'you take me for?' She pokes out her tongue after sucking on the question like a sherbet lemon, making Jamo laugh a bih too hard fuh comfort.

'No, no, you goh me wrong. I mean whas the story wi you both down yur out the blue?'

Becca rolls out the old change-uh-scenery line buh Jamo ain' having ih, keeping on until finally she spills the beans abou Mucksy an the bar. 'There woan be no trouble, though,' she adds at Charmaine's concerned clucking. 'They'll never find me down yur.'

'I knows tha Mucksy, he was in Portland in '91. Skinny little gypo, spent half his sentence crying in his cell an the other half joeing for every focker who raised their voice. Nothing to stress abou, Jam, trust guy.'

'I dunno – mixes wi some proper characters these days – big-timers from Birmingham an ah.' Why Becca's willing to make her case worse just to save face over Mucksy's anyone's guess – I've given up trynuh figure her out.

'Well if he comes calling at this door wi some Brummie dickheads they'll be gehrin this up their fucking arses,' Jamo goes, waving around the big kitchen knife he's been cutting up the dope with.

'Believe ih!' Shifty says wi tha mental giggle.

Me, I'm hoping Becca's right. I mean, there's no chance of um catching up with us, is there? Without saying a word, everyone's agreed noh to mention ih again. Booze is always handy for a spot of amnesia so we down our cans an crack open more, pretty soon they're reminiscing abou old times, snatches uh memories like:

'Wha'ever happened to Carter?'

'Over the wall, he is. Armed robbery with a chair leg, the dopey get.'

'Always was thick, tha one – member he convinced himself his flat was haunted – run over our place in his bare feet refusing to go back home. Reckoned he could yur voices an things kept switching umselves on an off? Turned out the silly bastard ud lost the telly remote down the settee – every time he sat down he thought he was gehrin visits off the dearly departed!'

'Yeah, wen on fuh days like ah, didn he? Nearly signed himself into the nuthouse by the end of ih! Best place for him!'

'Oh, tha reminds me. Becca doan know abou Acton, does she?'

'Who?'

'Stevie Acton – used to DJ all over.'

'Oh yeah, tha poor fucker. Lost ih completely. One too many microdots, now the boy's on a permanent trip. S'posed to be sectioned off up Whitchurch buh I've seen him a couple uh times in central station, fucking body popping in some bogging carpet coat asking fuh spare change an ah. Sad state, man.'

'Orr, I knows him breh, focking wicked on the decks, he was – goh offers to play the big raves – Fantazia, Helter Skelter, all of um.'

'Did he fuck! Wha you on abou Shift, you never even hung round with us back then. Stop bullshitting.'

'Wha d'you know abou ih? Kiss my arse, Char. Yuh bumbaclart!'

'Bumbaclart? Check you out. You ain' from Jamaica, yuh family's Maltese, yuh silly cunt!'

'Closest Shifty ever goh to the Caribbean was when we done over tha travel agent's in Albany Road!' Jamo says, making everyone laugh, an if there was any bad vibes they're gone in an instant.

'Still cahn believe Acton's ended up like tha,' Becca goes, shaking her head. 'He was a nice looking guy an all. Used to have a little thing with him at one point.'

'You used to have a little thing with half uh fucking Cardiff!' Jamo says, ducking as a cushion goes spinning past his head.

Anger flares deep in my belly an I desperately try to quench the flames wi more beer. Noh my business really buh the thought of her with anyone else drives me mad.

'Nah, serious though, Acton was safe as fuck. Took us to tha banging warehouse party in Swindon, member? You two girls was up Fairbank Grove at the time – had to sneak out the window wi bed sheets so the carers wouldn miss you. Nothing buh kids back then, wadn we?'

I'm feeling a right dumpling yur, listening to the good times they've shared, the laughs they've had. Stupid, like, cos the Cardiff crew been cool as fuck to me to me buh the jealousy uh being an outsider's eating me up like never before. I thought I was gehrin close to her buh they knows more abou Becca than I ever could, she likes um more than she'll ever like me, they goh memories an friendships an stories tha I can only dream of. Seems I ain' the only one feeling uncomfortable, though. Over in the corner Charmaine sucks at her teeth to geh everyone's attention, couple uh the wasps she's been chewing on escaping as she does so.

'I never went, remember?'

'Shit, thas righ. You goh caught by tha big bulldyke!' Jamo goes, enjoying himself too much to clock Charmaine's daggers. 'Who was ih again, Bec? Me, you, Stevie Acton an . . . ?'

'Leighton Saunders. Brought those speckled doves with him. Best pills I ever had.' Becca's eyes go all gooey an I wonder wha exactly she's thinking abou. The last uh my beer goes down the hatch an I crush the empty can with a bih too much venom, flecks uh foam spraying the others nearby. Nothing's said buh I realise I need to geh a grip on my emotions cos if I fuck this up I'll only have myself to blame an I dun need another failure on my conscience. Look how far I've come in a day – imagine the Francis twins an Stacey Evans seeing me now, partying wi genuine Cardiff crew an noh even gehrin picked on or nothing. Things are going great.

'. . . man, me an Acton was dancing wi these two girls – looked like sisters they did, both in army combats an tiny little vest tops, orr man, you shoulduh been there, Shift!' The two of um pounds fists, Shifty squealing at the thought an Jamo staring off into space wi this look uh sheer bliss plastered over his face.

'Like you'd have a chance! They were probly taking the piss out uh you,' Charmaine goes, sucking louder on her teeth buh Jamo either dun yur or dun care. Still cahn figure Charmaine out. Is tha attitude fuh real?

'Tell um wha happened when we left, Jam,' Becca says.

'Yeah, yeah. Check this. We goes outside abou six in the morning – pure fucked. Pilling our tits off. There's this big crowd gathered in the car park watching these guys screw their cars, wheel-spinning an doing doughnuts – puhrin on a proper show, like. We were loving ih, cheering an laughing when all of a sudden Leighton nudges me, going: "Oh, Jamo, I'm sure thas Acton's motor over there." I has a closer look an he's right! Some cheeky cunt's doing handbrake turns in our fucking ride home! Couple uh massive Rastas tried charging us fifty quid to geh the car back – thing wadn worth tha scrap!'

The whole place rocks wi laughter, even Charmaine in spite of herself. Big toothy grin wider than ever, Jamo's pure lapping up the laughs an why noh? He's the man, you can tell the way everyone looks up to him. I cahn hate him for ih.

All night there's been a steady stream uh people to the flat, buying off Jamo. Mostly he deals with um discreet in the passageway buh this time the punter comes right in, a young flustered guy who removes his baseball cap to reveal a glowing red mark branded on his forehead.

'Whoa! Whas happened to you, Chris? Looks like you been scrapping down the Grange End!'

'I needs a draw – fucking head's bumping, breh. Some short-arse round by the shops accused me uh robbing his van.

Never seen the cunt before in my life, I swear. Just pulled up out uh nowhere giving ih lip – next thing I knows he's come at me with a fucking wheel brace. Lucky my father was outside the pub with his mates at the time – they run over an pasted the guy. Coppers turned up an all sorts, there was murder out there.'

Fuh some reason Shifty's climbing up the back uh the settee, fiddling with his cap an giggling more than usual. 'Orr . . . thas – thas pure mad, tha is Chris. Hwahahaha!' Now he's biting his nails, twitching – fuck's wrong with him?

'Ih's noh funny Shift, the guy nearly knocked me cold. Fuh fuck all, like. Shouting abou hairspray or summin . . . doan think he was playing with a full deck, truth be told.'

Finally the penny drops, slow as I am. Subtlety ain' in Shifty's vocabulary mind, making a right song an dance abou gehrin a squad together an sorting this guy again, doing a proper job on him cos no one goes around hitting his oldest bestest mate Chrissy – focking disgrace is wha ih is! He shadow boxes his way round the room on a vigilante recruitment drive, giggling to himself all the while.

'Sit the fuck down, man.' Jamo goes, trynuh cool Shifty before he gives the game away. 'Guy could be anywhere by now, in ih?'

'Coppers took him off,' Chris goes with a wary eye cos Shifty's performance is fooling nobody.

'Well then, there you go. Problem solved, in ih? Now everyone take ih easy. You are Chris, have a can, mate.'

'Nah, I'm going for an early night. Catch you later.' He takes his draw an leaves, giving everyone another puzzled look on his way out.

We've all gone quiet, waiting fuh Shifty to speak. 'Wha? ' he says, eyes wide. 'How was I s'posed to know?'

'Chrissy's dad's warm as toast, Shift. He finds out yur at the bottom uh this an ih's lights out, man.'

A flicker uh doubt's quickly nipped by a wild click uh the fingers cos fretting ain' really Shifty's style if you know wha I mean. 'Ah, fock him! Long as you soppy cunts can keep ih shut he's noh gunuh find out, is he? Safe? Safe! C'mon, leh's puh some tunes on. S'posed to be a party, in ih!' He produces a cassette from his pocket an blows on ih like a smoking revolver. 'This one'll take yur heads clean off!' He ain' wrong either, pressing play to an instant blast uh bass tha shakes my guts an rattles the empty tins off the coffee table. Maybe ih's the beer or the dope or just being in a different place buh the sound affects me like nothing else before, total hook. Shifty notices me nodding my head an comes over.

'Like this tune, Marv?'

'Yeah, brah,' I says, feeling a bih daft buh saying "butt" down yur dun seem to fit, do ih?

'Hwaha, g'waan wi yuh Cardiff lingo an ah! So yur a little junglist, is ih?'

'Huh?'

'You into jungle?'

'Er, I dun think I been . . .' I goes, making out I cahn yur him properly over the pumping music.

'No,' he shouts, pointing at the speakers. 'Jungle. Ellis Dee at Dreamscape. Dog's bollocks, in ih?'

'No, ih's just bollocks,' Charmaine goes, turning the stereo down.

'Orr, wha d'you know abou music, Char? Doan listen to her, Marv. She thinks Take That are underground.'

'Shurrup yuh dick! All I'm saying is nothing these days can touch rave. Proper hardcore was much better than jungle.'

'Maybe so buh yuh living in the past, sister – gohruh geh wi the times, yeah? Yeah! Happy hardcore's gone shit, jungle's the way forward. End of.'

'Noh in my book.'

'Well, we all knows abou your book, doan we Charmaine?' Shifty says wi the cockshewer sparkle of a man abou to play his trump card. 'If ih ain' in the charts, you doan wanuh know. Funny how jungle was origh wi you last year, in ih?'

'I've never liked ih.' Charmaine's prickles ain' as sharp as before, Shifty well aware as he goes in fuh the kill.

'Bullshit, Char. You rewound tha General Levy cassette so many times the focking tape snapped!'

Jamo an the rest stifle knowing sniggers behind cans uh Carling while a speechless Charmaine rumbles like a boiling kettle. Shifty dusts himself down, game, set an match, too disgusted to look at his vanquished foe a second longer. 'Forgeh these philistines, Marv – uncle Shifty'll educate you in the ways uh real music, yeah? Yeah! Cahn believe you never yurd uh jungle. Fock they listen to up the valleys then, uh?'

Wha I know abou music you could fit on a postage stamp wi room to spare, buh I'll be begging for a piss-taking if I keep schtum. Only records I've ever played are my father's back home so I ends up blurting out: 'Er, mostly rock an ah, you know – heavy metal.' Straight away I realise I've fucked up, face flushing hot as Shifty's mouth twists in a mischievous grin.

'Hea-vy me-tal is ih, butt?' he sings, pure Welshy accent which I dun even talk like really. Some mug, me, in I? Actually believed things ud be different this time, buh wherever I go people'll pick on me. Ih's as though there's this flashing neon sign over my head screaming "target!" tha only I cahn see. 'Ro-cken all over the va-lleys, is ih boy bach!' he's going buh I roll with ih, knows the drill, leh him geh ih out his system while I find an excuse to leave.

'Stop being a dickhead, will you?'

'Orr, yur we go, the valleys girl with a stick up her arse!' Shifty rounds on my unexpected saviour buh Becca ain' the sort to go red over no one.

'I'm noh from the valleys, yuh fucking cretin, I'm from Barry. An the valleys ain' tha bad, origh? No worse than Llanedeyrn-kick-yer-'ead-in!'

'So you admit you goh a stick up yur arse, then?'

'You'll have my boot up yours in a minih, yuh cheeky cunt!'

'Hwahaha! Nothing like a bih uh healthy debate,' he goes, gleefully rubbing his hands together like a naughty monkey.

'Yeah, well doan be picking on younger kids, thas all.'

'Picking on – wha d'you mean, picking on him?' Shifty's eyes go wide again, this time seeming genuinely shocked. Maybe I'm being too much of a fanny buh ih's hard to know the score wi people sometimes, you know? This is the longest he's kept quiet all night mind, so maybe he really is puh out.

'Listen,' Jamo says. 'There's summin you gohruh understand wi Shifty; if he's giving you shit ih means he likes you. Just his way, he doan mean no harm.'

'Yeah, nice one, Jam. Safe, guy, safe.' Shifty wipes a mock tear, injured expression morphing into his trademark wild eyes as he leaps on top uh me, cwtching me tight wi kissy kissy lips, telling me I'm his spar an his breh an his bro, how he'd never do me wrong. Half-heartedly I struggle to geh free, embarrassment noh enough to wan him to stop cos even though I'm noh queer or nothing ih makes me feel nice being held.

Finally he breaks off, going: 'Reckon ih's abou time we initiated Marvin into the crew proper. Boy goh potential, like, buh we need to be sure he can keep the pace, yeah? Yeah!'

'Orr, Shift, leave the man alone, will you?' Jamo laughs. 'Yur scaring him. No, fuck tha, yuh scaring *me*!'

'Listen, breh, ih's our Cardiff duty to break this boy in, an we both know there's only one way to do ih.' His eyes shine bright wi the pure solid gold of his idea. 'Buckets!'

'Buckets?'

'Yeah, c'mon, Jam. We havn done buckets fuh years,' Charmaine chips in, every fucker suddenly sold on this bucket thing.

'Wha you saying, Marv?' Jamo flashes tha toothy grin an I know I'm in whether I like ih or noh.

'I s'pose, buh—'

Shifty waves his hand to shush me up. 'Doan talk, just listen. Yuh my bredrin now, so I gohruh train you up right, yeah?' He drags me through to the kitchen, giving step by step instructions as he's hacking at this empty pop bottle with a knife an doing weird shit wi tin foil. Then we go through to the bathroom an fill the tub halfway wi water, me wondering all the time wha I've gotten myself into. Now the others have gathered round, this real buzz of excitement in the air. My gob's dry as an Arab's dap, tongue stuck like Velcro to the roof uh my mouth. Sandpaper lids rasp my red raw eyeballs as I blink at the eager faces surrounding me. Well, eager except one.

'You loh are mad.' Becca stands in the doorway, arms crossed.

'Whas the marrer, hyng, scared you'll go under?'

Wrong move by Wonk Eye. I wince as Becca lehs him have ih full blast. 'Fuck off yuh goggle-eyed prick. I was doing buckets when you were still wanking off to She-Ra!'

Poor Wonk Eye, he wadn to know. There's no point trynuh be smart when Becca's goh her arse in her hands. Tha mouth can shrivel yuh balls up from twenty paces, pure hit you where ih hurts, like. Ih's a talent really, just noh one you wanuh be on the wrong end of. Wonk Eye's podgy gob drops like a stone an you can tell he never meant nothing by ih. He's a weird-looking fucker buh when ih comes down to ih he's alright. Thas wha I wanuh say, I wanuh stick up for him as he's mumbling an apology, buh nothing's coming. Suddenly I doan feel so good.

Shifty's first to the bathtub, crumbling the brown soapbar on the pop bottle's tin foil gauze. He holds his lighter to ih, slowly drawing the bottle up out the water till ih's full uh thick swirling smoke. I watch on, stomach dipping. Shifty undoes the bottle top an with a Geronimo! in the form of one of his mad giggles, slams his head down to hoover the chamber clean. He holds his breath, eyes bulging like he's abou to keel over before reeling back an fist pounding a heavy grey thundercloud from his chest. 'Whoo! Thas the shit!' he croaks. 'Who's next?'

Jamo takes a turn, then Charmaine, then Wonk Eye. Now all heads turn to me, an dun I fucking know ih. I kneel at the side uh the bathtub like old Amber Lynne, head on the chopping block sortuh style. A drip from the tap rings like gunshots round my empty head. Shifty's standing over me, sorting the works an grinning like some mad axe man while he does ih. My stomach churns at the pissy yellow bathwater, chunks of ash an fag ends an fuck knows wha bobbing abou on the surface.

'Quick, yuh wasting ih!' Shifty nudges me forward so I goh no choice buh to do the deed.

'Urgh!' I pull back, coughing an spluttering, dribble falling out uh my open gob. I wen too hard, sucked up a load uh the bathwater along wi the smoke an now yur comes the buzz, head rush like no other, pressure rising till my noggin's abou ready to pop. I fall back on the cold tiles, breathing hard. Shifty looms up in front uh me, proudest maniac you'll ever lay eyes on.

'Wha d'you reckon? I told you, breh. Buckets are a whole nother level!'

I try to force a smile buh my clammy lips can only quiver. My heart, ih's beating too fast. This ain' right, I'm having a fucking heart attack. I gohruh geh out, need fresh air. Standing up is impossible though, arms an legs completely gone. I manage to wipe a shaky hand over my cold sweaty forehead buh the battle's already lost. As soon as the stench uh stale piss an beer hits my nostrils an unstoppable jet uh puke screams out towards the toilet bowl.

'Eurgh! White fever, man, he goh white fever!'

'Quick, leh me out before he spews on my Karl Kani's! Brand new, these are breh! Hwahaha!'

As I listen to um scramble for safety behind me I know I should feel ashamed, embarrassed buh trivial shit like ah dun marrer when yuh dying. The only thought in my mind is to make this horrific feeling stop, please make ih stop – oh fuck, ih's never gunuh stop. I clench my eyes shut as the room starts to spin, clinging to the porcelain lifebuoy an hoping, dreaming, praying fuh death's quick release.

16

Ooh, yuh cunt! Pure brilliant light floods my eyes like a gallon uh raw bleach, hospital white, heaven white cos I might just be the first person in history to die uh white fever. A new low, even fuh me buh my blushes are spared by pain so savage I cahn possibly be dead. Seems I've spent the night on an upholstered wheelbarrow full uh bricks. Little scraps uh yesterday leap out like muggers from the corners uh my mind; Becca. School. Mam. Buckets. Fuck me, those buckets . . . I need water. Standing up sends a shockwave through my whole body, arm uh the settee the only thing keeping me on my feet. One step towards the kitchen an I freeze cos out in the passageway a door's creaking open. Being caught creeping round the flat half-naked is the last thing I need, especially after last night's shenanigans so I slip back under the covers an pretend to be asleep. Footsteps pad over the tiles in my direction. Summin soft brushes my face an when I take a peek Charmaine's stood over me, no flicker of emotion.

'Brought you another pillow. Probly noh much use now, buh wha'ever.'

Flashbacks uh hugging the toilet, crawling out into the passage, collapsing down down down . . .

'I – I'm really sorry abou last night. Didn upset no one, did I?'

'Cup uh tea?'

'Water,' I croak, inwardly cursing her attempt to make me sweat. Dun need ih, noh today. She hands me a glass an slumps into an armchair, a shut-up shop I havn goh the energy to try crowbarring open. Out in the kitchen the kettle's bubbling, shewer there's a sizzle uh bacon too. Hope to fuck

I'm right – nice bacon sarnie'd do me the world uh good right abou now.

'Have fun yesterday, then?' She waits patiently for an answer, playing with her cigarette smoke like she's playing wi my mind.

'Well, up until the buckets, like. Wen a bih downhill after tha . . .'

'Surprised you goh the balls to stick around. The stuff you said to the boys was out of order, mate. Lucky I held um back, else you wouldn be yur now.'

'I'm sorry, I'm sorry – cahn remember a thing, honest.' I know she must be messing buh ih's so hard to tell wi tha poker face of hers an a pasting's the last thing I need in a state like this.

'Noh me you need to apologise to, an anyway, ih'll take more than sorry after wha you done. Gun have to beg, I reckon.'

Charmaine snorts an disappears into the kitchen, leaving my brain to dissolve like Alka-Seltzer sludge in my skull. When she comes back she's carrying my last meal: a mug uh steaming tea an a bacon sandwich dripping wi brown sauce. Wi the reaper on my back, I dig right in, tearing strips off the sarnie while Charmaine casually pulls open the curtains an tidies a few things up. Her breakfast seems to be a cup uh coffee an another Regal. We sit quiet a bih longer, her fiddling absently between remote an fag, fag an remote, finally stubbing one an settling fuh the prancing TV weatherman wi the other. I stare at the screen, usually enjoyable possibility of him falling off his floating map ruined by Charmaine's lurking words.

Bored uh my fretting she finally says: 'Christ, I'm only yanking yuh chain. You puked up a bih an fell asleep. Told Shifty you loved him when he puh you to bed on the settee. Thas ih.' Her eyes never leave the screen.

Hope she's lying abou the Shifty thing buh ih's still a step up from the shewer fire kicking I was on course for. 'Well, thanks fuh stringing me along.' I say ih joking buh with enough weight to geh my point across. Noh tha she gives a shit.

'Doan piss yuh pants – happened to all of us at one time or another. Take ih yuh noh much of a smoker then?'

109

'I was okay until those buckets . . .'

'Yeah, they can creep up on you if yuh noh careful.'

There's silence again while the both of us concentrate on the programme. Lonely water pipes clang an clank in the distance like the chains of hungover ghosts banished by the bright morning sunlight. On the telly the weatherman's busy stating the obvious – today's gunuh be another scorcher.

'Where's the hairdryer, Char?' Becca drips in the doorway, tiny pink towel the only thing between me an heaven. Tantalising curls like creep like fingers from her neck down to her tits, jet black wi moisture. Every time I pull my eyes away they're drawn straight back, moth to a flame cos she's so lush ih's unreal, pure dream woman style. The inevitable result is a raging hard-on tha I do everything possible to hide under the duvet. Had enough shame fuh one lifetime, thanks all the same.

When Charmaine gehs up to show her where the girlie stuff is I almost spunk myself wi relief. She tells me we're going uh town soon so I best jump in the shower an I'm happy to oblige, knob twanging like a diving board now their backs are turned. As the boiling water rehumanises the freeze dried husk inside me I think abou everything thas happened, how mental ih all is. Leaving Dad, Darren an the rest uh the pricks – there's no regrets there. Mam? Now thas a different story. Reckon the way she reacted was due to shock. My own fault really, showing up unannounced buh in a few days she'll uv calmed down loads – enough to see how much I've changed. Especially if she thinks me an Becca are an item. Only one glaring problem wi tha plan, buh the fact tha Becca brought me this far means there's at least a little spark, deep down, like. Just my job to bring ih to the surface. There's a more pressing matter to deal with first though cos I'm soapy an stiff wi thoughts uh my future mrs in tha towel, out uh tha towel, in the shower wi me . . .

17

'Iqbal Malik! Iqbal Malik to desk four!'

This jobcentre's pure *Mad Max* wi giros, a nuclear wasteland crawling wi mutant refugees an inbred outlaws. Heads down we weave through the huddled masses, extra careful round a gang uh fully qualified skull crackers just itching to geh back to work. Either the cleaners Shake'n'Vac wi parmesan or more than one bogging cunt's goh their shoes off. Distracted by the stink, I'm caught off guard by this random hand shooting out uh the crowd to greet me. I instinctively go to shake ih, thinking the greasy old fucker ih belongs to might be one uh Dad's mates or summin buh Becca yanks me away, shouting loud enough fuh the mackintosh man to yur: 'Fucking pervert! Watch out fuh the creeps in this place, Marv.'

Dun need to tell me twice.

'Iqbal Malik! Desk four!' Bloke behind the counter finally gives up on the AWOL Malik an searches fuh the next lucky contestant, stilton stench worsening all the while. Heat's beyond stifling. Cahn wait to leave.

'Yuh noh listening! I needs my fucking money!' Some ginger ninja springs to his feet at one uh the nearby tables, face like a wrung-out dishcloth. The little round-eared mouse he's screaming at casually bats him away with her well-worn script. 'Mr Morgan, I've already explained, there's nothing we can do unless you have the relevant docum—'

'Fuck yuh relevant documents!' ginger shouts, making a grab fuh the dole woman over the desk. These two guys rush an bundle him towards the door while he screams threats at anyone who'll listen. I shuffle a bih closer to Becca who's sitting with a deadpan, another morning in front uh the telly sortuh expression. Charmaine's name's finally called buh brief

111

hopes uh gehrin out are soon dashed when she returns with a handful uh forms.

'Fuck's sake! They wants me to go fuh some interview thing – reckons they might stop my money, the cheeky cunts! Gohruh hang around till they can fit me in. Fuck!' She boots the seat next to her an the big lump sat on ih spins round ready to start. Luckily, one look at the raging pineapple makes him think twice.

'Listen, Char, I cahn handle much more uh this place,' Becca says, standing up. 'I'm gunuh take a walk, origh? Needs a spliff.'

'Serious? Cahn you hang on a bih?'

'We been waiting ages as ih is. Meet you back yur in an hour or so, yeah?' Becca says as she moves off, pointing to her lug hole like ih's too noisy to yur the choice words Charmaine's shouting after her.

18

The Taff. Taffies, English people calls us buh ih's weird cos as I dink another stone off the shipwrecked shopping trolley out in the shallow waters ih occurs to me tha up until a few days ago I never actually saw the river in real life. Never seen any English people in real life, come to think of ih, 'cept maybe snooty fuckers like teachers an social workers. They dun count though, they're noh human, they're an alien species; spies planted to make notes an keep tabs, mark us down fuh the way we behave, way we talk, way we feel. We fart an burp emotions too honest an too raw fuh those elbows-off-the-table sorts to deal with. If we're happy, we leh the world know. If we're pissed off, we leh the cunt who upset us know. Tha sort of honesty frightens the shit out of um so they try to turn ih around, make out like there's summin wrong with us. Buh we dun need their amateur psychology or even professional come to tha, we just need people like us, people who understand wha ih's like to have everyone against you an still stand tall. People like Becca. She busily works the skins on the wall next to me, oblivious to the truth thas gehrin laid on her when the time's right. An when the time's right, I know she'll feel the same. Way she stuck up for me in front uh Shifty last night tells me all I need to know.

I aimlessly fire another rock across the water, impossible notions uh breaching the Arms Park fortress on the far bank. The stadium which looks so cool on the telly takes a sinister air close up, ihs high spiny girders folding inwards like the legs uh dead spiders Darren used to leave under my bedcovers. I batter the unwelcome thoughts from my mind rolled-up magazine style, blurting out a distraction wi the first thing tha comes to mind. 'Horrible in tha jobcentre, wadn ih?'

'Uhuh,' she goes, running her tongue along the Rizlas.

'I feel bad for Charmaine, having to stay there . . .'

'Hmm.'

'Dun think she wanted us to go. Reckon she's pissed off with us?' I'm shewer Becca yurd Charmaine's grumbling. She must've.

'Doan worry abou Charmaine, she's always goh a face like a smacked arse.' She smiles at me buh this time I dun smile back. I wanuh know the score.

'Listen, Marv, me an Charmaine goh history, origh? Ih's nothing to stress abou.'

'Wha sort uh history? D'you have a fight or summin?' I brace myself fuh the crashing shutters buh she just laughs an shakes her head slowly like I wouldn understand.

'Silly sod, you makes ih sound like we're in the playground.'

'You did though, didn ew?' Pushing my luck yur, buh fuck ih. You dun ask, you dun geh, as Buncy always says.

'Listen . . .' She pauses for a minute, debating whether to leh me in cos I couldn be knocking any louder. 'I used to go out with her brother, years ago. Life was a bih crazy back then an things ended badly.'

'Was tha why you come to live up Pengarw wi yuh auntie an uncle – Scott's parents, like?'

'Yeah, sort of.'

'Becca . . .'

'What?'

'Whas Fairbank Grove?'

'Uh?'

'I yurd you talking last night. Jamo said you an Charmaine had to sneak out of a place called Fairbank Grove.'

'You knows wha ih is, so why you asking?' The edge in her voice ain' enough to dislodge my foot from the door cos I'm almost there, almost inside.

'Ih's the homes, in ih? They were gunuh puh me in the homes, before . . . never, in the end, like, buh I shit myself when they said ih.'

'Yeah, well. Ih ain' the nicest place in the world.'

'Bec–'

114

She seems to sense whas coming an nips ih in the bud. 'Give ih a rest, Marv, I'm trynuh chill out. Talk abou summin lighter, yeah?'

Alright, ih can wait. She's leh me further than I expected. Pretty soon she'll be holding the door wide open. In the meantime we sit there, her smoking an me scratching brick wi stone. MARVIN 9T5. Noh bad fuh a quick throw-up. As I stand to admire ih I catch sight uh two scruffs over Becca's shoulder, sort uh cunts who'd have Stig uh the Dump selling up if they moved next door. Summin tells me these fuckers an their Happy Shopper white cider ain' planning on strolling by. Knew ih!

The one with a greasy ponytail an thick Oasis monobrow beelines fuh Becca, sniffing at the spliff over her shoulder like a stray dog at a bone. 'Alright der, are ya?' he says, catching her off guard.

'Yeah, I'm origh,' she spits, shooting him a filthy look.

'What ya got, love?' His accent's pure weird buh strangely familiar, summin in the back uh my mind screaming: *'Accrington Stanley? Who are they?'*

'Fuck all fuh you, pal.'

Ponytail shoots a black-toothed grin to his sidekick; this stocky guy with a pure square head like a fuck-off loaf uh Mighty White. 'Looks like we've got a lippy one here, Marco!'

This Marco sortuh sniggers an takes a seat on the wall. Ponytail follows suit. I keep my head down an check um out from under my eyebrows. Both been battered by the ugly stick, crags an creases telling war stories way beyond their years, impossible though ih is to guess their actual ages. Ponytail catches me looking an goes: 'Y'alright, ked?'

I give him a quick nod an move closer to Becca, tugging on her sleeve cos we should really geh going.

'Gonna let me have a toke on dat after you, then?'

'Noh likely, mate. He's already called,' Becca points towards me. 'An anyway, I'm noh into dishing out freebees to any old fucker who comes along.'

'Less of the old, if ya don't mind.' Ponytail raises his bushy monobrow at Marco an grins again. 'No, no, fair enough. You've gotta be careful who you're dealing wit' these days.

Bugh still, if yer gonna come and sit on our wall, it'd be polite to offer us a toke, dat's all.'

'Your wall? Funny, I cahn see yuh name on ih.'

'Ya don't even know what me name is, do ya?'

'Har fucking har.' Becca passes the spliff to me an I goh no choice buh to take ih even though I swore off the dope after last night.

'It's Kenny, by the way.' He twists the cap off his bottle, takes a gulp an offers ih over to Becca. She looks at ih for a long moment before accepting an swigging ih back.

'Marvin, give um some uh tha, yeah?'

I cahn believe wha I'm yuring. These dodgy fuckers could be anyone. They'd make some uh the maniacs back at the jobcentre cross the street buh she's expecting us to be best pals with um just cos they goh a bottle uh booze. I hand the spliff over at arm's length, feeding time at the zoo.

'Ah, nice one, ked. Dat's it, eh? Share and share alich. So you're Marvin, right?'

'Yeah, he's Marvin, I'm Becca.'

'Well pleased to meetcha, then. Y'aving some ciader, Marv?'

I take up the bottle an knock ih back cos I might need some Dutch to survive this encounter. Kenny has a few more puffs on the spliff, nodding his head to himself. 'Yeah, not too bad, dat. Alright if Marco here catches on?'

Becca nods an swipes the cider back out my hands.

'Well, me name might not be on this wall, bugh we sit here every day. Can't say I've ever seen you around, dough. So where ya from?'

'Well there's no need to ask where you're from, is there? Sounded like Cilla fucking Black was creeping up on me! *Surprise surpriiise!!*'

This is insane! She'll geh us both fucked up, talking like ah – or just me, more like. Kenny laughs, buh I'm ready fuh the cunt to switch at any moment. I knows his sort.

'Can ya believe dat, Marc? Cheeky mare! Well dat's noten, I thought for a moment we had Tom Jones skinning up on the Taff embankment! And dat was *before* you opened ya mouth!'

'Silly get!' Becca laughs an swings a playful punch at the guy. My guts twinge again cos she should be doing stuff like ah wi me, noh some psycho from cardboard city.

'Don't dish it out if ya can't take it bach!' Kenny teases. 'Nah, you're right, I'm Scouse and proud. Been down Cardiff way for years now, dough.'

'Yuh mate doan say much, do he?'

'I do enough talking for the both of us. And anyway, I could say the same about your man over there, couldn't I?'

'Marvin's origh, in you, Marv?'

'Yeah, yeah, course I am,' I say, breaking my back wi the effort uh sounding cool.

'So seriously now, where are you two from?'

'He's from the valleys. I'm from yur, there an everywhere, in ih?'

'Oh right, like dat, eh? Youse lot sleeping rough then, are ya?'

'No we ain't, yuh cheeky bastard. We're staying with a friend uh mine. Wha you doing round yur, anyway? Bih far from home, in you?'

'Like I said, been down this way on and off for years. Met a girl here bugh things went sour and I ended up on the streets.'

'Wha d'you mean?'

'Smach. Bad, bad news. Was the eighties dough, every cunt was doing it.'

'An wha abou now?'

'Nah, been clean for yonks. Never walk dat road again, let me tell ya. Stick to the bevy now, you know. And, of course, a little smowch if it comes my way. Speaking of which, you got any more of dat hash?' He drains the last uh the cider, cracks open a new bottle an offers ih to her, swapsies style. Becca smiles to herself an pulls out the Rizlas.

19

'Whas she wan, a fucking picture or summin?' Becca slurs, holding another silky top up against her body. The fart-faced assistant wi the Deirdre Barlow glasses coughs an pretends to sort some coat hangers on the rack buh we both know she's been following us ever since we come in. Charmaine was long gone by the time we goh back to the jobcentre so Becca insisted on dragging me round these fancy shops, even though we havn goh ten pence to scratch our arses with. I knew ih was a bad idea buh you cahn reason wi Becca when she's in a state like this. Deirdre's giving me the heebies buh Becca's too pissed to care as she admires herself in the mirror, clothes pressed tight against every inch of her curves. Thas the problem wi window shopping – just a cruel reminder of all the things you havn goh buh on the plus side there's tha determination to succeed. Wan summin bad enough an you'll geh ih, an I wan her more than anything else in the world.

Suddenly I'm blindsided by the creeping buzz an for a second another white fever situation's looking dead cert. Somewhere in the distance Becca's still rabbiting abou halter necks an boot cuts buh I'm deep in the twilight zone between life an white death, fighting with all my might to keep ih together. Gohruh stay cool. Cahn leh myself . . . leh myself . . .

'Marvin! Wha you doing over yur, yuh little perv!'

I find myself crash landed in the middle uh the women's lingerie section, a frilly maze wi no way out in my wasted state. Then darkness closes down over my eyes an I'm shoved flying into one uh the naked dummies. By the time I've goh the big yellow knickers off my head the only trace uh Becca's her shrieking laughter still hanging in the air.

'Becca. Becca, where to are you?'

She jumps out from behind a rack wearing dark glasses an a pudding bowl wig. 'Hey baby, you looking for a good time?'

Personally, I'd still fancy her if she had a pink Mohican an leg callipers buh best play along till the time's right. 'Eurgh, no thanks!'

'You better give me some action, lover boy!' She comes after me an I scramble away, straight into the arms uh Deirdre Barlow.

'Excuse me, but I'm going to have to ask you to leave. This isn't a playground.'

'Wha you gunuh do, call Ken?' Becca goes, clearly on my wavelength. 'Or maybe tha foreign stud – thas who yuh knocking off these days in ih, yuh dirty hussy!'

'I beg your pardon!'

'Orr, lighten up love, fuh fuck's sake.'

'Are you going to buy those?' Deirdre says, pointing at the wig an glasses Becca's still wearing.

'Nah, they'd look better on you,' she says, casually dumping the loh in the shop woman's hands an adding the big ball uh chewing gum from her mouth as a cherry on top uh the pile.

Deirdre does her nut. 'You can't do that! You'll have to pay for the damage.'

'Yeah, origh, I'll go an geh some money from the Cashpoint,' Becca calls, backtracking on her heels towards the exit.

'Wait! Come back!' the woman shouts buh we're already out into the busy street, surfing on waves uh shoppers an euphoria, Becca piggybacking me through the crowd, barely managing to swerve a pair uh mothers wi prams before we collapse in a shop doorway.

'Haha! Wha a mission! Cardiff doan know whas hit ih, eh Marv?'

'Yuh nuts, Bec! Pure nuts!'

'Fucking right! Only way to be, in ih? Hey listen, listen . . .' She pulls me close, big brown eyes looking right into mine. 'I been thinking abou you lately.'

I gehs tha tingle inside cos this could be ih – the moment I been waiting for. 'Wha? Wha you been thinking?'

'I been thinking . . .'

'Yeah?'

'. . . tha pretty soon yuh gunuh start to stink!' Flecks uh cider-spit tickle my lips as she falls into me buh there's no danger of her discovering my hard-on cos along wi my face ih's dropped like a stone.

'Aww, doan look so sad!' She pinches my cheeks like Nan used to years ago. 'Wha I mean is, you didn bring no clothes wi you. We gohruh geh you kitted out, mate.'

'Yeah, buh how?' Shoulduh know better than to ask really. Without a word she drags me back on the rollercoaster thas become our life.

*   *   *

Becca's strutting around like she owns the place. Reckons ih'll be a piece uh piss, buh this ain' the tuck shop or Hooley's. There's security guards an cameras – the whole setup screams "dodgy". Even the shop girls goh this creepy vibe, pure painted orange drones gliding silent surveillance missions around us. I spin left an right, trynuh catch one spying buh they're playing ih well too smart.

'See anything you like?' Becca goes, breathing booze at me an swaying into the racks uh clothes. Even if I could see straight, this sortuh stuff all looks the same to me. Flashy shit fuh blokes wi trendy haircuts an white teeth. I'd be hard pushed to remember the last time I wore anything noh out of a catalogue or a charity shop. Becca clocks my cluelessness an decides to help, shoving me towards the changing rooms with armfuls uh randomly selected shirts an jeans.

'Listen, I've done ih before, loads uh times. All you gohruh do is puh the new stuff on under yur old then walk back out. Easy.' The old butter-wouldn-melt card might be more convincing if she could keep tha wonky grin off her face.

I was all set to tell her where to go buh somehow find myself standing in the changing rooms, knowing full well I'll most likely end up locked away cos of her mad schemes. The first thing the attendant gives me, apart from a dirty look, is a token thing saying how many items I'm trying on. So much fuh

120

Becca's big plan. I curse silently in my cubicle for a few minutes before returning to find her stumbling round a rack uh shoes, so arseholed she seems to think ih's a coffee machine. Amount uh cider those tramps give her, summin like this was bound to happen. Now ih's up to me to tell her straight before we geh into real trouble.

'Yuh full uh shit! You havn done this before, uv you? They checks how much stuff you goh, fuh one thing – an there's alarm tags on the clothes.'

'Take a chill pill, Marv, fuck's sake. Yuh too high strung, thas your problem. C'mon, gimme a smile, I doan like ih when yuh grumpy.' She tries to tickle me buh I break free.

'No, this is serious. We're gunuh geh caught.'

'Marvin, uv I ever leh you down?' she says like we're life-long pals. I've only really spent the last few days with her an I'm still noh shewer uh the answer. As ih turns out, a reply's noh needed cos she's too busy ranting abou how she never breaks a promise, how she's gunuh geh me some new clothes come hell or high water.

'Wha you doing?' I say as she drops to her knees an begins tugging at my shoes.

'C'mon, geh um off. If they wants uh play funny fuckers, so will we.'

'No chance! Yuh mental!'

Wi one already gone, I'm locked in a battle fuh my last remaining trainer an any sense uh sanity we might have left. Determined as a subs-bench flanker she tackles me to the floor where I scramble hopelessly from her giggling horror show loony advance. 'Stop struggling yuh little fucker!' she laughs through mouthfuls uh swept hair. By now I'm a sweating, knackered heap, too weak to resist.

'Stop . . . stop . . .' I croak as she devours the other shoe an hoists a pair uh jeans up over my trousers.

'Fucking things are gunuh fit whether they likes ih or noh,' she says, buh these jeans ud be tight on an anorexic flamingo.

'No, you dun understand . . .' I eventually manage, pure hysterical. 'I'm gunuh pi – piss myself!'

Now the both of us collapse, rolling round in streams uh tears. People are beginning to notice – these two faces appear overhead, a mother an daughter, the pair of um pure horrified.

'Ih's origh, I works yuh! Just dressing the dummy, see?!' Becca wheezes as the two of um scoot off sharpish. Wi my legs waving in the air like an overgrown baby she manages to pull the jeans as far up as they'll go before popping my shoes back on an lifting me to my feet. 'Come on, ih's time we wern yur.'

'Buh you havn taken nothing.' Fucked if I'm going ih alone.

She throws a few t-shirts over her head an pokes her tongue out as if to say, *Happy now?* I try to follow as she heads fuh the door buh the jeans are so tight I can barely move.

'Yuh s'posed to be playing ih cool,' she goes. 'Stop walking like you've shit yuhself.'

'Noh my fault – these jeans are pure nutcrushers!'

Tha sets her off again, laughing so hard she cahn stand up. When I try to help her I lose my balance an we both go down, taking a rail uh trousers with us. Laying in the jumble pile another thought strikes me. 'Wait! We havn taken the tags off.' This seems to tickle her even more, buh ih ain' a joke, like.

'Too late fuh tha now, Marv. Look over there.'

Across the shop the mother an daughter are stood wi this big fat security guard, pointing our way.

'Shit, wha we gunuh do?'

The answer's obvious, really. 'Run!'

Everything breaks down into freeze-framed madness, strobe effects an jittery insect movements as I force my limbs to comply. I goh a vague sense uh the shoppers standing aghast buh the whole situation's so daft I just wanuh piss myself laughing, especially when Becca trips over a display up ahead an tumbles across the finish line like the winner uh some kind uh mad-cap charity fun-run. I'm abou to claim silver when an iron hand grips me from behind an pulls the bottom out uh my world. All the booze an dope an adrenaline roars from my body till the only thing left is stark reality. We've fucked up. Bad.

20

Where's Becca's smart mouth when you need ih? Before now I thought she could geh us out of anything buh her lips are solid stone as we're taken through to the staff area an sat down on some upturned crates. Knew this was a bad idea – I fucking told her. Now wha? Geh sent back home, maybe prison, maybe they'll take my prints an link me up wi the fire at the Handies . . . I could go away fuh years!

Uv I ever leh you down?

Yeah, you fucking have!

I wanuh scream buh I'm hog-tied, apple in my gob ready fuh this fat security guard an his hulking sidekick to chow down. This ain' quite the fancy set-up I was expecting mind – no clinical interrogation facilities, no magic mirrors, no tape recorders – just a bigger version uh my mitching lock-up back home, junk an cages an crates full uh fuck all.

'Ughh, phww right . . . right you two . . .' The more white foam Fatty dabs from the corners of his mouth the tighter my fingers cross cos a timely heart attack could be our ticket out uh this mess. Unlucky! A few popped shirt buttons release the pressure from his plum tomato cheeks an suddenly against all the odds ih's looking like the selfish old cunt's gunuh live to spite us. 'You two, get those – phww phww – get those clothes off, now. We've, ugh, got, phww . . . it's all on camera . . . so don't try any tricks.'

Ih's the Pengarw High changing rooms all over again, tha same sinking dread at wha comes next. The task uh removing jeans is summin akin to undoing ship rivets with a pair uh chopsticks, an my nervous struggles dun go unnoticed.

'Tsh, tsh, what is wrong with you?' the other guard says, patting his radio like ih's a truncheon. This one's a mean mother, big an black with a foreign accent, a whole different ball game to Fatty. I'm dreading Becca giving him any lip, honest to God.

'Look at the – ugh, guh – look at the state of um. Off their heads – must've been to pull a stunt like that.'

'We're noh off our heads!' Becca goes, like she wouldn know a spliff from a candy stick. Fatty ain' going for ih, mind.

'Quiet, you! Bloody waltzing in here high as kites, helping yourselves.'

'Buh we nev–'

'Save it, son. Names. Now.'

We both sit there, silent. I'm grabbing at false names buh every one I choose sounds obvious, pure John Smith or Phil Collins, like.

'Alright, you want to play dumb, that's fine. You can talk to the police instead.'

'Ih's Lee. Lee Bray.' I bite down on my lip, trynuh avoid Becca's evils cos I had to tell, didn I? They call the coppers an thas us truly fucked. Guaranteed she wun see ih tha way, though.

'Rebecca Bray – I'm his sister. Please, we were only messing around. We didn't mean to cause trouble, honest.'

Fuck me, this is a turn-up fuh the books. No chops, just shining eyes an trembling lips, the hardest girl in the world abou ready to burst out crying.

'Listen, I've heard ih all before, love. You been caught bang to rights, so save your whining for the courts.'

'Buh you doan understand!' She's full-on blubbing now, real tears an everything. 'Ih was only a dare! Our mum's in hospital, ih'd kill her if she found out wha we done!'

I swear, if I didn know her I'd buy ih hook, line an sinker. Just a shame Fatty's a tougher nut to crack.

'You must think I was born yesterday. Right, now – addresses.' When he pulls out the notepad Becca cranks ih up a notch or ten buh she's going too far, ruining everything with her amateur dramatics.

'Ih's . . . ih's true-hu-hu,' she's sobbing with her head in her hands. 'Our mum's really ill, we only come to town to geh her a present an–'

124

Fatty slams the notebook on the counter. 'I haven't got time for this, I'm going to find Geoff. We'll let management deal with them.' Once he waddles off the nerves really creep in cos we're left wi the Mean Mother, his stare alone enough to peel paint. Becca's wisecracks are shewer to anger him buh does she keep quiet? Does she fuck.

'You understand, doan you? Tha guy thinks he knows ih all, buh I can tell you're different. You can see we're only kids who made a mistake, cahn you?'

'Tsh, Billy is a cynical man, but what more can you expect when you act in such a manner?'

'Yuh right, yuh so right,' Becca says, wailing again. 'Ih's totally my fault, I've leh everyone down. You must think I'm a silly little girl.'

'I think you are on the wrong path. Now come, I need to know exactly what is taken.'

'Yeah, course,' Becca goes, piling the clothes up on the counter. 'I'm so sorry, ih's just things are really tough right now. I feel like I'm falling apart – need someone to help me.'

'People can help, but first you must help yourself. Your address?'

Becca rattles off some bollocks abou Aberdare: 'We live there with our mother – well, we used to before she goh taken ill. I been thinking uh moving down here to be closer to her buh I doan know my way around. Do you know Cardiff?'

'Yes. I live here some years,' he goes, face buried in the notebook.

'Bet you geh out a loh.'

'Not really.'

'C'mon? Good-looking guy like you? Probly goh a different girl every night uh the week.'

'That is not the way I live my life. Your date of birth?'

'Doan worry, I'm noh too young,' she says, giggling all coy. 'So you gunuh take me out, or wha? '

He shuts the notebook an kneels down to her level, looking her right in the eye. She leans forward to meet him, the little girl lost from two minutes ago nowhere to be found. Now she's fluffing her hair an poking out her lips like Jo Guest in my *Razzle* back home.

'I would like to take you somewhere, yes. I see something of myself in you.'

'You doan waste no time!' she goes, pretending to be shocked. 'I was thinking more like a drink to start things off, buh you never know yuh luck.'

My stomach prickles deep inside. This ain' fucking acting, I'm noh tha stupid. Fancies the cunt, dun she!

'Tsh, if you are seeking help, this is not the way to find it. Throwing your body away is sinful, but I would still like to take you somewhere. My church group holds meetings every Wednesday. It would be good if you could come along. '

'Uh?'

I was expecting Becca to flip at the sinful jibe buh she's too taken aback to notice. Neither of us seen this one coming – he's a fucking Jehovo!

'If you are serious about changing your life, Jey-sus Christ can help. I was not so different from you until I found God.'

'Right, yeah – yeah, okay. Yeah, I'd like tha.'

'Good, but first you must face the consequences of your actions. No more deceit.'

'I know, I will. Buh this isn't anything to do wi my brother. I led him astray, ih's my fault.' She nods over to the fire exit. 'Cahn you leh him slip away?'

'That is the old you talking. You have to be true to yourself and others if you want forgiveness. I must finish taking your details and you must not tell any more lies. You will find honesty brings understanding and compassion.'

Compassion, my arse. Fatty ain' gunuh swallow this hallelujah bollocks, an neither's the manager, most probs. We share a look between us as Jehovo's rummaging around in his locker for some pamphlet. Ih's now or never. My boot smashes open the fire door an we're gone, out into the back alley easy as ah.

'Spin, yuh limp-dicked Bible-basher!' Becca calls to the guard as he's shouting after us abou choices an conscience an all the rest of ih. He goh no chance uh catching us now, mind. We've done ih. We're free. Summin's still niggling me though, an when she tries to ruffle my hair I shake her off, noh in the mood to play her games.

'Whas the marrer wi you, stroppy? Goh us out uh trouble, didn I?'

'You?'

'Well, you know wha I mean.'

'Hmm.'

'No, come on, droopy drawers. Whas yuh problem?'

'I dunno, ih's just the way you was wi tha security guard . . . did you – well, did you like him?'

'Behave yuhself, Marv. Fuck's sake.'

'Buh the things you said, I thought–'

'Well you thought wrong, didn you?'

'So you never really liked him?'

She pats my head again, good little dog. 'Marvin, mate, you goh a whole loh to learn abou women.'

No shit, I say to myself as she marches off. Sometimes ih seems like I goh a whole loh to learn abou everything.

21

'Wakey wakey! Ih's like *Dawn of the Dead* in yur, breh!' Shifty skips across the room an whips the curtains open, causing us to hiss an recoil in pain. Another heavy session last night has left everyone fragile, bathing our sore heads in a balm uh darkness an weed smoke.

'Easy, Shift, fuck's sake.' Charmaine croaks from the armchair in the corner. 'Where'd you spring from, anyway?'

'My mother's fanny, if I remember right!' he goes, clicking his fingers together triumphantly. 'Nah, one uh you bumbaclarts left the front door open. Focking spongies, the loh uh you.'

'I'm gunuh kill Jamo. Dun no how many times I've told the useless twat abou tha dodgy latch!'

'Yuh lucky an upstanding member uh the community was passing, in ih?' Shifty goes, splashing down between me an Becca.

'Really? You should've invited him in,' Becca says, reclaiming her patch uh settee wi the help of a well placed elbow.

'Harsh!' He nods to me with a wink. 'Loves me really, doan she, Marv? Safe? Safe! Hwahaha! So anyway, whas everyone been up to? Was gunuh pop over yest'day buh the community service done me in.'

'These two wen thieving in town,' Charmaine goes, clucking like a mother hen at her naughty chicks. 'Almost goh done an all.'

'Is ih?' Shifty leans forward, intrigued.

'Security caught us trynuh run,' Becca says like ih happens every day. 'Goh out of ih in the end, though.'

'Raz, didn they call the police?'

'Nuh, give um a sob story, didn I?'

Notice she leaves out the part abou practically throwing herself at tha Jehovo.

Shifty raises an eyebrow. 'An they fell for ih?'

'No,' I pipe up before she gehs too carried away. 'Her sob story nearly goh us signed up to the God squad! The guard was a full-blown Bible-basher! I had to boot the fire door through to escape.'

Shifty's pure lapping ih up, snapping his fingers an bouncing off the walls wi delight. 'Focking rarers, guy! Wish I was wi you – they'd be kipping before I confessed half my sins, we coulduh just breezed out uh there, pure dappa don, breh. Praise the Lord!' He stamps his feet an spuds fists wi me an Becca. The only one noh laughing is Charmaine.

'Shoulduh known you'd find ih funny, Shift,' she says. 'We're s'posed to be grown up these days, noh running round nicking like a load uh kids.'

Becca's lips slide into a wry smile. 'Fuck off, Char! Since when did you become goody two-shoes? I remember when you woulduh been first in there for a laugh.'

Charmaine puffs on the spliff an stares at the telly, some proper heavy thunder clouds in the air now.

'Anyway, I was only doing ih for him.' Becca eases the tension by giving me a shove.

'Hey, dun blame me!'

'Well, if you'd uh brought some fucking clothes wi you–'

'Whoa, whoa, hang on,' Shifty cuts in, decking himself. 'You telling me Marvin ain' even goh a change uh scruds or nothing?'

'I been washing um out!' I lie, buh somehow tha sounds even funnier an we all crack up again.

'Why didn you come to me, breh? You'll never go without when uncle Shift's about! Hold tight, I'll be back in a minih.'

'Watch you doan slam my fucking . . . door,' Charmaine calls as the whole block shakes.

Five minutes later a life-sized mcing Mr Messy comes waddling in, armfuls uh clothes dropping to the ground almost as quick as our jaws. Charmaine breaks the stunned silence.

'Best you doan go bringing no trouble to my yard, Shift, I'm telling you now.'

'Relax woman, ih's all safe an kosher, in ih? You are, Marv. Problem solved!' He parachutes towards me with a massive pair uh nearly-white boxer shorts.

'There's no way thas legit!' Becca says, examining the pile. 'Look, this one's still goh the fucking clothes pegs on!'

An injured Shifty clasps the dagger from his heart. 'Well wha d'you expect fuh fock all?'

'I'm noh wearing someone else's boxers,' I say.

'Okay, puh these on instead.' A pair uh frilly black knickers land on my shoulder an I brush um off quick smart. Wha is ih with everyone throwing their knickers at me lately? Last week I couldn geh near a pair, now I cahn geh away from the fucking things. Just a shame they ain' the one person's I'm interested in.

'We'll geh you some new ones over the shop later. Doan stress,' Charmaine says to me. 'As fuh you, Shift – geh this crooked shit out my house, now!'

'Cahn take ih back, I lost the receipt. An I ain' no crook, I'm an entrepreneur, I'll have you know. Pure Richard Branstones in the house, yeah? Yeah! Believe!'

*   *   *

I'm kicking Shifty's arse on the Mega Drive when the door knocks. The comings an goings in this place ain' remarkable buh on this occasion summin abou the voice out in the passage causes my hands to freeze stiff on the controller.

'Ah! Gutted. Fatality, motherfocker!'

Shifty might be gloating buh I goh bigger fish to fry cos the lounge door's just opened to reveal my worst nightmare – Brian Harvey from outside the chippy the other day, an leh's just say he's still goh one massive chip stuck on his shoulder.

'Sit down, Russ,' Charmaine says, smiling fuh the first time in wha seems like years. 'Jamo's still out buh you can hang on yur till he gehs back.'

'Origh, safe.'

'So how's yuh sister doing wi the baby? Been meaning to visit for ages.'

'Yeah, yeah, she's origh,' he tells her, eyes fixed on me an me alone.

'Beat you again, breh! You knows you cahn test!' Shifty taunts cos my concentration's shot to shit.

'Yes Shift, fuck him up man,' this Russy says with an empty magpie laugh. I wish the cunt a slow death, I really do. The whole atmosphere in the room has changed an ih dun take Charmaine long to notice.

'Whas up with everyone all of a sudden? Why's ih gone so quiet?'

'Dunno,' Russy shrugs, trynuh snatch the controller out my hand. 'Gimme a go, kid. Yuh shit.'

I grab on tight, fucked if I'm lehrin go. No way.

'Oi! Fucking cut ih out! Still havn learnt yuh lesson, uv you?'

'Wha you on abou, Bec?' Charmaine goes, puzzled. 'You loh knows each other, do you?'

'This little thug tried robbing Marvin the other day. He's a nasty piece uh work.' Becca's chipped sabre-tooth glints under her raised lip, itching for a shot at the boy's jugular.

'I was *jo-king*,' Russy goes, as though we're all thick.

'Like fuck you were. I knows your sort, mate.'

'Durr, I was only messing around, how many more times? Wadn I, kid?'

'Nuh,' I goes, an he shakes his head in disbelief at my betrayal.

'You shouldn even show yuh face round yur,' Becca goes, wrinkling up her nose like she's smelling shit.

'Hang on a minih. Russy been calling over yur for ages an we've never had no trouble before. I'm good friends with his sister as ih goes, an she's never said nothing abou no bullying either. Maybe Marvin just took ih the wrong way.'

Russy's loving the support, pure playing up to Charmaine like no one's business. 'Doan listen to um Char, they're full uh shit. Ih's me tha should be moaning. This bitch threw a full bag uh chips at my head. Skanked my lift home, too – had to walk all the way from town.'

'Didums!'

'Oh, doan start on him, Bec. Yur out of order.'

'So yuh gunuh take his word over mine? Some fucking friend you are!'

'Hark who's talking! You doan give a fuck abou anyone buh yuhself, so doan gimme this best buddies bullshit.'

'If ih's like ah I'll geh my bar off Jamo an go elsewhere, no worries.'

I'm shewer there's a glint in Russy's black pebbles at the mention uh the bar. Becca an Charmaine are too angry to care, mind.

'Well ih's gunuh happen sooner or later, in ih? Cause mayhem an fuck off; why break the habit of a lifetime? You've never paid yuh dues!'

Shifty's up off the settee trynuh calm things down, handling ih surprisingly well for a guy who usually cahn do his laces up without a song an dance. Charmaine an Russy end up in the kitchen while we stay in the room to cool off.

'If they comes out starting I'll bang the cunts!' Becca goes once the door's shut.

I'm shaking, fists clenched ready to show Becca I'll always have her back.

'Listen, calm down, people, calm down,' Shifty goes, ushering us into our seats. 'I know wha Russy's like, buh Charmaine's well in with his family an she cahn see no bad in him. Just leh ih slide, yeah?'

A few minutes later the kitchen door opens an there's a square off as we wait to see who makes the first move. 'Everyone safe now then, or wha? Shifty says, buh before we goh a chance to answer in walks Jamo, his smile disappearing at the sight tha greets him.

'Fuck's going on yur?'

'Ih's Becca – she's stirring some shit up wi Russy. Never took her long to start, just like I told you.'

'Just like I told you? Been talking behind my back is ih? Tell her, Jam. This prick was well out of order in Chippy Lane, wadn he?' She's puhrin Jamo on the spot yur, buh fair play to him, he tells ih like ih was. Russy visibly shrinks while Jamo's

132

laying ih on, his puffed up budgie chest plucked bare by the damning testimony.

'Thas righ, stick up for her, woan you?' Charmaine spits.

'I'm noh sticking up fuh no one. All I'm doing is telling the truth.'

'Truth doan do you a loh uh good wi Becca around.'

'Right, forgeh ih, I'm out uh yur!' Becca picks up her stuff buh Jamo catches hold of her arm an swings her round.

'You doan have to go nowhere,' he says. 'Ih's abou time you two properly puh all this behind you. No good dwelling on the past fuh the rest uh yuh lives, is ih? If anyone needs to leave, ih's Russy.'

'Doan worry, I'm going,' Russy sulks. '. . . only messing abou.'

'Yeah, I knows your version uh messing abou,' Jamo says. 'Yur a bully, Russ, an you'll end up gehrin ih back one uh these days.'

'Wha you gunuh do, Jam? Touch me an I'll geh my brothers over yur to fill you in.' He sweeps round the room pointing at everyone in turn, bar Charmaine. 'I'll geh my brothers to fill you all in. Cunts!'

The door slams an we're left looking at each other as if to say, *Wha now?*

Jamo speaks first. 'Should knock these girls' heads together, eh, Marv?' His grin shines like a beacon around the room, cutting through the poisonous vibes an bringing us to our senses. Becca an Charmaine exchange sheepish glances.

'C'mon, I ain' telling you the good news unless you both make up.'

'Forgeh ih, Jam. Ih's obvious she ain' gunuh trust me. I'm better off leaving.'

'Well be fair, Bec. You have goh a habit uh jetting wi the loot, so to speak,' Jamo reasons. If anyone else said tha she'd be freaking, buh with him she just drops her head an gives a little sniff.

'Buh there again, you come back to make amends, like you said, in ih?'

'Yeah.'

133

'Well then, ih's only fair we give her a chance, ain' tha right Charmaine?' He peels a wad uh notes from his pocket an begins to count before thinking twice an handing the loh over to Becca. 'You are. Yur's wha I made off the weed so far. So whas ih to be, Bec? Cut an run, or pay yuh dues like you said you were gunoo?'

'Thas wha I come yur for,' Becca says, passing a pile uh cash to Jamo, then a pile to Charmaine. 'Thas fuh Gavin.'

Charmaine inspects ih, hesitates, then puhs ih in her pocket. 'Thanks,' she says quietly.

'Origh. So now you two can start fresh, yeah?'

'Yeah.'

'Yeah.'

'Wicked. Cos there's some good news I been itching to tell you.'

'Whas up, Jam?' Shifty says, glad of a chance to lighten the mood.

'Saw a man abou a dog today.'

'Orr yeah. Pleased fuh you breh – really made up.'

'Origh yuh sarky cunt. This man happened to have on him summin I think you'll find very interesting.' Jamo plucks a packet out uh thin air wi the flair of a TV magician, teasing his captivated audience before finally letting the little white pills tinkle out on to the coffee table.

'Pukkas!'

'They're noh, are they?'

Everyone crowds, excitement brewing.

'An they are, nice one!'

'Check ih out, Marv – mitzi's. Pure clean too,' Shifty says, holding one up to the light.

'Dun no wha you're gehrin excited abou, Shift. Still owes me fuh tha draw the other day.'

'Doan go all Scrooge McDuck on me, Jam. I gehs my giro next Tuesday, you knows ih's there, breh.'

'Yuh lucky I'm feeling generous,' Jamo goes, clearly enjoying the wind up. 'Buh I s'pose there's been enough bad vibes round yur today. Time to spread a bih uh love, wha d'you say, Marv? You up fuh some ecstasy?'

'I'm noh taking no ecstasy!' I says. 'I seen in the papers, tha stuff can kill you.'

'Media hype breh! Media hype!' Shifty's singing, clicking his fingers an giggling. 'D'you think we're gunuh kill our focking selves, yuh bumbaclart? The government spreads lies cos they ain' creaming no cash off this shit, thas all.'

'Well, I dunno . . .'

'Up to you,' Jamo goes. 'No one's forcing you to do nothing, buh we been taking pills fuh years an none of us uv croaked. Shifty might be brain dead, buh he was like ah in the first place. Honest.'

'If yuh gunuh do pills only take half, okay? You goes green off a smoke, fuh fuck's sake.'

I think thas Becca's way uh looking out fuh me buh the others ain' having ih.

'Bollocks! Either he does a pill or he don't. So whas ih to be?'

I can yur Mr Hooley in the back uh my mind: . . . *dirty druggies . . . killer pills . . . a cabbage fuh life* . . . Then I think abou some uh the other crap he's come out with over the years an realise people like Hooley dun know fuck all abou anything, just sit on their fat arses badmouthing stuff tha scares um. I wanuh live, do exciting things with exciting people, find out wha ih's all abou an I'm gunuh start right now. I grabs the pill out uh Shifty's fingers, puhs ih on my tongue an swallows hard.

'Hwahaha! So much fuh being nervous, Marvin's first to drop! You were winding us up, this ain' yuh first time is ih? Yuh some hardcore cheesy quaver on the quiet breh!' He grips my shoulders an shakes buh ih's nice an safe an proud, noh like Dad's rough hands. I'm buzzing already an the pill havn even hit my stomach.

'Right then!' Jamo claps his hands together. 'We ain' gunuh geh hype hibernating in this fucking hovel. Leh's geh out there people. Barry Island, wha d'you say? We goh some cash, leh's go down to the shows like we used to.'

Ih's stupid, buh my first reaction is *no way*, cos the only time I been to Barry was wi the youth club an I ended up gehrin my bag thrown in the sea by a gang uh kids. Then ih dawns on me – thas wha this whole thing's been abou, this

135

whole journey. I didn come to Cardiff just to find my mother. I come to find myself. The kid who wen to Barry Island last time's long gone. This is the new Marvin, Marvin wi friends, Marvin wi balls, pure ready for anything. An I'm loving every minute of ih!

22

We stop in Ely on the way through, cos apparently the probation uv sent Wonk Eye to stay with his nan an grampy away from Llanedeyrn. By the time we pull up I'm convinced these pills are bunk, noh even the faintest tingle of a good time on the horizon. I'd like to yur Shifty's opinion buh he's far too busy muttering sweet nothings to himself, sweating deep breaths into cupped hands like a winter's morning on planet Mercury.

'Proper breh, focking proper. Safe? Safe!' His eyes bulge as he pokes an prods, checking to make shewer every facial feature's still intact. Answers my unspoken question, I s'pose. Jamo kills the engine an we sit in the ceasefire silence uh this war torn Ely street taking stock of our casualties. Apart from Shifty who's now doing some sortuh weird Mr Miyagi routine, everyone seems fairly normal.

'Wonk Eye's nan's house is over there,' Jamo says. 'Becca, you'll have to give him a knock. She knows our faces. Reckons ih's us tha leads him astray. If only she fucking knew!'

We watch through the bushes as a reluctant Becca gehs verbally power slammed by Big Daddy in a tabard. Big bones must run in Wonk Eye's family buh unlike her grandson, this old battleaxe dun take no prisoners. 'Mouthy old cow, she is!' Becca tamps back at the car. 'Swore he wadn there buh I seen his coat on the banister. She's full of ih.'

'Fuck ih, leh's go,' Charmaine says. 'Cahn say we never tried.'

'Nah, I ain' leaving him out, ih's rude as fuck. Hang on, I'll be back now.'

Jamo's gone less than twenty seconds before Shifty starts to fidget. Ih dun take him too much nagging to persuade me to follow cos fuh some reason I've started to feel a bih antsy myself. As we creep through overgrown gullies the tingling I initially thought was nerves suddenly explodes into pulses uh pure sweetness as though somewhere deep inside my belly ten thousands sherbet bombs have exploded all at once. I'm sideswiped by this warm fuzzy feeling which massages every muscle in my body an coaxes my jawbone out of ihs socket. So this must be coming up.

Shifty ain' slow to notice, either. 'Raz, Marvin – yur eyes are like focking dinner plates breh! Hwahaha!'

There's a rustle in the bushes an Jamo pops his head out. 'Wha you two doing yur? I thought I told you to wait in the car.'

'No can do, Jam. The beans uv kicked in an we needs a mish. So whas g'waanin?'

Jamo ain' abou to piss into the wind by trynuh reason wi Shifty so he decides to make best use of us now we're yur. 'Thas Wonk Eye's window up by there, I think. Maybe if we give ih a knock we can geh his attention.' He finds a few little stones lying around an taps um on the window buh there's no signs uh life.

'Fock this. I'll show you how ih's done!' Shifty picks up summin resembling half a house brick an cocks his arm back.

'No!' I shout, cos if tha hits the glass ih'll puh ih through, no doubt.

'Warghhh!' Shifty drops the brick an almost ends up on the roof. Ih's noh me who's spooked him though, ih's the two giggling, flushed faces emerging from the bushes wi the same dinner-plate gaze I've apparently goh.

'Girls – orr, fuh fuck's sake man, ih's like a family reunion. Well, try to keep quiet, yeah?'

'I seen him breh, I seen someone up there – Wonk Eye! Oh, Wonk!'

'Shhh!!'

Everyone dives behind the outhouse, hoping we havn been spotted.

'Shifty, wha did I just say? You'll have his grampy out yur in a minih.'

'Sorry breh, I forgoh.'

'C'mon, Jam,' Charmaine goes. 'We cahn stand out yur all night. We've tried our best.'

'Nah, fuck tha. I told you, I ain' leaving without him. Ih's noh right. Wha we need is someone to climb up there. Who's the smallest?'

This is my time to shine so without missing a beat the new Marvin's straight across the garden, shimmying up the drainpipe to the muffled cheers uh my new friends, my real genuine friends, fingers trembling an heart racing. They love me an I love them, these thoughts all tha keeps me going cos ih's higher than you'd think up yur an this iron drainpipe's rusty as fuck round by Wonk Eye's window. A final leg thrust tugs the fixings from their berth an for a moment ih's looking like I'll be kipping on the concrete tonight.

'Hwahaha! He's gunuh go, he's gunuh go!'

Yuring Shifty crack up sets me off, nervous giggles tickling my fingertips, grip weakening more with each second tha passes. Still, I somehow reach the window an peer in. Wonk Eye's there alright. Sat with a big pair uh headphones on, lost in the music. When I bang on the window he spins round, screams an falls backwards off his chair. Like a chain reaction I balk too, an with an agonising creak ih dawns on me tha the drainpipe's finally given up the ghost. There's literally milliseconds between grabbing the window ledge an the rusty pipe crashing to the floor.

'Fucking help me boys, help me!' I'm going, struggling to keep hold uh the ledge. Shifty's trynuh help, buh he's laughing so much he can barely stand. Then there's a rattling at the backdoor. Someone's coming! Everyone scrambles for a cover, leaving this dead duck dangling right above Wonk Eye's nan's head.

'Who's there?' she calls, buh no one's moving a muscle. I pray she dun look up. 'Frank! Frank, come quick. There's someone in the garden.'

The old boy appears, big an bald in a white vest an slippers. Coulduh been pretty tasty in his day. Few too many Clark's pies in the fucker now mind, buh on the upside, tha belly might make for a soft landing when the inevitable

139

happens. 'Someone out my garden, is it? Thieving bastards, I'll put you through the wall.'

'Maybe it's those tinkers from up the road,' nana says.

'Tinkers!' the old man roars. 'C'mon out yuh stinking gypos, I'm noh too old to thrash you!'

The weight uh my burning bladder slowly pulls me down like thick treacle from a spoon, fingernail after fingernail eliminated from the ledge until shewerly . . .

Ffrrrrt!

Time stands still. Nana turns to her husband, mouth open. 'Ooh, Frank!'

I yur someone whisper, '*Por, ih fucking stinks, Shift!*' an then Shifty sniggering in the bush. Now I really goh the giggles there's no chance uh keeping grip. I land in a heap in front uh the two fogeys, thanking my lucky stars the old boy's too stunned to react cos he looks even tastier from this angle. Everyone breaks from their hiding places, shrieking laughing over hedges an fences in the mad scramble back to the car.

We pile into the motor an Jamo revs hard, Wonk Eye tearing out to flag us down as we pull away. 'Stop, Jam – wait!' we call, opening the door so the big man can squash onto the already rammed back seat an then we're off, screaming an joking, claiming glories an savouring the victory.

'Wonk Eye! Nice uh you to join us, man.' Jamo passes the bag uh pills over his shoulder.

'Hyng, yes guys! Cahn believe you showed up – thought I was gunuh be stuck up yur forever.'

'Wadn gunuh leave you stranded wi no mates while we go on a mad one, was we? Wha sort uh daft fuckers sends someone to Ely to geh straight, anyway?'

'In ih? This was my last chance to clean up my act,' Wonk Eye says, looking back through the rear window at his grampy out in the street. 'Tried my hardest buh ih's boring being good. I doan care no more, they can tell the probation officer. Couldn handle another day there. Whas the point uh living if you ain' having fun?'

23

Soft colours meld on the dusky horizon, pinks an blues an greens swimming together to the sound uh pumping dance music as we sail down the yellow brick road towards our very own Emerald City by the sea. My tingling stomach takes a dip in time wi the log flume in the distance, every muscle in my body pulsing hard wi the ecstasy tha feeds ih. A thousand crystal clear thoughts flash through my mind at once, pearls uh wisdom brought to the surface by the giant thas awakened within me. Guilt an worry fall away as I reach fuh the stars, finally free, finally understanding. I remember a quote this supply teacher once told us – there's nothing to fear buh fear ihself, said ih more to himself than the class as we puh him through the wringer buh I'd shake his hand if I saw him right now. Hug those kids who threw my bag in the sea too cos I'm noh scared anymore an I truly hope they ain' either. Nothing can harm you when you ain' afraid, when you ain' ashamed to look the world in the eye an say this is me, take ih or leave ih.

I drift out the car pure fresh air on legs. Ih's only Becca grabbing my arm tha keeps me from standing there all night, just drinking in the sights an sounds. We follow after the beckoning house beat, Shifty leading the way like a deranged Pied Piper, ripping the piss out of everyone as he goes. I dun escape a tongue lashing buh now I can laugh cos I know the score – a wind up merchant buh one uh the best really, deep down.

We bounce from one ride to another, the dodgems to the waltzers to the pirate ship, screaming laughing as we're thrown upside down an all around. Flashing bulbs print luminous patterns on the backs uh my eyelids, machine grease an chip fat linger like danger an excitement on the cool night air. No chance to gather myself, the safety bar clicks into position on the rollercoaster cart, Jamo's big massive grin to my left saying everything's alright. The chains clank as we climb higher an higher, soothing breeze sending mad shivers along my spine while I look down at the hoardings, paintings uh vipers an big muscle-man barbarians wi long hair an glinting axes. I'm reminded uh my father's heavy metal records back home, his prized possessions – them an his guitar, his stupid fucking guitar which I never even touched no marrer wha Darren says buh the records I couldn deny, caught red-handed when Dad come home early from the pub bruised an angry an looking fuh someone easier to pick on so the phone cord cracked an the tears fell, usual story, fighting to hold um in never worked, Darren leering through the gap in the door, snivelling shithouse glad ih was me an noh him gehrin hiding off the cunt yuh CUNT, YUH FUCKING BULLY CUNT buh I cahn hate no more, dun have ih in me, dun wan ih in me cos I love um, I honestly do love um buh sometimes ih's better to love from a distance till one day when the time's right to come back an see um, when I'm sorted an I know who I am an wha I'm doing an I might even have a job an some money, money to buy Dad new records, to fix the string I snapped on his guitar, the string tha goh Darren battered buh I never meant to break ih, I swear, an I'm sorry buh in a way I'm thankful cos if ih never happened maybe I wouldn be yur wi this loh having the time uh my life, reaching the peak, as high as we can go an now ih's down, down a hundred miles an hour, Jamo screaming summin in my yur buh all I geh is the rush an ih dun marrer anyway, wha'ever he said, I know ih was good so I hold on tight an shout back, noh even words, just feelings like, an as we twist an turn water stings my eyes buh I wun pretend they're from the wind cos they're tears, real tears leaking emotions I've never dared face before an now I know, truly know why they call ih ecstasy.

24

Shows worn out, we pile back into the car wi the aim uh continuing the party at some seaside park the boys know of. As soon as we set off Shifty's acting up, swinging from Jamo's headrest like a hyper young brat nagging Daddy fuh ice cream an pop an Rizlas. Stocking up's noh a bad idea so we pull over outside a row uh rough an ready shops, Charmaine tossing Shifty a single twenty-pence coin fuh rolling papers cos at this precise moment ih's revealed he's actually brassic till giro day. She stays puh buh the rest of us troop in, rising above the stares from the gang outside cos we're untouchable tonight forever. Inside, everyone drifts their separate ways, chatty an mellow an easy, browsers in a department store looking fuh Pringle sweaters an scatter cushions. A single blink launches me one thousand years into the future, snapping to consciousness inside the mother ship's engine room, rows uh radioactive Lilt an Fanta capsules glowing luminous in their stark white chiller cabinet. The humming fridge motor's infectious rhythm syncs wi my body sparking small belly vibrations which grow into full blown rushes by the time they reach my arms an legs.

Wonk Eye's big clumsy body knocks me back down to Earth as he rumbles by, giggling a selection uh five-finger discounted items into his pockets. I wanuh tell him to stop buh I'm no more than a floating flake uh dandruff on his vast shoulders, debris to a gentle giant in the zone. Shifty's at the counter, rabbiting away to the shop owner in tha mad Cardiff accent, part jungle MC, part platform announcer wi sinus trouble. Sounds mad to me like, buh there again everyone down yur thinks I sound weird too. An thas wha ih's all abou really – accepting differences an enjoying um instead uh taking the piss out of anyone different. I wanuh spill this revelation to Shifty cos he's right on my wavelength, especially wi these pills. Thing is, the boy's on a roll an I cahn interrupt as he's going: '. . . orr yes breh, I knows, I knows! People doan realise wha a hard job you goh sometimes . . . like those little fockers out there, 'scuse my French an ah . . . causing trouble for everyone, an people says you're the problem, you know, coming over yur taking our jobs buh the end uh the day why should you be the one to geh hassle when ih's them loh smashing up the place every night? Serving the community, thas wha yuh doing buh these scumbags doan wanuh see ih tha way – rather blame someone else fuh whas wrong in their lives instead uh making the effort to fix themselves. D'you geh wha I'm saying, breh?'

The shopkeeper eyeballs Shifty like he's just stepped out of a flying saucer. Shifty's noh stopping fuh no one mind, words just pouring out.

'Orr, wicked! I knew ih breh, I knew you'd geh ih. Some people thinks I'm daft when I tries to explain myself, buh you're on the level man, you knows the score. Cos the end uh the day, life's too short in ih? Too short to go around giving other people grief. Gohruh focus on the good stuff. Ih's like my auntie Pam, wicked woman, swear to God – always bought me presents an sweets when I was young. Havn spoke to her fuh years now, none uh my family have since she married tha copper. My father wouldn leh us go to the wedding or nothing. I mean, doan geh me wrong, I hates the police as much as the next man buh the end uh the day he's serving the community an all, in he? Just a question of how you looks at things, thas wha I'm saying, yeah? Yeah! Been approaching life the wrong way before today, time to build some bridges, do the right thing. Wha d'you reckon boss, should I phone my auntie Pam tomorrow? Think I will, you know. I will do ih breh. My auntie Pam. Short fuh Pamela, like, buh she ain' short – lanky if anything – husband's six foot three though so ih all works out in the end. Like life really, buh only in fairy tales if you see wha I mean cos you never know when ih's all gunuh end, do you? Like little Deano, died last year, only fourteen years old. Joyriding. Hit a tree an BAM – game over! In the *Echo* an everything, pure tragic. Read abou tha, did you? Terrible in ih? Boss . . . boss – I'm saying abou little Deano–'

'Leave the guy alone, Shift,' Becca cuts in, walking up to the counter. 'There's people trynuh geh served yur, fuh fuck's sake.'

Shifty takes the hint an pays up buh ih still takes Becca to frogmarch him out the door cos wisdom like his just wun't stay contained.

Back in the car Wonk Eye marvels his ill-gotten gains. 'Hyng, check ih out! Four Walnut Whips, biscuits, a tin uh peas–'

'A tin uh peas?' Becca goes. 'Fuck d'you wan wi tha?'

Wonk Eye shrugs off the stupidest question he's ever yurd in his life an Becca might be abou to say more when Shifty busts in with an agonising 'awwwww . . .' which builds to an eventual: '. . . wwww breh, I cahn believe wha you've done! Tha guy in the shop was safe as fock an you've gone an skanked the cunt right under his nose.' He lunges for the steering wheel, forcing Jamo to swerve across the road.

'Whoa!'

'Shifty, wha you doing?'

'Mad cunt's trynuh kill us!'

Shifty's noh listening though. 'Turn the focking car round, Jam,' he pleads, grabbing the wheel again. 'C'mon, we're taking ih all back. Tha guy was safe, he'll understand. I'll explain everything.'

Jamo pulls an emergency stop an everyone turns to inspect the three extra heads Shifty's shewerly sprouted. Charmaine's first to speak. 'Take ih back? You listening to yuhself, Shift? Coppers'll be round there before you can say a word. Pff – *take ih back*. Lay off the pills man, they're frying yuh brain.'

'No, you doan geh ih. I made a connection wi tha bloke. Building community bridges an ah, breh. He knew the score, he would've understood. We gohruh stop living like this.'

'Fuck off! You're the world's worst to talk – thieved anything tha wadn bolted down since you was in juniors!'

Shifty's chewing hard, looking for a chink in Charmaine's flawless comeback an I gohruh speak up cos he's reading my thoughts, pure *Twilight Zone* style. 'Shifty's right. Ih's noh on, ripping decent people off all the time. We gohruh start living right – going back to tha shop might be the first step for us.'

His face instantly brightens cos he knew he could count on me an he dun wan me ending up the same way as him, in an out uh prison an all the rest of ih. Makes a good case too, cos the piss-taking eases up an when he feels he's properly hammered the point home he sits back an cracks open a can uh pop, pretty damn pleased with himself.

'Blurgh! Cherry coke? Wha' the fock?' he spits through a jet uh fizzy brown liquid.

'Where'd you geh tha from?' Becca says. 'Thought you didn even have twenty pence fuh Rizlas.'

Shifty frowns, proper stumped, like. 'Orr yeah, yuh right . . . wha the . . .'

'So wha else you hiding in yuh pockets?' Becca frisks him down an next thing they're both pulling out all sorts; chocolate, chewing gum, drinks, the loh. By now everyone's pissing umselves an I gohruh admit I'm laughing too cos ih's like one uh those magic acts – all thas missing is the white rabbit. When he's finally finished he snaps his fingers together an gives his mad giggle.

'Raz, even when I'm trynuh be safe I'm still a cunt!' he says, an everyone cracks up again.

'So much fuh the hippy bullshit, Shift! You'll never change, man. Born tea leaf, through an through!'

As we drive off again I snatch glances at Shifty, noh quite able to believe tha whole thing just happened. He's playing ih off, laughing along wi the others, buh laughing a bih too hard if you know wha I mean, a wild-eyed hyena laugh, actually more of a scream an thas when I notice the fingernails clamped deep into his forearm, clawing an scratching an twisting the scarred flesh into knots.

25

I sit staring into the flames, jaw working overtime as crackling bonfire sparks dash themselves into oblivion against the inky blackness above us. The extra pills tha did the rounds either minutes or decades ago have made my mind fly buh my body slow so I lay back an leh the night wrap around me . . . No sooner uv I closed my eyes than a bass quake erupts from the boot uh Jamo's car an someone tugs on my arm – Jamo, is ih? No, ih's Shifty an now Becca's flanked my other side an they're pulling me to my two left feet.

'Doan flake out, Marv, have a dance with us,' Becca says, dragging me to a clearing where Wonk Eye shuffles in tha Spliffy jacket, his big round face glowing post-box red. I've never even danced in a disco, leh alone some field buh ecstasy wipes ihs arse on the yuh hang-ups an before I know ih I'm up on my heels, bobbing an weaving to the jungle beat. Shifty lehs out this primal scream an jumps in front uh me, waving his arms in time, motioning fuh me to copy an pretty soon we're both hooked into the groove, wired into the mains cos this music's doing things to my body I never knew possible.

Charmaine an Jamo retreat to the other side uh the fire, hugging an smooching like ih's the last dance in one uh them stupid American films leaving me, Shifty an Wonk Eye in a ring throwing out our best moves. Becca winds her way between the three of us, flashes uh smooth white belly under her crop top as hypnotising as the rhythm. When she coils up close my heart's ready to give out buh nothing can prepare me fuh wha happens next. Round she spins, wiggling her arse abou half inch from my dick, closer an closer till those smooth round bumps knock into my groin sending my stomach into orbit as the beat goes on an on. The message is clear – she wants ih! After all the hoping an wishing, my dreams are coming true. I start to move in time with her, almost like we're fucking there an then buh just as I'm going in fuh the kill she's off, snaking her way over to Shifty, grinding him the same way while he whoops an shouts, moving with her much better than I was an there's a pang uh jealousy tha even the lead-lined ecstasy buzz cahn deflect. Wonk Eye's in for a turn next buh suddenly Jamo butts in out uh nowhere all joking an laughing buh I can see the way he looks at her an the way she looks at him an I reckon Charmaine can see ih too, even though she's dancing wi Shifty pretending noh to notice.

After a while the music fades an everyone seems to slink off into the shadows till there's only me an Shifty left sat by the fire. My eyelids begin to drop buh Shifty nudges me gently an when he speaks there's this sortuh urgency abou him. 'Noh kipping on me, uh you, Marv? Doan fall asleep breh, I'm – you know . . . I wanuh talk, yeah?'

'I wadn sleeping, Shift, I was thinking things over, thas all.' I says ih pure soft for some reason, like I'm trynuh reassure a frightened kid.

'Safe, breh, safe . . . so wha you been thinking abou?'

'Dunno, all sorts, I s'pose.'

'Abou life an ah?' he goes hopefully.

'Yeah, mayb–'

'Funny, tha thing wi me nicking from the shop earlier, wadn ih?' He does his little *hwahaha*, buh his eyes are lost at sea, searching fuh some beacon in the distance. 'Ih's true wha they said in the car. I am a born thief. Been doing ih so long I doan know anything else. Mad in ih, breh? Twenty-two years old an all I done wi my life is nick an geh locked up, nick an geh locked up over an over. When I come out last time I swore tha was ih buh I focked up again. Same old story, hwahaha.' He's chewing his face like a cow in a meadow, fixing me wi those big dark saucers. 'Promise me you woan go nicking no more, Marv. I knows ih's a mad laugh buh – well, like I said before. Doan wan you ending up like me. Try an do summin good wi yuh life.'

'Buh yuh noh tha old. You still goh time to change.'

148

'Nah, I'm focked. Made a name fuh myself now an ih's all downhill from yur. People . . . people woan leh you forgeh who you are. Noh talking peer pressure from other crooks neither, I'm on abou people in the community – neighbours, teachers, coppers, every focker. They say they wan you to change buh the truth is they're desperate to keep you the same. Think abou ih – wha ud happen if we really did suddenly turn into saints? Who would they have to look down on? To make umselves feel better? They needs us to be fock ups! These people, respectable cunts an middle-class cunts an the rest of um – they're just as messed up as us buh they're sneakier, thas all. Instead uh taking their issues out on the streets they found a way uh making other people feel like shit – sortuh diverting the attention, yeah?' He looks up at me again, almost begging now. 'You knows wha I'm talking abou, doan you? I mean, ih makes sense, righ?'

I geh tha shiver up my spine cos ih's like the guy knows me better than I know myself, words connecting like a mental dot-to-dot, giving some vital structure to the mass of orphaned thoughts scrabbling abou inside my mind. I wanuh hug the fucker buh I'm no poofter so I just looks him dead in the eye an nods pure deep to make shewer he knows I'm on the level.

'Thas why ih's so important you listen to me, Marv. You're a good kid, man. Sometimes I feel like if I can just geh one person to change ih'll make up fuh the mess I've made uh my life, you know? Ih's wha the God-botherers calls redemption . . . atonement, like buh I'm noh interested in no fairytales, I just needs peace uh mind, yeah? So promise me, breh, promise me you'll geh straight before ih's too late, before tha prison door slams on yuh future. Listen, I'm gunuh tell you summin I never told no one–'

'Shifty! Whas'appening rude boy!' Charmaine bombs up out the shadows an lands on his lap, fucked off her trolley.

'Shift!' I says, cos I cahn leave ih like this, noh when I'm so close to finally sorting this jumble in my head. 'Shift, you was abou to tell me summin . . .'

'Huh?' The old mischievous Shifty turns back to me, no trace uh the tender soul tha possessed his body for a few sweet moments. 'Orr yeah, ih was – uh – argh, fock knows, Marv. Probly bollocks anyway!'

'No "probly" abou ih if ih come out uh your mouth!' Charmaine goes an now he's wrestling her to the ground an she's shrieking an he's blowing raspberries on her neck an I'm left there holding an empty sack wondering if I'll ever geh the answers I'm searching for.

Autumn 2018

Somehow the girl with the thick fringe and dark eyes is back in his bed. This shouldn't have happened. After he forced Karen away he swore never to get involved again. Strictly no strings from now on. Easy. Safe. Fun. The way he used to be. But then, from the way she's lolling, right breast half exposed on the crumpled sheets, his 'n' hers bathrobes and Sunday trips to IKEA seem to be the furthest thing from both their minds. As if to sooth his unspoken anxieties she rolls over to his side of the bed, teasing him back to life first with her hand, then her tongue. He sighs with pleasure, rising to the occasion and enjoying not only the sensation but the fact that at thirty-eight going on eighty he can still get female attention. Young, fresh female attention, not fat and frumpy like Karen, more like . . . needful kisses smother distant memories, bodies meeting as he pins and mounts, arched back shielding them from the outside world, forcing everyone and everything from his mind for this short while.

Afterwards they lie back exhausted, taking turns to drag on the poorly constructed spliff the girl pinched off one of her flatmates. The smoke makes the man splutter, not having used weed since his teenage years, since the YO unit a lifetime ago. One of the few pleasures they'd sometimes manage to get hold of, smoking around the tinny pocket radio that picked up pirate stations full of jungle, hardcore and garage. He pulls up a few old tunes on the laptop, dismayed as the girl crinkles her nose in disdain at his supposedly hip musical tastes. She switches to some new deep house thing created by two twelve-year-olds with designer salon haircuts, if the accompanying artwork is anything to go by. He tries to tell her it's rubbish, and worse still, rubbish which samples an old garage record but she's impervious to his criticism, wrapped snug in her own youthful sense of cool which draws simultaneous resentment and admiration. He chides her again about learning the roots of her music, but secretly quite enjoys the track and makes a mental note to pick up some hair gel when next at the supermarket. Maybe it's time for a new look to go with his new, fun attitude.

Now she's talking about some weekend rave the two twelve-year-olds are playing, moaning how little her bar job pays and it doesn't take a genius to see where she's heading with this one. He duly obliges, feeling quite the smooth operator as the girl melts with excitement. She rattles off all the different DJs she wants to meet but the man is busy indulging in his own fantasies, imagining the swathes of pretty young things, easily impressed by an older guy with a flat and a car and a few quid in his pocket. He's absent-mindedly wondering whether eyebrow piercings are in when his mobile buzzes on the bedside cabinet.

Shit. The school play. He forgot about the fucking play!

He tears out of the flat, trying to straighten out his shirt while prising the car door open. Even with his foot right down, he knows it's too late. At the school gates a tsunami of costumed children engulfs him, stripping his trendy pretensions right back to the bone and exposing the insecure fuck up cowering underneath. Where are they? Where are Karen and the kids? There – evidently already aware of his presence, his wife bundles the children into the car so fast bits of crêpe paper cobweb and Halloween bunting break off and tumble forlornly to the ground. When he approaches she turns on him with a ferocity that buckles his knees, screaming about how he promised, how he couldn't even keep a simple promise to his kids and he's screaming back how she never wanted him there anyway, stopping mid-stream at the sight of the kids' frightened faces, staring through the window at some safari park beast, a sad, middle-aged orang-utan ready to pull their windscreen wipers off any second now. As always, she doesn't miss a trick, instantly clocking that he's high on weed. He tells her to go back to her clean cut fancy man, Bob the Builder or whatever his name is, if she can't handle it because he's a free spirit who doesn't have anyone telling him what to do but she laughs and lets him know that he's a pathetic shithouse, and he's the only one who can't see it. She tells him Rob is a shop fitter, not a builder and that there's nothing going on between them anyway. Rob's just been a friend, a huge support to her and the kids, doing a damn sight more to provide stability than him with his mood swings and nastiness, throwing teenage wobblies every two minutes. And talking of teenagers, who's this young girl he's been seen around with, young enough to be his daughter, and just what the hell was he thinking wearing those jeans with his arse hanging out?

When she's thrown everything but the kitchen sink at him she turns away, sobbing now, her voice softer. She tells him she never wanted him to go, tells him the kids miss him and that none of them understand why he left. He wants to explain, wants to lay his insecurities bare but his brain simply can't articulate such complex emotions so he breaks down too and they stand there, yards apart but a chasm between them, both crying out of frustration and genuine despair for the implosion of their family.

Part III : Going Down

26

Fuck knows how long I'm out for or whether I've even slept at all buh when I open my eyes the whole atmosphere's different. Noiselessly we drift back to the car, shell-shocked pill-poppers stewing in a rumbling silence tha keeps up right along the pitch black lanes. I wish there was summin to say, some magic spell tha could zap back the perfect vibes we shared buh ih's hopeless, pointless, useless. The last tingle of excitement I'll ever feel has drained from my guts like piss down a plughole, replaced by pure lead, full blown dread. *Lead, dread.* I'm a poet an I dun know it. Thas noh funny. Ih means nothing, an I hope to fuck I never said ih out loud cos who can guess how these zombie ravers are gunuh take my wise cracks. Look at um, sitting there scheming, itching for a pick uh my brains, a slurp uh my blood, a ride on my carcass oh no oh no oh noooo! I shrink back into the seat, fall out through the boot uh the car, bounce down the road, sit bolt upright, sweat trickling off my nose. Fuck, wha uv I done? Wha uv we all done?

The nagging paranoia refuses to take a breather all the way back home, an as we mount the concrete steps up to the flat I just know fuh shewer summin ain' right. Then ih happens.

'Orr my God!'

Everyone rushes Charmaine to find the front door swinging loose an a few things turned over inside, except the flat was a bih of a state in the first place so telling messed from trashed ain' as easy as ih seems. Jamo barges his way to the front, checking fuh stragglers wi some wild Hollywood door kicks.

'Cunts!' Charmaine goes. 'Whas been taken?'

'Fock all by the looks of ih – telly an stereo both untouched,' Shifty says with a sense uh certainty tha woulduh stopped me reeling if ih wadn fuh the anguished cries coming from the kitchen.

'The bar's gone! They've taken the ganja!'

'Nor breh, nor – this ain' right, ih's noh right,' Shifty mutters, pacing the floor in disbelief. Wonk Eye's sporting his trademark five-hundred yard stare. Only Becca's acting out uh character, finger-tapping her sourpuss very casual fuh someone who'd happily wipe out a continent over so much as a missing cigarette. The weirdness dun stop there though. Charmaine starts to cry. Shifty an Jamo are up over to her in an instant, swearing revenge an rewards if only ih'll shut her up buh Becca ain' having none of ih.

'Boo-fucking-hoo! You must think I was born yesterday.'

Everyone spins around, jaws on the ground.

'Oh, noh being funny Bec, yur out of order, yeah? They've had their door kicked in, fuh fock's sake,' Shifty goes.

'Yeah, right. Some burglars magically burst through the door *without smashing the lock*, missed the fuck-off telly an stereo an wen straight fuh the secret stash uh ganja no one buh us loh knows abou? An *I'm* out of order?'

This pained, scolded-dog look spreads across Shifty's face as the cogs go round, noh shewer wha to believe any more. Him an me both, butt. Telling ew. The surprises keep on coming, now from Wonk Eye who breaks the habit of a lifetime by talking some sense.

'Hyng, doan forgeh Charmaine's always on to Jamo abou leaving the door open. An there's people after tha bar, from Birmingham you said.' The simple truth in his words sizzles on Becca like spit on a hot stove buh the logic's air tight.

'Yeah, Wonk's right. If anyone's goh a motive ih's those Brummies you ripped off. Maybe they tracked you down.'

'No chance! How could they?'

'You tell me. Only gohruh leh slip to one person – word always gehs out in the end.'

'Bollocks! Summin's dodgy yur.' She swallows a gobful uh phlegm an creeping doubt, in way too deep to back out now. 'Cut the waterworks Charmaine, you goh five seconds to gimme my weed back or I'll turn the place over.' Chest heaving, she's ready to rumble an believe me ih's a sight to behold.

Charmaine bites back like we knew she would, shouting through her tears: 'Yuh sick in the head! Really think I'd rob my own house for a little ragga like you? If I wanted summin uh yours I'd tell you to yuh face, noh weasel round on the sly – thas more your style, in ih?'

The details are lost on me buh the gist is clear, blood thumping through my eardrums to the schoolyard echoes of *fight fight fight!*

'Origh, you wanuh talk straight, you wan the truth – Jamo never looked at you twice till I left. Face ih Char, yuh second best. Always have been.'

Talking's over. Charmaine rises from the chair like some mechanical ghost train ghoul, arms outstretched, claws at the ready. Becca's reflexes are spot on mind, clocking her coming in with a solid closed fist an using the few stunned seconds she's bought to latch on to the peroxide pineapple fuh maximum leverage. *Thud thud thud* the punches rain down in sickening hi-fi until Jamo an Shifty can wrestle Becca away. The girls' combined fury proves too much to contain though, breaking free in a cartoon cyclone uh random fists an feet demolishing everything in their path. Ih's all I can do noh to collapse cos this is too much, too raw, this shouldn be happening buh there's no way to stop ih. Noh just the fight buh the rot, everything's fucked. Nothing's gunuh be the same after this.

Finally Jamo manages to prise um apart, fronting up to Becca wi such hostility ih's hard to believe he's the same guy thas held us all together to this point. 'Out, now! I'm serious, you berrer fuck off. Yuh nothing buh trouble.'

'Orr, yur we go. Check out the knight in shining armour,' she laughs through mouthfuls uh hair. 'Wanuh tell her the truth then, Jam or wha? Ih's the least she deserves. All ah talk abou running away wi me – load uh bullshit to geh into my knickers, was ih?'

'She's lying, Char,' he says in a tone tha guarantees she ain't.

'Shoulduh known ih was empty words. Shame, you sounded so convincing wi yuh tongue hanging out,' Becca goes, taunting the pair of um with a devious smile.

'Jealous bitch!' Charmaine's up again buh Shifty catches her an Jamo takes the opportunity to puh a proper end to the matter.

'Out. Now,' he goes, shoving her back towards the front door.

'Geh off me! Get the fuck off meee!' She breaks free, determined to leave wi some sense uh dignity an a couple uh well aimed parting shots to boot. 'Origh, I'm going. You two are welcome to each other. Yuh both full uh shit. Jamo, yur a spineless cunt, an Charmaine, I knows you goh my ganja an you will pay in the end, trust me.'

'Out!'

Ih's crunch time fuh me too, cos obviously this ain' my argument buh there's no way I'm gunuh leave Becca. Buh do she wan me to follow her? One step outside an the door slams shut behind me, so I s'pose thas my dilemma figured out.

'Wha you doing out yuh? Ih's fuck all to do wi you.' She blinks as though waking from a vivid nightmare. I must still be stuck in mine.

'I – I wanuh make shewer yur alright.'

'Yeah I'm fucking origh, an I doan need you or any other little dickhead flapping round me.' She starts back towards the flat then seems to think twice, elbowing past me into the night muttering: 'Cunts! Cunts!' to herself over an over. When she disappears from view I shit ih an give chase.

'Cahn you take a hint, Marv? Go back inside or go home or summin.'

'Buh we come on this mission together . . . I thought we were friends!'

'Ha! Some dreamer, you are,' she goes, picking up a brick an taking a few cool steps towards this car parked nearby.

SMASH!

She's straight in the motor, tearing at the cover under the steering wheel an I'm in the passenger seat before she's goh a chance to stop me. Shewerly there's no way the car will start buh fuck me if the engine ain' revving like a tank in under thirty seconds an then we're gone, pinned against my seat by a mixture of horsepower an horror.

Through the streets, she's bombing ih. Didn even know she could drive buh yur she is taking corners like Nigel Mansell. I sneakily pull on my seatbelt cos ih's clear we goh a good chance uh hitting a wall any second. There ain' much need to be sly, mind cos she's lost in her own world, muttering an banging on the steering wheel, even clawing at her hair every so often.

'Slut!' she's going. 'Dirty little slag, in I? A fucking ragga.'

'No – no, yuh noh,' I says buh ih sounds weak an half-hearted cos I realise I'm well out uh my depth yur.

Now she's laughing an screaming, eyes blazing. I honestly think she's flipped this time, babbling abou being trapped, needing to escape an make everything better. If the words are scary the driving's absolutely terrifying, houses an bus stops melding into a white hot blur, sixty, sixty-five, seventy scorching the glowing speedo. I shrink back while angry demons roar through the broken window, my fingers embedded in the seat fabric as though thas gunuh do a fucking thing to help when the moment of impact comes.

Houses an streetlights finally trail off an we're out on pitch black tarmac, eating up cat's eyes like a big metal monster as the engine strains to ninety-three, ninety-four, ninety-five. Oh my God. I havn even considered where we might be heading, apart from into a fucking ditch like, buh now some familiar signs loom up: *Barry 5 miles*. I kid myself she must've left summin on the Island earlier, or maybe there's friends we can stay with buh one look at her twisted features as we roll into a newish housing estate tells me this definitely ain' no friendly call. Becca kills the headlights an we glide up to a row uh detached houses, semi-secluded by rows uh giant fir trees.

'Where are we?'

She says nothing, staring straight ahead wi those glazed eyes. I go to ask again buh she cuts me off.

'Know who lives in tha house, there?'

'No.'

'My mother an my sister,' she says, leering at the dashboard.

'Bih late to go bothering um now,' I say, amazed how summin so sensible can sound so absurd in a situation like this.

'Noh their house, mind.'

'Uh? Well, whose is ih? Yuh dad's?'

She turns with a weird little chuckle tha makes me shudder. 'No, ih's noh my dad's. Belongs to a bloke called Derek. Owns a garage down by the docks. Nice guy he is, or so everyone thinks.'

Blood drains from my face as the pieces click into place – Frank Butcher. Creepy Frank Butcher. Summin's brewing yur, a big bubbling shit storm just waiting to go off.

'Oh . . . probly in bed now though, in ih?' I say cos wha'ever she goh planned, however gross he is, this ain' the time for more insanity. Without another word she's out the car an disappearing up the driveway, leaving me with only the buzz uh the engine fuh company. I chew my face off in the darkness, trynuh convince the shadows in the rear-view mirror tha she's just gone to collect a few toiletries buh even on drugs we all know thas a load uh bollocks.

Fuck's sake, please hurry up. Great! Now the lights are coming on, first one then two, filtering through the thick branches. Bet they'll hit the roof when they finds us two outside, bombed off our nuts in a nicked car at stupid o'clock in the morning. Call the coppers most probs, unless I can geh her out uh there in time. As I step out the car more lights come on, strange lights, flickering lights, noh like electric bulbs at all, more like – oh fuck, no!

My fried head cahn process the scene tha awaits me up the driveway, six foot flames licking out uh Frank Butcher's shiny Audi an Becca stood near the open garage, tin uh turps or petrol or summin next to her on the floor.

'Wha you done, Bec? Wha uv you fucking done?'

She sortuh screams, so loud an twisted I cahn quite tell if she's laughing or crying an those eyes – fuck me, like an injured animal, pure wild. There's no chance uh gehrin any sense out of her so I turns my attention to the fire, hoping to somehow smother the flames with a dustsheet in the garage. Uh course, the fucking thing whooshes up like tissue paper, searing heat driving me back an I suddenly realise the car could blow any minute. Becca's only interested in snarling at her handiwork, oblivious to the fumbled bedroom lights as she dances round the lawn like some whacked-out Amazon warrior. As if summoned, a face appears in the upstairs window, young an pure enough to banish the demon thas possessed my partner in crime. 'Aimee!' Becca goes, glaciers behind her eyes instantly thawing at the sight of her younger sister. 'Aimee, I've come to rescue you. Believe me love, he's evil – sick in the head. I woan leh him hurt you like he hurt me . . .'

There's an almighty roar from the next window over as creepy Frank makes an appearance, all hairy chest an comb-over, doing a pretty solid impression of Animal off *The Muppets* at the sight before him. Clearly time we wern yur, buh try telling tha to Becca. 'Aimee, please, Aimee, please!' she's going, coaxing her frightened sister like she's a lost puppy. The girl's transfixed though, too gobsmacked to move even if she wanted to, unlike me who's determined to geh going even if ih means dragging Becca along by the hair. Turns out there's no need cos she's snapped out of her trance an legged ih down the drive, leaving me to make my excuses.

Back in the car she's on top uh the world, pure Jekyll an Hyde whooping an cheering like she's won the pools. 'Whooooo! Whooo, burn yuh cunt! Yuh dirty cunt! Happy now? Yessss, hahaha!' I try to laugh along at the unfunniest joke in the world in the vain hopes uh maintaining her high spirits for as long as possible. As ih happens, the festivities end two blocks away when she pulls over an issues me my final orders. 'Out, now.'

'Uh?'

'I said jump out. Things are gehrin serious, this ain' a game no more so go home, take yuh bollocking an forgeh this whole mess ever happened, origh?'

'Buh I cahn go back. I – I dun care wha happens, I ain' gunuh leave you.' Maybe ih's the pills or just the whole emotional rollercoaster buh my voice is cracking yur cos I'd do anything for her, I swear I would. Nah, this ain' the drugs talking. No way. This is real. Her reaction ain' exactly wha I was hoping for, though. Anyone else woulduh learnt by now.

'I'm noh asking you, yuh stupid little cunt!' she shrieks. 'Geh out uh the fucking car, geh out, geh out!' Tears prickle as I'm forced up against the door buh I hold on tight all the same, determined to see this through till the bitter end.

'No, I'm noh leaving. I can help you geh away, Becca, please!'

'Yuh pathetic. Still havn goh a clue whas going on, uv you? I doan need you, Marv. I. Do not. Need. You. Yuh purpose is served, now yuh just extra baggage. So do me a favour an fuck off.' She leans over an pulls open my door an I'd be flat on the pavement if ih wadn fuh the siren tha rips the sky in two, blue lights swooshing past a hundred miles an hour. No prizes fuh guessing where they're headed buh if they've spotted us they could be making a swift detour any second now. Becca's obviously on the same page cos she floors ih wi me still halfway out the car an we're off again, away from the blue an orange madness an into the endless, terrifying night.

We're back in Cardiff somewhere when the inevitable moment comes. She's took one too many corners on two wheels an the best I can do is try to keep my brain from falling out my nose as we slam broadside into a garden wall. The steady blare uh the horn brings me back around, although I'm more dazed than sparko an all in all I'd say I goh off lightly. Good. Okay. Where's Becca? The open driver's door makes me assume the worst buh my fears are misplaced cos she's alive an kicking alright, arse-end shifting down the street at a rate uh knots. I follow on hob-nob legs, down through a dingy subway tha brings me out into this weird concrete park wi motorways running above an below. I call her name first left then right buh this place is a maze an pretty soon I'm gassed, coughing up a lung at the foot of a giant floodlight. Ih's hopeless. She's left me. Desperate an deserted, I curl up in a hedgehog ball, listening close as the lonely wind whistles between the concrete pillars. Stupid as ih sounds, I honestly believed when ih come to the crunch, she'd stick by me. Dad always said I was soft in the head.

Grey dawn snuffs streetlights like candle wicks as I sit debating my next move when suddenly there's this strange sound, a sortuh yelp coming from somewhere past the bushes.

I'm up an running again, tired legs an arms feeling no pain cos I know instinctively she's in trouble. The footbridge across the motorway. She's stood there, wrong side uh the railings, edging her way along the ledge with her back to me. Right, think fast, Marv. How do I play this one? Any sudden movements might send her over the edge. There again, if I dun do summin quick she might send her fucking self, like.

'Becca.' I cahn give more than a whisper cos my heart's in my mouth. Ih's no good though. The wind's blowing up, whipping hair around her streaked cheeks as I move closer, gently gently as though trynuh catch a butterfly. 'Becca – Becca, wha you doing?' Ih sounds pathetic buh wha you s'posed to say? She dun seem to uv yurd anyway, staring blankly at the road below, knuckles white on the railings behind. Another streetlight waivers in the corner uh my eye, countdown to the unthinkable. Should I make a grab for her? 'Come back from the edge, Bec.' Ih's weird, cos after the stillest uh summer nights a hurricane's sprung from nowhere, swallowing my every word before they've even left my lips. This time her eyes flick in my direction, even if the rest of her stays rigid an outstretched like Jesus on the wall uh Buncy's house back home. 'Please, this is stupid. I'll help you back over, yeah?'

I take a step towards her buh she recoils, going: 'Fuck off, Marv! I'm serious, just leave me alone.'

'Buh this dun make no sense . . . ih's noh worth ih.'

'An wha d'you know abou ih, exactly? Fuck all!'

'I know this ain' the answer. Look, ih's been mad lately, things goh out uh control buh you still goh people looking out fuh you – still goh friends, in ih?'

'When you gunuh geh ih through tha thick skull? Friends? No such thing. There's people you can use an people who use you. End uh story.'

The next streetlight dies, closer this time.

'Ih's noh true. Wha abou me? I never wanted to use you . . .'

'Course you didn't. Staring at my tits every opportunity buh you never wanted nothing off me did you? Wake up.'

165

I must be the worst Peeping Tom in history cos I genuinely never thought she realised. Least uh my worries right now though. 'Ih's noh abou tha, I swear. Yur a great person, tits or no tits . . . maybe, I dunno, maybe you've had some bad experien–'

'Stop trynuh figure me out, kid. You doan know the first thing abou anything.'

'I know tha I need you. Noh how you thinks, buh I need you.' Fuck knows where tha come from buh the more I leh ih sink in, the more I realise ih's completely true.

'You ain' gunuh talk me out of ih. I'm in control. I decide wha to do wi my life so doan think you can bullshit me into coming back over.' All the bitterness in the world cahn conceal the note of uncertainty playing in her voice. She's starting to give way. Now ih's up to me to keep pressing.

'Buh I do, I need you. Please dun leave me on my own – yur all I goh, Bec.'

'Fucking shurrup, will you? Just shurrup!'

Another streetlight goes an I know ih's now or never. I make a lunge for her buh she wriggles away so I back off, worried I'll do more harm than good. Time seems to stand still as I watch her fingers loosen on the railings buh the blaring horn of a passing lorry provides the momentary distraction I need to grip hold of her jacket an drag her back over the metal barrier using strength I never even knew I had. First she lashes out, calling me all the cunts going buh eventually the punches trail off an summin happens tha I've been dreaming of forever. Her lips meet mine an just like tha we're kissing, full-on tongues an everything. I pull her close an try to tell her again I need her buh my words are muted by our clashing teeth, hair an spit an salty tears all mixed up in a hot heavy mess. She takes me down to the grass, her epileptic-style shakes rousing a little voice in the back uh my head cos maybe this is wrong – maybe she ain' in her right mind, like. When I pull away she grabs my wrist, stuffing my hand inside her legging wi such force I'd be too scared to refuse even if I wanted to. As ih is, my dick's pitching a tent to rival anything Zippo's circus could come up with so there's no way I'm backing out now. Electric sparks make my stomach dip an twinge as she undoes my fly, so much juice running down there I'm convinced fuh one horrible second tha I've spunked in my pants. I goh no idea wha to do next buh Becca's firmly in control, tugging off her knickers wi one hand while pulling me down on top of her wi the other. The grass is cool an prickly on my hot skin, perfect contrast as she guides me into the softest, warmest place anywhere on planet Earth. Best stay utterly still cos one wrong move'll see me blowing my load yur an now buh Becca's goh other ideas, clamping tight an bucking her hips till I abandon the lost cause an leh ih all go inside of her in ten seconds flat. She sortuh groans an rolls away, leaving me to wrack my brains for a suitable apology buh the moment's already passed. I turn onto my back, catching my breath as deep red welts rise up on the neck-white skyline. Directly overhead, the last streetlight flickers an dies.

27

'Cahn sleep yur, fella. My gaffer'll be along soon,' some grotty old moon face shouts over the din of his motorised leaf blower. Fat chance uh any cunt sleeping wi tha racket going on so I peel back my eyelids an sit up, only fuh Worzel to recoil in horror. 'Bloody druggies,' he mutters an I dread to imagine the state uh my face if ih can give a hi-viz bog man like him the heebie-jeebies.

'We ain' druggies!' I protest through crusted lips buh he's already moved on, zapping at random bushes like some carrot-crunching version uh the *Texas Chainsaw Massacre* an anyway, I s'pose to the likes of him we are druggies. Buh drugs are the last thing on my mind right now. Like a jumble-sale t-shirt, I'm worn an knackered, stretched too far out uh shape to ever geh back to a presentable condition. So much has changed, so much I've lost. Except fuh one thing, one precious special person who could still save me if only I can save her. Last night was just the start of ih. Now we're officially an item there's no telling how far we'll go.

I spark up a fag an watch her sleep a while longer, the two of us all alone now in the middle uh this strange concrete jungle, peaceful an calm in the eye uh the gritty traffic hurricane tha rages outside. She looks so peaceful an perfect, her dirt-streaked face framed wi twigs an leaves like an innocent forest maiden buh when I reach over to brush her cheek the spell is instantly broken.

'Doan fucking touch me! Doan touch me!' she shouts, scrambling back from my hand with her eyes still half closed.

'Okay, alright, I'm sorry, I'm sorry,' I say, feeling like some dirty park-bench pervert.

Finally realising who I am, she groans wi relief an draws her knees up to her chin, her glazed eyes fixed on the busy road below. The danger of her finishing wha she started last night flashes by me buh I'm noh too concerned – she's goh no reason to has she? Noh now we're together.

'How you feeling, Bec?'

The big phlegmy gremo she's sent sailing over the railings tells me all I need to know. 'Any fags left?'

I fling her the packet, itchy with unanswered questions. 'Wha we gunuh do? We goh nowhere to stay . . .'

She inhales half a cigarette in one drag an spits again.

'Reckon the coppers are still after us? Yuh family's bound to uv grassed – we might be on *Crimestoppers* – photofits on the telly an ah.' Fuck me, my brain's pill-pickled, racing with a million spazzy thoughts a second. The trouble we've caused, the bad things we've done. Sooner or later ih's all gunuh catch up with us.

'Fuck the police an anyone else who's looking for us,' Becca goes, her fag butt exploding in a shower uh sparks on the windscreen of a passing car. 'There's only one thing bothering me. Those cunts in Llanedeyrn goh my ganja an my money an I'm gunuh geh ih back.'

Her scowl screams the kind uh trouble my aching bones dun need an my comedown head cahn hack. I wish more than anything we were back in Jamo's, smoking an dancing an having a laugh cos they were good times wi good people an wha'ever happened last night, I just cahn believe they woulduh ripped us off. No way. Surprise surprise though, Becca's having none of ih.

'Doan you dare gimme tha soppy look,' she warns before I've even said a word. 'They took our shit.'

'Yeah, buh how can you be shew–' Talking sense only seems to disgust her even more.

'Orr, wake up fuh fuck's sake!' She taps a finger on the side of her head. 'They tucked us up an I ain' gunuh sit around an take ih. I'm tired uh people ripping the piss out uh me. C'mon, leh's go.'

*　　　*　　　*

169

As usual, I'm clueless buh Becca's well on top uh the situation an before long we're back in the thick uh the city, surrounded by wheezing double-deckers an tongue-twisting *Echo* sellers. 'Now wha?' I say cos the little money we had goh blown on the shows an everything else was tied up wi the soapbar back at the flat. Noh even shrapnel left, bar fuh Mam's lucky penny uh course, fuh wha ih's worth.

'Watch an learn,' she says, eagle eyes zeroing in on this couple uh doddery old coffin-dodgers on a bench. A quick makeover courtesy uh spit-soaked eyes followed by an even quicker rehearsal an ih's show time. I wait in the wings wi my mop an bucket, ready fuh the big clean up once the inevitable ton uh shit hits the fan.

'Please, please, you gohruh help me – my baby's been taken ill!'

The unsuspecting pair freeze, dentures hovering over their homemade sandwiches.

'I needs four pound for a train to Merthyr. Please, ih's urgent!'

'We haven't got any money, love. We're pensioners, see?' the old lady goes, her saggy neck jiggling into overdrive like some built-in bullshit detector. 'Why don't you go to the police station?'

Becca tries her luck wi the old boy instead. 'Please mister, there's no time fuh the police, I need to catch the train. Asthma, he goh, he's had an attack.' Her blubbing's so convincing I'd empty my own pockets if only there was anything in um. These old cunts ain' so easy to fool mind. 'My son! My son!' Becca's going, cranking up the desperate decibels as they pack away their things. 'Please, I only needs three pound.'

'I thought you said four?' the guy snaps, spotting a chink in the armour. 'We've already told you, we're retired pensioners. You're better off asking someone else.'

Never in a million years are they gunuh fall for ih buh Becca cahn see when she's beaten. Blocking their path is the final straw – the old boy grabs hold of her, examining her face

170

with hundred watt intensity. 'What's wrong with your eyes?' he goes like a snotty head teacher. 'You're on drugs, aren't you?'

'No, I ain't!' Becca shouts buh ih's funny how the waterworks uv stopped so sudden. Demon Headmaster's clocked ih an all.

'You're not really upset, you want money for drugs! Someone call the police – this girl's on drugs!'

People are beginning to stop an take notice, whispers wildfiring through the shoppers as I exit stage left. The crafty old codger's playing Becca like a fiddle, kicking up a proper commotion, barking orders at anyone who'll listen. Yur's where I'm s'posed jump in like the hero I dream I am buh old habits die hard an pussying abou on the sidelines is really more my dap. Thankfully this random man-mountain emerges to save the day, our second coming dressed head to toe in sportswear all held together by a bulging bumbag fresh out uh nineteen-eighty-summin. You'd swear he was some bona fide yankee doodle tourist took a wrong turn on his way to Disneyland buh fuh the accent, pure dumb dumb valleys drawl.

'Hey-yey-yey, whas going on yur now, butt?' he goes, unpeeling the old man's bony fingers with his own humongous shovels. 'This pewer girl's in trouble, you cahn go treating her like ah. Where to is it yewer trynuh geh, my love?'

We cahn believe our luck, an neither can the fogeys judging by the hundred-metre dash they've broken into. Becca's turned the taps back on, subjecting dumb dumb to the full force of her hard sell routine. Coulduh saved her breath cos all ih takes is a couple of her standard whoppers to have him eating out the palm of her hand, fighting back the big dopey tears in his big dopey eyes.

'Dun't you worry about a thing, my lovely. We'll get you home in no time.'

Becca's licking her lips as he unzips the bumbag buh I feel nothing buh sheer relief cos against all the odds we might actually come out uh this whole sorry mess unscathed. As he rifles his tatty plastic wallet I'm suddenly touched by how kind an pure some people can be, even if they are too daft to know when they're being swindled. My other half clearly ain' sharing the sentiments cos her determination to fuck everything up's taken another surprising twist. There cahn be a sadder sight in history than Dumbo's confused expression as Becca yoinks the whole wallet from his hand in one swift movement buh the sympathy can go on ice for a minute while we make like a pair uh serious shepherds an geh the flock out uh yuh. A shout goes up as we duck an weave through the crowd uh shoppers, some trynuh grab, some trynuh trip, most too stunned to move a muscle. In truth, I probly coulduh slinked off undetected buh I said I'd stick by her an I meant ih. Thing is, Becca cahn half shift, an she's had a head start too so I'm left fuh dust at the mercy uh the baying mob. The desperate struggle to keep pace soon collapses into a lost cause as she takes side street after side street without missing a beat. Lost an alone, I dart from left to right trying hopelessly to pick up her scent buh relieved to find Dumbo an the rest uv given up the chase. I crouch an gasp, hands on knees when a lanky bolt from the blue with NHS specs almost catches me sleeping. There's still enough fumes in the tank for a last ditch escape attempt buh this geek's unshakable, obviously some have-a-go hero with an axe to grind. My chest's fit to burst as I swerve into a dead-end alleyway, prepared to face the music after falling flat on my face in a pile uh shitty bin bags. An iron grip on the scruff uh my neck hoists me to my feet an I'm thinking this speccy cunt must be harder than he looks buh somewhere along the line wires uv been crossed cos when I turn around the nerd's stood directly opposite me, minus the big-I-am attitude.

'Y'alright, ked?'

I recognise the voice instantly – ih's Kenny, the Taff embankment ponytail. Noh hundred percent sold on him, I only stop struggling when Becca an Kenny's mute sidekick poke their heads out from the shadows. All together, our attentions turn to the nerdy hot shot who's managed to back himself into a corner, beseeching the tramps in a vain attempt to avoid an arse kicking. 'They've – they've stolen from a disabled man,' he's whimpering. 'The police will be here soon – you'll be accessories if you stand in their way.'

He's stretching a bih yur cos no way the pigs are on to us tha quick, an ih's noh like the tramps give two fucks either way. As we close in I gehs this surge uh blood, itching to paste the clean-cut cunt all over the alley, pure stamp him into the ground. He sees whas coming an charges us, squealing wi fear as he scrambles out into the street. The others jeer after him buh me, I wanuh give chase an finish the job. Maybe I'm tired of always being the one running, having people like him thinking they can hunt me down without asking questions. Ih's abou time they had a taste uh their own medicine.

When the tension's died down Becca throws her head back, laughing like a loony – noh a care in world. Who the fuck's she think she is? Ih was her who took ih too far, she's the one who gehs us into this shit an all she can do is act like ih's one big joke. I'm gunuh puh my foot down soon – things are changing now she's wi me. Telling ew.

'Well, fancy meeting you two again,' Kenny grins, all black stumps an stubble. 'Could easily have got yourselves caught, pulling a stroke like dat.'

'Just another day on the streets,' Becca laughs. 'An anyway, I was home an dry – ih was this little divvy tha nearly goh his collar felt. I'll have to start puhrin you on a leash!' She mushes my cheeks like drunken auntie buh I twist away, temperature rising in frustration. I'm sick of her acting up to her audience, making out like everything's a game. She's just the same as Mam.

'Well I'm glad you find ih funny,' I say. 'You nearly goh us done, an fuh wha? Fuck all. Never know when enough's enough, thas yuh trouble.' Ih's surprising how spiteful I sound buh the end uh the day summin's gohruh be said. As her boyfriend I need to start setting down rules. She shoulduh took the money an left ih at tha.

'Orr yur we go, Mighty Mouse uv found his voice at last,' she sneers, curling her lips up like I'm shit on the bottom of her shoe. 'Who goh us this far, Marv? Me! If ih was left to you we'd still be sat in Pengarw crying abou how unfair everything is so spare me the lip now you've had a little fumble. If you doan like ih you know wha you can do. No one's forcing you to stick around.'

She gives Kenny the nod an the three of um set off, her exaggerated laughs ringing echoes uh Mam in my yurs as she holds on to the tramps, weak with amusement at their wise cracks. I follow after um like a ghost, sick wi regret fuh opening my mouth. Never meant ih really, an when I try to tell her as much she gives a tight little smile an orders me to hurry up if I'm coming. Turns out Kenny an the quiet one, Marco I think ih is, uv been staying in this derelict place round the corner from where we met um. Ih's like an old room above a shop buh the shop's long gone now, a burnt out blackness lurking beneath the gaps in the floorboards. There's shit thrown everywhere an graffiti covering the walls buh according to Kenny no one ever comes yur no more, bar fuh them. We sit round this metal dustbin full uh smoking ashes, Becca flicking through the stolen wallet an cursing when all she finds is six pound twenty-three, a train ticket an an old video card. She takes the cash an throws everything else into the yawning depths below. 'Fuck loh uh good thas gunuh do me,' she spits, as though Dumbo was the most inconsiderate cunt in the world fuh noh having more money on him at the time.

'So where were you two headed, anyway?' Kenny goes, squinting through his rollie smoke. 'You're looking a bit worse for wear, compared to the last time we saw ya. No offense, like.'

'We've had a fucking mental night. Some cunts uv done me wrong an I'm gunuh geh back whas mine. After tha I'm gone up to London. Had enough uh this shithole already.'

London, is ih? First I've yurd of ih. I ain' gunuh bite though, cos Buncy warned me abou the stupid games girls plays when you go out with um. She'll have to try harder than tha to do my head in.

'What you gonna do up there? Know people, do ya?'

'I'll find people,' Becca goes, sucking on her lips. 'I can take care uh myself.'

'I know you can, love. I'm just saying, London ain't all it's cracked up to be. So anyway, what's this trouble you've been having?'

Becca studies him sidewards for a minute. 'Listen, d'you two fancy earning yuhselves a drink or wha? '

Kenny an Marco both swap glances like, *Uh course we fucking do.* 'What ya got in mind?'

'We were ripped off last night – couple uh ounces uh ganja. There's a chance ih might come on top an I needs a bih uh back up. I'll make ih worth yuh while.'

This is sounding a bih too heavy fuh me. Whas she mean, "back up"? Cahn actually be planning on fighting ih out wi Jamo an Charmaine, shewerly noh. They're s'posed to be our mates, in they? The way Becca can switch, I dunno. Ih's pure cold. There's no proof they even nicked the dope buh in her mind she's judge, jury an executioner all rolled into one. I'll stick by her no marrer wha buh she dun make ih easy, leh me tell ew.

28

There's an eerie silence as we walk through the courtyard, tumbleweeds rolling past cos this is injun territory an ambush is on the cards. Becca leads the troops, woman on a mission wi no time to debate. Believe me, I've tried. A little kid playing in the hallway lehs us in the main door an we file up the steps, my whole body prickling wi nerves. There's disaster written all over this situation buh wha say uv I goh in ih? Wha say uv I goh in anything? I think Kenny's nervous as well, cos he keeps scratching an sniffing an fiddling with his belt. Marco's steady an quiet as always, his little dark eyes taking everything in. None of us are prepared fuh wha we find at the top, mind. The flat door's swinging loose, exactly the same way we found ih last night an I'm struck with a spooky sense uh déjà vu, like this all might be one endless drugged up nightmare looping over an over on repeat. Buh when we step inside the place is a mess, much worse than before. There's noh one thing in the whole flat tha havn been trashed – tables, chairs, stereo, telly. There's broken glass over the floor an blood too by the look of ih. We swap confused glances, trynuh make sense uh the carnage when a muffled sound draws our attention to the bedroom. I cautiously open the door, braced fuh bloodied hostages, bound an gagged buh all thas waiting is a withered version uh Charmaine, tidying the wreckage between heart-wrenching sobs. She screams when she sees us an before I know ih she's thrown herself at Becca, going: 'You! This is all your fault – we should never uh leh you back in our lives!'

Maybe Becca's in shock cos she dun even try to fight back – just tucks up tight to weather the storm while Kenny plays peacemaker an catches a smack in the mouth for his troubles. In the end the girls split an Charmaine falls back on to the bed, crying through her curls. Becca straightens herself out, checking her gob fuh blood while the rest of us stand round like spare pricks. When the silence becomes too awkward to bear I pipe up: 'Whas happened yur, Charmaine? Where's Jamo an Shifty?'

'Ask tha dirty ragga!' Charmaine goes, channelling all her rage through a single quivering finger.

'Dunno wha yuh talking abou,' Becca says buh her voice is quiet now, lacking her trademark chopsiness. Even she's come to her senses. This is fucking horrible.

'Tha junkie boyfriend uh yours. Turned up with his Brummie mates looking fuh you an their drugs – tore the place apart when they couldn find either. I told you we never took yuh stuff buh you had to stir shit up! Ih's you! You're the cause uh this, wherever you goes, always in the thick of ih. An we all know why. Yuh trouble. Why d'you think you goh no proper mates, no proper boyfriend? No family? Ih's you!'

I'm waiting fuh Becca to freak buh this time she stands there like a statue, the verbal blows bouncing off her chiselled granite chin.

'Where's the boys?' I ask again.

'Shifty goh beat up pretty bad. One uh the Brummies had summin in his hand. I didn see properly buh Shifty's face is busted up. Should be going uh hospital buh he's out wi Jamo picking up boys an looking fuh revenge instead. All cos of her!' She screws up her mouth to Becca: 'You deserves every bad thing thas ever happened to you, I hope you know tha.'

Without another word Becca turns an leaves, shrinking six inches with every step.

*   *   *

'Oi, hang on a minute! What about our money for booze?'

Becca keeps walking.

'Oi! I'm talking to you!'

She breaks into a trot, noh looking back.

'Fucking nice one,' Kenny mutters, pissed off buh resigned, never truly expecting anything else. 'We did you a favour.'

'I'm sorry, origh,' she shouts in a fuzzy voice. 'Wha d'you wan me to say, I fucked up again. You goh knocked. Serves you right fuh listening to me, doan ih?'

'You've got issues, you girl, d'you know dat? You can't even tell when people are on your side.' He shakes his head after her an even wi black stumpy teeth an tha greasy hair he looks sortuh righteous, like even he's disgusted by us.

So Kenny an Marco go off in a huff leaving the two of us on our own, me an Becca together again, the way we started. Buh summin's changed an no marrer how much I wanoo I dun see her the same way no more. Ih sounds daft buh I genuinely believed she could sort anything, thought nothing was so serious Becca couldn find a way out buh last night on the motorway bridge I realised I cahn go relying on her for everything. Ih's time I took control, supported her like a proper boyfriend should.

'Wha we gunuh do now?' I says after wracking my brains for a good ten minutes. Ih's okay though cos uh course Becca's cooking summin up, an as usual, ih's gunuh be a pain in the arse.

'How abou trying back at yuh mother's?'

I'm noh into this. I wanted to go back to Mam when I'm sorted, noh show up on her doorstep in a worse state than before. 'Well, whas the point? You seen how she is, she's noh gunuh be able to help us . . . if anything, I need to help her. She cahn be stressed out, ih's no good for her.'

'Well, wha abou this bloke she's goh? This fucking Tony or wha'ever his name is.'

'Terry.'

'Yeah, well . . . he's s'posed to have a few quid, in he?'

'I dunno. So wha if he have? Noh gunuh give ih to us, is he?'

'Listen, Marv, you gohruh start learning to make the most uh opportunities. You're the kid in this whole mess, remember? So we need to lay ih on thick, give um a proper sob story. Yuh mother owes you, noh the other way round, righ? An anyway, I thought you said last night you'd do anything fuh me? Or was you just bullshitting like every other guy I've ever been with?'

29

Becca snaps her fingers an I find myself once again on Mam's doorstep, hoodwinked an press ganged by my girlfriend's irresistible gob. This time ih's Terry who answers, looking every inch the prick I knew he'd be. Beer belly, open shirt, hairy chest – this guy ticks all the boxes fuh the sleaziest swinger in town. Goh a right face on him too, obviously ready to tell us where to go until Becca works her magic an then ih's all smiles an jokes an JCB-strength handshakes. Fucking sovereigns on those fingers, mind – Becca was right abou one thing, at least. Cunt must be loaded.

'Come in, come in, make yuhselves at home,' he goes, leading the way through to where chip fat an stale smoke still linger. 'Sorry I missed you the other day, Lee – yuh mother said you dropped by. She's out wi the girls tonight buh yuh more than welcome to wait.'

'Well, we dun wanuh be no bother,' I say, taking the seat nearest the door cos this creep's nice-as-pie act ain' washing wi me.

'Ih's no problem, no problem at all. Yur, leh me geh you two a drink. Scotch origh?'

We both nod.

'Yuh mum'll kill me if she finds out I've given you booze, mind. How old you now then, Lee?'

'Fifteen.'

'Ah, old enough, son, old enough, eh?' He hands me the glass with a big phoney wink. 'I used to drink at your age, never did me no harm. Practically a man now, anyway.' He directs the last sentence at Becca an they both laugh like they're sharing some big fucking joke. Knew ih was a mistake coming yur. Wha a scumbag.

179

'I been hoping you'd call over again, to be honest – wanted to clear the air abou yuh mum's reaction last time. See, well – she's under a loh uh stress buh ih is gehrin better, slowly buh surely. Talks abou you loads, she do. Misses you, you know.'

I nod an take a sip uh my drink, almost heaving, as much at his syrupy sentiments as the sickly sweet whisky-lemonade mixture in my mouth. Gunuh take more than a few soppy words to win me over butt, no marrer how genuine they sounds.

'So who's this, then?' Terry goes, nodding to Becca. 'Yuh girlfriend is ih, Lee?'

While I'm busy fighting the urge to puke Becca jumps straight in with a bombshell answer. 'No, we ain' together, Marvin's just a mate, like.'

Why's she being like this? I know the score, this is more mind games like Buncy warned me. Well two can play, believe me. Just gohruh bide my time. Terry dun seem to uv clocked the tension anyway. He's still struggling wi the basics.

'Hang on a minih, who's Marvin? You mean Lee, doan you?'

'Yeah – no one calls him Lee, though. He's Marvin. See if you can guess why.'

Great. She's really pushing ih lately, trynuh embarrass me an make a scene.

'Come on, look at him – whas the first thing tha springs to mind?'

Terry's still blank. 'Christ knows, someone off *Neighbours*?'

'No,' Becca laughs, 'look how skinny he is. Ih's rhyming slang. He's Hank Marvin!'

The good old chuckle I expect from Terry never arrives. Instead he rubs at deepening frown lines before finally saying: 'Hank Marvin? Bih cheeky, in ih? How d'you feel abou tha, Lee?'

I shrug. 'Used to ih now, like. Dun bother me.'

'Well ih'd bother me. Hank bleeding Marvin! Wha do they call you then?' he says to Becca.

'Nothing . . . Becca, thas my name.'

'Oh yeah, whas tha slang for?'

'Nothing.'

180

'Ih's alright, Terry, I dun mind ih,' I cut in cos he's taking things a bih to heart like.

'Origh, origh, I know how ih is mate. Buh I doan like people having the piss taken out of um, thas all. Had ih myself when I was younger. Might be just another old grey sod now buh I was only nineteen when my hair started losing ihs colour. Copped no end uh stick for ih. People still call me Fogey to this day.'

'Honest,' I says, 'I know wha you mean buh ih's really noh a problem. Everyone uses Marvin, even me!'

'Yeah,' he sighs, senses returning. 'Gehrin a bih lairy yur, in I? Doan mind me folks, been on the pop all day. My day off, see? Serious now, I'm glad you called over. I'm just off to the bog, help yuhselves to another drink while I'm gone.'

'Silly cunt!' Becca goes, scowling towards the ceiling where you can yur Terry's piss clattering against the pan. 'Fogey? More like Geri-fucking-atric! Leh's see wha he goh yur.' She rifles the drinks cabinet, taking a half bottle uh vodka from the back an sliding ih into her bag. Then she skips over to the fag packet on the arm of his chair an swipes a handful.

'Becca, stop! Yuh robbing my mam's house,' I says, gobsmacked.

'Behave. I'm noh robbing yuh mother, I'm knocking tha fat prick up there. Doing yuh old dear a favour, if anything.'

'Buh he dun seem tha bad, do he?'

'You changed yuh tune,' she sneers. 'Thought you wanted nothing to do with him.'

'Yeah, tha was before . . . maybe I was a bih hasty . . .'

'Geh real. Still daft as fuck, you've learnt nothing. Take wha we can an hit the road, right?'

Heavy feet clump on the stairs.

'I said right?' she hisses between gritted teeth.

'Oka–'

'How you two gehrin on down yur?' Terry slurs, bursting in through the door more sauced than I thought, although at least he's smiling with ih. Luckily he dun seem to notice the missing stuff an he's noh too nosey with his small talk, even though he's probly figured out things ain' exactly rosy for us right now. The whisky keeps flowing an I gohruh be honest,

I'm starting to enjoy myself. Terry ain' so bad – down to earth like, noh the nasty cunt I had him pegged for. Seems to have my mother's interests in mind an all.

As the night wears on he starts to flag, slumping further an further into his chair with each passing hour. Finally, with an almighty yawn he gehs to his feet, eyes pure piss holes in the snow. 'Christ, I'm out on my feet yur. Been a heavy few weeks in work.'

'Listen, we'll be on our way,' I says, noh wanting to outstay our welcome.

'No, no, you two stay the night. Yuh mother shouldn be too much longer, she's only out wi Sheila from round the corner. Might even be back at Sheila's house by now, having a nightcap, if I know yuh mum. I would give her a ring buh they've had the phone disconnected. Come to think of ih, maybe you could go an give her a knock, Lee. Ih's only a couple uh streets over – number forty-seven, ih is.'

I'm in a bih of a position yur cos I'm feeling the worse fuh wear an I ain' really in the mood to go wandering abou in the dark buh I cahn look a sap an say no either, can I? 'Coming wi me, Bec?'

'Where's yuh manners, son? Cahn ask a young lady to walk the streets this time uh night. You can take care uh yuhself, cahn you? I'm ready to crash out . . . Becca can wait yur to leh you in.'

Becca's never give a fuck abou being out on the streets before buh I keep my thoughts to myself fuh the sake uh peace. So instead I pull on the jumper Shifty nicked fuh me an step out into the empty night. Fresh air knocks me sideways, fuel fuh the whisky flames belching from my stomach as I repeatedly try an fail to puh one foot in front uh the other. Somehow I manage to stagger my way to this Sheila's house an knock on the door, only to be greeted by the one person in Cardiff more drunk than me. Sheila clings to her doorframe for dear life, cackling wi delight an insisting I come in for a drink once I've explained who I am. She wun take no for an answer, an I'm happy to oblige if only to see my mam buh when I geh inside I'm surprised to find Sheila's home alone. A sober doubt cuts through the alcoholic haze cos summin dun add up yur. In the end I almost gohruh shout in her face to geh my message across buh all I'm offered in return is a blank look cos apparently my mother havn been round her house all week. Bollocks! I push my way past her, panic beginning to rise. I gohruh geh back to Terry's.

When there's no answer I really start to freak out, banging on the door an spying through the letterbox fuh signs uh life. Shewer I yurd summin smash in there. Whas going on? A scream! Tha was a definitely scream. Becca. There's more crashing an a light flickers upstairs, erasing any doubt from my mind. I'm going in. With ihs rickety old door the place ain' exactly Fort Knox buh ih seems to take a hundred kicks before the frame gives up the ghost. I take the stairs in two strides, heart thumping loud as Jamo's bass cannon. When I geh to the top I freeze for a second while my mind tries desperately to make sense uh the scene playing out in front uh me. The bedroom door's half open an Becca's on the bed, Terry on top of her writhing round like a beached whale. She's kicking frantically buh the big bastard's goh her pinned fast wi those shovel hands. Ih's one uh those weird sensations, like a realistic dream tha dun quite make sense buh her screams shatter the illusion an I know I gohruh do summin fast.

Instinct picks up a big bottle uh perfume off the dresser an launches ih at his big fat head. Ih's glass buh ih dun break – just sortuh *dunks*, causing his wild eyes to swivel round in my direction. Fuck. I try to run buh he's on me in a flash, size an strength too much to resist. Becca manages to wriggle off the bed as I'm battered into the corner, rag-doll mauled by a sovereign-wearing grizzly bear. He's goh his powerful hands round my neck, ranting abou Becca trynuh rip him off, claims he caught her stealing buh I knows he's full uh shit cos his pants are loose an his hairy cock's flopping abou an even I ain' tha stupid. He squeezes tighter, raging red blur of a face the last thing I see as my vision starts to fade. This is ih. I cahn fight him off, he's too strong. I yur Becca scream in the background an then there's a shower uh glass an coins an the hands loosen their grip on my throat. He hits the deck like an oak tree – swear he was dead if noh fuh the weird snoring noise coming from the depths of his throat. Catching forty

183

winks after taking a penny jar to the swede might sound strange buh nothing makes sense no more, an from the way the blood's lashing out on the peach carpet he might noh be snoring fuh too much longer. I look over at Becca's cos we both know wha to do now. The same thing we always do. Run.

30

Tap tap tap.

Focus on the sound, shoes on concrete, count the steps, dun lose ih now, gohruh keep going, gohruh geh away. Becca! Where's Becca? As soon as I stop my legs go completely an I fall to my knees, raindrops an blackness rushing all around in a whirlwind of hot tarmac an cold terror. This is too much, this ain' real. I'm suffocating . . .

Hyurghhhh.

Before I've even goh a chance to wipe the puke off my chin a thundering shadow catches my arm an scoops me up, knowing just as much as I do tha stopping now is fatal – no, no noh fatal, noh like ah, please noh like ah . . . Becca. Concentrate on Becca. She's alright. I'll make shewer she's alright. As long as we keep running, gohruh keep running. Buh some things you cahn outrun. Some things are too big to escape. Like murder. This is ih – no kids' games, no mischief. If tha cunt croaks we're murderers, plain an simple.

Splash splash splash.

Our feet rip through neon puddles as we bomb past pubs an takeaways. Music pumps, people spill out onto the street dancing an laughing cos they dun know wha we've done, they couldn give a fuck abou the trouble we're in. Outcasts like us dun belong in the normal world wi families an friends an lives anymore, we're ghosts, running scared uh the living. I think I'm gunuh puke again.

A blue flicker washes over the night sky like the shadow uh some winged demon, forcing us to dive fuh cover in a shop doorway just as a speeding ambulance swishes by. 'Is tha fuh . . . is ih fuh *him*?' I yur myself saying through clay lips buh the pair uh wide eyes staring back speak only raw fear. 'We need to

185

make ih to Kenny's squat,' I say, trynuh reassure her with a knotted smile. 'At least we'll have time to think there.' No sooner have I coaxed her from the doorway than we run smack bang into this group uh posh students struggling to handle their lager-tops.

'Halt, ye travellers!' This one bellend in a cloak an traffic cone hat steps forward, barring our path while his toffee-nosed fan club mill around behind. 'I am the High Wizard, Sir Stella of Artois. I demand a toll.'

Me an Becca share a quick glance before ploughing straight through um like a row uh skittles.

'Toby,' I yur this one girl shrieking over my shoulder. 'You are so off your head! Absolutely mental!'

Mental? Those rah-rah fuckers couldn spell ih. Try spending five minutes in our world – then you'll know mental, an ih'll wipe the smile right off yuh sappy spoilt faces.

*　　*　　*

We slam the hoardings shut an stand there panting an shaking in the pitch dark, neither of us able to speak a word for at least fifteen minutes. When my breathing finally returns to somewhere near normal I manage to croak out the unspoken fear on both our minds. 'W – wha if he's dead?'

'He cahn be – he was making tha noise.'

'Buh the blood – ih was everywhere. If no one finds him he could bleed to death . . . wha if he's lying there dead right now?'

More panting in the dark. I reach out for her buh she ain' there. My heart thumps in a panic an I call out pure frantic: 'Becca! Becca!'

'I dunno, Marv. Wha d'you wan me to say? I don't fucking know, origh!'

'We're going uh jail, in we?' I try to hold my voice together, only glad she cahn see the tears rolling down my face.

'Noh if I can help ih. Fucked if I'm doing time fuh some pervy old cunt. He deserved wha he goh.' She makes her way up the stairs buh I hold back, scrubbing at my cheeks to hide my shame cos I'm determined to stay strong for her. When I finally follow she's stood over by the broken window, watching as the rain beats heavy on the empty street. Fuck knows whas happened to Kenny an Marco buh they ain' around. Good. Less people who know abou this, the better. 'I gohruh geh out uh yuh,' she goes. 'I'm gone uh London – no chance uh the police finding me up there.'

'Buh how? We goh no money, no car – fuck all!' I bite the bullet an ask the dreaded question. 'Yuh noh planning on leaving me, uh you?' Ih comes out a bih more desperate than I wanted buh fuck ih. The time fuh games is long gone. This cards on the table time.

'No,' she goes, like I'm annoying her. 'Shurrup, will you? Gimme a minih to think.'

I know in an instant I'm gehrin ditched. I've always known ih deep down. Might as well give up now cos there's no way I'll geh through this without her. The waterworks surge again buh I leh um flow cos there's nothing left to be embarrassed abou. When she takes pity an wraps me up like a babe in arms I completely dissolve, chest heaving wi gut-wrenching sobs.

'Come on, stupid. I promise I woan leave you, okay? Doan go gehrin upset.'

'Upset? We done someone in, Bec! Tha bloke could die cos of us. An we'll end up going down for ih an all.' I'm drowning in snot an dribble, cahn catch my breath – she releases me an I run over to the window, gulping in fresh air like I've risen from the depths uh the ocean. My head's spinning yur, I'm trapped in a bad dream wi no way uh waking up. 'Wha if . . . wha if we go to the police, tell um everything, like – tell um wha he tried to do. They might go easier on us.'

'Geh a grip, fuh fuck's sake.'

'Well, whas waiting for us up London? We dun know no one there – probly end up on the streets gehrin into all sorts, always looking over our shoulders fuh the pigs. At least this way we might geh a better deal.'

'You still havn cottoned on, uv you? People doan believe trash like us. If we was snobby little rich cunts like them loh wi the traffic cone maybe we'd have a hope. Buh us? Pfft. We'll be on remand as soon as we step through the door an they'll throw away the fucking key. Case closed.'

187

'Buh–'

'Listen, Marv. I'll geh us out of this. I always do, doan I? This time tomorrow we'll be miles away, having a mad one an forgehrin any uh this ever happened. Just sit tight an wait fuh morning – we cahn do nothing till then.' She faffs around with her bag, pulling out the vodka she nicked off . . . him. If I've ever needed a drink ih's now buh I'll be lucky to geh a look in, the way she's downing ih. At last the bottle's passed an I knock ih back, savouring the bleachy burn as ih strips all thas rotten from my insides. We sit in silence for a bih, glugging away an trynuh geh our heads round everything thas happened. Ih's all such a mess buh I still goh Becca an thas wha I need to focus on – sticking with her, no marrer wha. Best to keep her talking, give her no chance to forgeh I'm yur.

'Wha did you mean, Bec? When you said no one believes people like us?' I know full-well wha she meant buh I wan her to say ih.

'Doan play dumb. Noh exactly Janet an fucking John, are we?'

We sit quiet for a bih longer, lehrin the alcohol numb us through.

'How come we're like we are, though? How come we're always gehrin into trouble? Reckon we're just bad people?'

'Fucked if I know.' She lehs out a long sigh, hunched in the faint light from outside pure gaunt an weary – a bag uh bones. Like Mam. I wonder wha my mother wen through to end up how she have. Maybe she was a bad kid too, maybe thas how ih happens. I dunno. She'll be a fuck load worse when she finds out wha we've done. Oh my God. I feel the dry retching come on again buh Becca seems to sense a freak-out an cuts in with a question.

'So wha abou you then, Marv? Ever wondered why you acts the way you do – mitching an thieving an all the rest of ih?'

'Who knows?' The more I mull ih, the more I realise I actually havn goh a clue why I do anything. 'Just cahn seem to behave how they wants me to – brought ih all on myself, really. In the beginning, at least. I mean, no one forced me to go nicking or lighting fires, did they? Buh Shifty reckons once

188

you've goh a reputation you'll end up doing wrong cos thas wha everyone expects of you, like. Ih's true in a way, cos now even when I try to do the right thing I make more trouble for everyone. Ih's as though I'm jinxed – I've caused so much shit you cahn imagine.'

'Like wha?'

'Well . . . ih's my fault my parents split up.'

'Doan be so fucking daft. How'd you figure tha one out?'

'Cos I always had teachers on the phone, the boardie man an coppers round the house an ah. Goh so bad my mother couldn handle ih no more.'

'So? Wha did she expect? Both yuh parents are steaming alchies, fuh fuck's sake. You were never gunuh be teacher's pet, were you?'

'You dun understand, there's more to ih. Ih *was* my fault. I knew bringing trouble to the door was doing her head in buh I couldn stop myself. Then one time in school I wen too far an everything fell apart. Right after break time, ih was. The Francis twins ud been giving me shit in the playground an I just sortuh lost ih – next thing I knows I'm in the corridor spraying a gang uh year sevens wi the big red fire hose on the wall. When the teachers flipped they goh a soaking too – almost pissed my pants at the sight of um flapping abou in their nice smart suits. Only ih turns out I wadn laughing at all. I was crying – bawling my eyes out like a newborn without ihs bottle. In the end Mr Austin wrestled the hose off me an dragged me kicking an screaming into this empty classroom. Made a right show uh myself. The other kids were cheering outside, calling me psycho an stuff. I'm still noh shewer why I done ih. Only year eight then, though. You act daft when yuh young, dun ew?'

Right now the familiar prickle uh shame should be creeping over me buh the feelings tha uv held me prisoner fuh so long are suddenly nowhere to be found. Maybe ih's the vodka or the fact tha wha we been through makes everything else seem so petty, I dunno, buh I feel like I can truly be myself fuh the first time since forever.

'I thought they were gunuh gimme a bollocking an suspend me – you know, the usual. Buh instead they took me to this room wi comfy chairs an gave me squash an crisps. The headmaster comes in wi this soppy-looking woman I never seen before an they're asking me loads uh questions abou home an family. Wouldn uh told um nothing buh I'm so pissed off cos my crisps uv gone soggy wi tears tha I just starts pouring all this stuff out – everything thas been bothering me, abou Mam an Dad an all the murder they been having.'

'Sounds like yuh parents were fucked up long before you started causing trouble, Marv. Blaming yuhself is silly.'

'Yeah, buh everyone drinks an argues, dun they? Thas normal, buh me blabbing to these posh cunts – they didn understand. Sent Social Services round the house investigating my family. Mam almost ended up having a nervous breakdown. The arguing goh worse, the drinking goh worse. I started gehrin into more trouble, doing more bad stuff. Weird, in ih? They say social workers are there to make things better buh with us everything wen downhill twice as fast. Then one night there's this blinding argument. Screaming, smashing . . . everything goes quiet an when I look out the bedroom window the coppers are taking Mam into a police car.'

'They locked her up?'

'No, she wanted to go. Took her to some hostel or summin an thas the last I yurd till a few weeks ago.'

'So thas wha coming down yur's been abou – trynuh make ih up to yuh mum?'

'Yeah . . . I s'pose. I wanted to show her I can be good so she can come home, like. Fucking great job I done an all, didn I?' My voice cracks again cos the reality of whas happened comes rushing back to me. Fuck knows where I'd be without the vodka.

'Well, I'll tell you one thing; you need to stop wi this guilty shit. Ih ain' your fault mate, any mother worth a fuck ud realise tha. You thought you were doing the right thing telling the social worker. As long as you knows you done yuh best, thas all tha marrers. Serious, now. If she doan come back to you, ih's her mistake. People always try to blame you fuh their problems an you shouldn fall for ih. Trust me, I know.'

Creepy Frank Butcher looms large in the memory buh I gohruh tread careful yur. 'You had the same in yewer family, then?'

'No, noh the same,' she says, softly shaking her head. 'Ah, ih's pointless. Who gives a fuck at the end uh the day?'

'I do, Bec,' I says wi genuine conviction.

'I know you do, Marv. I know you do.' She's slurring her words, hand heavy on my shoulder. We've made a proper dent in tha vodka bottle buh I still dun feel pissed, just numb, an thankful for ih too.

'I was up on the mountain last week when tha Derek tried to pay you off in his car – I yurd everything.' Ih's possible she'll flip buh there dun seem any point holding back now. As ih is, she's barely listening, head lolling like a puppet on strings as she squints to focus on my face noh two feet away.

'Promise me one thing, Marv . . . if you ever haves kids, promise me you woan turn yuh back on um, okay?'

'I wouldn – ever.'

'Honest?' she breathes.

'Yeah.'

'Even if yuh daughter's a lying little bitch? You'd still know when she was telling the truth, in ih? Abou summin serious.'

'Er, yeah, I s'pose. Course I would.'

She leans back against the wall, wobbling on the upturned plastic milk crate. 'Leh me ask you a question, Marv.'

'Uh?'

'D'you think I'm a slag?'

'No!' I says. 'No, I dun't!'

'My mother thinks I am.' Her face is pure stretched heavy through booze, eyes spinning round like the reels on a fruit machine. 'In tha bad? In tha a terrible thing for a mother to think? Buh d'you know whas worse? She's right!' Becca necks the last uh the vodka an flings the bottle through a gap in the floorboards with a drunken violence tha causes me to tense up. 'Ih's all everything comes down to wi me. Always have done. My mother, my step-dad, Charmaine an Jamo, Mucksy . . . you. Fuck knows why, mind. Ih's noh like I'm much to look at, is ih? Probly gives off the easy vibe. Any old fucker can see they

191

goh a chance wi me.' She throws her head back with a gritty cackle. 'D'you know, I've never had a real friend in my life?'

'Buh you knows loads uh people.'

'Thas noh wha I said, is ih? I told you before, ih's a game. Use an be used.' She lights up a fag an takes a long drag, orange reflections skating on the glassy sheen of her bright brown eyes.

'Ih's . . . ih's noh true,' I says. 'Abou everything coming down to . . . *tha*, like. Noh fuh me, anyway.'

'Geh real, Marv. We been through this. You've leh me treat you like shit an we both know why.'

'Well maybe at first, buh noh no more. I've never met no one like you. I dun care if we never does ih again. Yuh still my girlfriend.'

Her eyes snap back into focus. 'Girlfr– wha the fuck you on abou ?'

'Buh I thought–'

'Come yur.' She plants a big smacker on my cheek an cwtches me again like Mam used to. We sortuh rock back an fore for a bih, looking down at the rainy street an wondering whas waiting for us when we dare to break cover.

'I wun leave you,' I says wi my mouth buried in her chest. 'I swear, I wun leh nothing bad happen to you no more. You can trust me.'

'Trusting people ain' my strong point.' She laughs a bih through her tears an pops me on the nose.

'Yeah, buh if we can at least rely on each other thas summin, in ih? Summin no one can take away from us. I'm noh asking you to trust other people. Just trust me.' I'm deadly serious an all. I've never ever felt this way – a surging, fierce pride tha flying bullets couldn tame.

'D'you know wha the mad thing is? I think I do,' she goes an we pull each other even closer, no longer cuddling buh clinging to each other with everything we goh left.

'I wish I could leave all this behind. Wouldn ih be wicked to uv been born somewhere else, been someone completely different?'

'Gohruh deal wi the hand yuh dealt. Simple as. Things woan always be this way, I promise mate. You'll be okay in the end. The world's a wide place an there's still a chance to start fresh somewhere else, in there?' She points over the road to a sign above one uh the takeaways – a corny painting uh the Statue of Liberty next to the words Hollywood Pizza. 'Thas the place for us. In America we could be anyone we wanted, in ih?'

'How the fuck would people like us geh over there?' I says, instantly regretting shooting her idea down.

'You always gohruh have a goal. Even if ih ain' easy, you gohruh keep trying. Otherwise you just give up on life.'

'Would you take me with you if you found a way?'

'Course I would. You'd be the first person I phoned.'

Suddenly I remember Mam's lucky penny. 'Have a look at this.' I hold ih up to the streetlight to show her. 'Ih's American – s'posed to be fuh good luck. My mam give ih to me. You are – take ih.'

'Marvin, doan be silly, I can't. Ih's important to you.'

'C'mon, I wan you to have ih. Maybe ih'll help you geh to America. Keep hold of ih till you make ih there.' I pass ih over in the darkness buh our jittery fingers fumble an somewhere along the way the coin goes bouncing across the floorboards an ends up fuck knows where. Becca groans like she's sorry an I wanuh tell her ih ain' her fault buh there's a lump in my throat an a sinking in my guts cos no marrer which way you spin ih our luck has well an truly run out.

31

Cruel morning light snatches away fading dreams uh freedom cos we're still here an we're still doomed, living off borrowed time an nervous energy. I protect Becca the only way I can now, by lehrin her sleep a while longer, oblivious to the crushing reality outside. Buh there's no escape from this nightmare, no amount uh running or chopsing or quick thinking tha can save us from having to face the music eventually. This is the end. Checkmate.

A last gasp memory uh Mam's lucky penny offers the only straw left to clutch so with a sore head an shaky hands I begin to scour the litter-strewn floor. The cracks an gaps leading down into charred black nothingness seem to multiply as I go, the hopelessness uh the situation soon following suit. When I stumble on a spray can with a few dregs I cut my loses an retreat to the safety of our corner, finding a strange comfort in the bold blue letters as they're spattered against the wall. BECCA. Then underneath: MARVIN. I leave a gap, debating whether to add 4 in between our names. Fuck ih. Wha else is there to lose? I've almost finished the 9T5 when she splutters to life, revived by the sickly sweet paint fumes. Any hopes uh continuing last night's cwtches are immediately dashed as normal service is resumed: 'Wha d'you think yuh doing, Marv? Uh? We're s'posed to be laying low, yuh fucking little retard!' She grabs the can an tries to cover up the letters, sinking to the floor with her head in her hands when she realises the paint's run dry. Me, I've goh my head in my hands for another reason cos I've gone an ruined ih again, pushed her away after gehrin so close. I wan the ground to swallow me up as paint letters trickle blue tears down the brickwork an I realise fuh shewer we're truly, truly fucked.

Winter 2018

The man brushes the curtain aside, sucking up deep lungfuls of frosty evening air while the sharp draught dissipates the heavy murk of sex and alcohol in the bedroom. A whimper over his shoulder is soundly ignored, too wrapped up in his own festering sense of guilt and self-loathing to even acknowledge the girl in his bed. He let it happen again, after all his intentions to break it off, to let her down gently, when it came to the crunch his dick had the last word. Talk about pushing his luck. She's becoming ever more insistent, pressuring him to follow through with rash promises made in the throes of passion, the loose words he draped over her like jewels in an effort to get what he wanted. And now, balls empty and senses restored, he assumes that cold, distant persona which inevitably comes to the fore when his relationships pass a certain point.

His phone bursts into life on the bedside cabinet and he dashes through a hail of huffs to retrieve it, devouring the text message from his vantage point at the window like a buzzard on a ledge. Secretly he's hoping it'll be that punky girl from the rave weekend but as usual it's Karen's name that flashes up on the screen. Good job, really. That weekend caused nothing but grief. He'd latched on to this punk or goth or whatever the hell she was and after a bit of bullshit a threesome was looking odds on. Till they get back to the hotel and what's-her-name starts getting cold feet, saying she feels pressured and she doesn't want to share him and she thought they had something special and blah blah blah blah blah.

At first he'd been angry. This was supposed to be no strings fun, wasn't it? That's what they'd agreed from the very start. But he held his tongue, sensing a chance to salvage the situation with a bit of drug-fuelled smooth talk and before he knew where he was he'd poured out all this shit about her really meaning something to him, how he'd never felt this way about anyone and maybe this experience would strengthen their relationship. Thankfully managed to stop short of the L word, although by then the damage was done. The punk got bored and fucked off and it took another barrage of drivel to blow his load at all that night, and ever since it was as though they'd passed a point of no return despite all his efforts to keep things strictly casual.

He considers pretending it's the punk girl on the phone, hoping to stir up the whole threesome debacle again but with some sort of inexplicable sixth sense, she already knows it's Karen. When he asks what makes her so certain she says she must be psychic. His snort provides the final straw and all the girl's pent up resentment comes gushing out in an ice cold torrent. She tells him she knows it's Karen because it's always Karen, ten times a day Karen, phone calls, texts – Karen, Karen, Karen! Weren't they supposed to be separated?

The man fires back that one day when she's old enough she'll understand that ending a marriage with kids isn't like dumping your little two-day crush after maths class. These things take tact and maturity, stuff she could do with learning a bit about. Shaking his head, he goes back to his text, freezing at the message that greet him. The phone goes down and he drains the dregs of the whisky bottle, buying time to make sense of the words on the screen. In the split second his guard's down she jumps at the phone, wrestling it out of his hand with drunken determination and reading the words aloud as though she's uncovered some great conspiracy. Karen's leaving – going to Ireland for Christmas with her family. Taking the kids. Looking into the possibility of a permanent move. The man's invited to meet up before they go.

Now the questions come. Does he still have feelings for Karen? Has something been going on, has he been stringing the girl along all this time? His bemusement turns to outrage as the girl proceeds to call him all the spineless cunts under the sun, saying all his sweet talk was bullshit, nothing but a big ploy to take advantage of her but she's forgetting one simple fact: it was no fucking strings! He'd laid it out as plainly as possible at the very beginning but still people read what they want to read into situations. He's had it all his life, in every relationship he's ever had – family, friends, women. Try to be straight down the line and people will still find a way to make it your fault. It gets so that you're too scared to make a move, too scared to build a relationship because they all seem destined to end in disaster.

So now here he is again, back to being the worst person in the world, upsetting people he never meant to hurt, unable to do right for doing wrong. Frustration gnaws at the straining guy ropes barely holding him together, fraying ever more with each insult the girl hurls. Selfish. Heartless. User. Finally he snaps. Yeah, he tells her, he is a fucking user, and she better get with it because the whole human race is the same way. Emotions and feelings and all this other shit – it's all just there to be manipulated. The smart people get what they want and the rest get left behind.

Her face crumples but he's not falling for that old trick. See, he tells her, she's doing it right now. Turning on the waterworks to get her way – she's just as much of a user as him when it comes down to it. And what about the car and the money and the freedom? It was all stuff she'd wanted and he'd had. Simple as that. Why else would she be messing round with an ugly old fucker like him?

She wails in exasperation, first pulling on her clothes and then gathering the various personal belongings that are scattered around the room. There's something wrong with him, she says, stomping down the communal stairway. He's damaged, not normal. He needs help. Out in the street she turns back one last time, bundles of possessions in her arms and black mascara spiders crawling down her cheeks. She tells him she hopes for Karen's sake that he's not going to their meeting, because his family is better off without him. Everyone is. He's pure poison. From now on he'd better stick to fucking himself because he's the only one he loves. Then she's gone, leaving the man to choke on the caustic aftertaste of her words. It isn't true, what she said. He doesn't love himself. He loves Karen, loves the kids. The girl's right about some things though. He is poison. And they are better off without him.

197

32

The vibes in this place are perfumed poison an if I could only catch Becca's attention I'd be heading fuh the door quick smart buh unfortunately fuh me she's too wasted to notice anything other than the smug-looking creep who's surgically attached himself to her left yurhole. Who are these people? Noh even shewer how we goh yuh – the whole thing's been a blur since . . . no, noh now. Take another swig uh my bottle, try to look like I'm enjoying myself. Tell ew one thing though, this flat is summin else. Massive fish tank, leather settees, cinema-screen telly – this Dane bloke must be loaded, which begs the question: wha are we doing yur? People like him dun wanuh know people like us, do they? Becca met him outside some bar I think, buh ih's all pure hazy, a mess, one big fuck off mess which is best left well alone.

I'm wedged between two uh the scariest, politest undercover jailors in the business, pair of um suited an booted an chewing gum with over-the-top enthusiasm. The one on my left looks like he might actually wrestle bears in his spare time, a big bald meathead wi tattoo ink crawling out from cuffs an collar like giant squid tentacles while to my right some slicked-back Mexican-type dude sits sporting a smile so thin ih could slit yuh throat. They've both been nice as pie so far buh make no mistake, if I try to run they'll drag me back kicking an screaming fuh shewer. The thick green Rizla-wrapped panic attack they're smoking's doing nothing to ease my mind either, weed so strong ih makes our soapbar look like Old Holborn by comparison. If I was jittery before, a couple uh tokes on tha thing goh me fit fuh the asylum an when the intercom buzzes I'm all buh ready to give myself up to the men in white coats.

'Jezz an Maandy.' The meathead rolls his eyes, clearly noh sharing my anxieties when in step two top class page-three stunners done right up to the nines. As soon as they see me the whispers start, pure shades uh Stacey Evans an the bitches back in Pengarw buh try as I might, there's just no chance uh catching Becca's attention while she's lost in this Dane cunt's eyes. The two girls start to giggle.

'What d'you keep licking your lips for, kid?'

Never even realised I was buh they goh me paranoid abou ih now.

'Fancy yourself do you, loverboy?' the other girl goes with a quick flick uh the tongue tha misses the sexy look she's aiming for like a cock-eyed marksman an instead ends up somewhere between gormless an retarded. 'Play your cards right and Mandy here might sort you out!'

Mandy shoves her. 'Eurgh, shurrup Jezz, for fuck's sake. You're the one who'll blow anything that moves.'

Jezz ignores her friend an sparks up a fag, rolling ih seductively between blood-red lips as she plans her next attack move. 'So where you from, kid? What you doing round here?'

'Been staying wi some mates, thas all,' I says, sticking to Becca's well-drilled script.

'Oh yeah? Where d'they live, cardboard city?'

'Stop being mean to him,' Mandy says through barely stifled laughs. Another look across the galaxy to Becca achieves nothing buh more unwanted questions. 'That your girlfriend, then, is it?'

Now I feel my face flushing buh ih's pointless trynuh explain summin complicated to morons like this. 'I dunno, noh really,' is the best I can come up with.

'Not at all, by the look of things,' Jezz snipes as Becca's best Mam-laugh rings out over the apparently hilarious Dane who's now holding my drunken soul mate steady with hands tha creep like the tide. A wave uh sickness pushes me back in my seat.

'Don't be such a pair o' facking bitches, you two,' the big bald meathead goes.

'Alright, Tone. Keep your knickers on!' Jezz huffs at him.

'You wanna take your own advice once in a while,' he goes, winking at his slick hombre.

'Cheeky twat!'

'Yeah, well how abaht you two make yourselves useful an get some more drinks? Facking dying o' thirst 'ere. Get one for the boy an all – he could do with a livener. Fack's sake, s'posed to be Friday night, init?'

When the girls go into the kitchen Meathead turns to me. 'Don't worry abaht those two, pal. They're still bitter cos their sister got to go to the ball without 'em, hawhawhaw!'

'I heard that!' Mandy goes, returning with armfuls uh chinking beer bottles.

'Oi, Tone, you gonna rack 'em up then or what?' Might be the first time I've yurd the Cockney Mexicano speak, buh there again ih might noh. Who knows? Who cares? Either way, Meathead takes the hint an spoons out a pack uh white powder with a credit card, chop-choping on the glass coffee table like a psycho chef behind schedule. Straight away Jezz's eyes light up.

'You gonna sort me out, Tony? I'm gagging for it, you know,' she goes, pressing herself up to him.

Meathead Tony raises a bored eyebrow. 'Yeah, when ain't ya?'

'Don't be like that.' She winces feigned offence. 'Everyone likes a little boost now and again, don't they?' She slides a sensual hand over his tentacled neck buh he's noh taking the bait.

'Get off, for chrissake. You can wait yer turn gel.' In a quick one-two combination white lines disappear up each nostril through a rolled up twenty note. As soon as he's finished the rest of um swoop like a pack uh vultures, practically fighting each other to geh to the goods.

'What d'you reckon, shall we give the little fella a line or what?' Mr Slick says once he's filled his boots. Meathead Tony laughs an hands me the note.

'Nah, I'm okay,' I says before Tony's big tattooed hand clamps over mine and directs me towards the table. Ih's noh rough an he's smiling while he does ih buh the message is clear. 'Go on, don't be a wimp. Get that up yer snozz and you'll feel brand new.'

Fuck ih, I'm too far gone to care anymore. Straight away a nasty drip uh chalky snot goads me into puking buh a moment later all the badness is swept away by an impossible wave uh confidence tha picks me out uh my dark pit an restores me to my rightful place in the human race.

'What you saying, kid?' Tony goes, his cratered planet of a head dominating my field of vision. 'Quality shit, init? Cor, fack me, that's not bad at all as it happens.'

'Of course it's quality, when have I ever given you less?' Ih's the first time in ages Dane's paid attention to anyone other than Becca.

'Nah, course not boss, but this is a cut above the usual, init?'

'What do you think, Marvin?' Dane goes, fixing me wi tha smug grin an ice-cold eyes. This guy's pure bad news. You can just tell.

'Yeah, ih's good – wicked, like.'

Mandy budges me up on the settee to do another line, tits practically in my lap as she leans across to the table top.

'Bloody hell, get a load of this fella. Finest weed, finest coke, girls all over him! You'll go far, Marvin. I can see that now.'

I try to act natural buh even through the sniff he's making me uncomfortable an I think ih's showing.

'Becca tells me you're looking to get out of Cardiff for a while, is that right?'

'Well, I s'pose. Been thinking abou ih, like.'

He waves his hand. 'It's okay, buddy. I know how it gets. We all need a change of scenery sometimes, yeah?'

I nod without saying a word, focused solely on avoiding his diamond-splitting stare. Whas this fucker's problem?

'I own a couple of bars around London. I've talked it over with Becca and she says you might want a job. Nothing major – collecting glasses, tidying up, running a few errands, you know. Plenty of opportunities if you're willing to take them. Don't answer now – think it over, yeah? We'll be leaving in the morning if you're interested.' He turns to Jezz an his tone's completely different. 'Hey, put some fucking music on, will you? Place is like a morgue. And get some more drinks, too. We're supposed to be having fun.'

The music goes on an more drink an drugs goes round an I throw back everything thas pushed in my direction cos there dun seem to be any other way out uh this shit. I wanuh talk to Becca, make her understand how important ih is to ditch these creeps buh tha Dane's making damn shewer I dun geh her on her own. When she finally do come over she's so fucked she can barely stand, wrapping her arms round my neck an breathing hot vodka breath everywhere. Been boozing even worse than me since ih happened – her head's gone proper.

'MARVINNN!' she goes, pure mushing her face right up to mine an I love her being so close buh I hate the way she's acting, like. 'Whas going on, Marv? You having a good time? I told you! I told you I'd sort summin out. Never leh you down yeh, uv I?' She leans back an almost falls off the chair. Gehrin through to her ain' gunuh be easy buh fuck ih – I gohruh try.

'Becca,' I says. 'Bec, I'm noh shewer abou this. Maybe we should–'

'Whooo! I loves this one!' she screams, jumping up to the beat uh tha Baby D tune, back out uh range as she sways round the room singing into her bottle uh beer. The others are swapping looks buh Becca either dun notice or dun care cos for all the states we been in, I've never seen her this out uh control. Ih's scary buh wha choice do I have other than to stick with her an hope for a miracle tha never comes?

*   *   *

I dare noh move a muscle fuh fear uh my burning bladder spraying like a cherub fountain all over this cold, tangled bed. Whose bed? Fuck knows. I cahn make out much buh I dun think there's anyone else in the room. Whose room? More importantly, where's the fucking bathroom? My mouth's full uh shag pile an battery acid burns the back uh my throat as I trace my way round the walls to freedom, pissing for an hour straight wi my eyes half shut when I finally find the toilet. Best noh flush cos shewerly everyone's sleeping buh on my way back to bed faint voices geh the better uh my curiosity.

'. . . facking silly little slag . . .' I yurs the meathead say while the slick fucker rocks wi laughter. '. . . only young kids an all, lambs to the slaughter . . .'

I peer in to the living room wi bated breath to find the two of um sitting wi their backs to me, watching this porno on the big screen. Whas going on? Where's Becca?

'Bit rough araand the edges, like, buh fackable all the same,' Slick says.

'. . . shame really . . . what a way to end up. Bit o' sweet talk and a coupla lines o' Peruvian and the next thing they know they're stuck in some bedsit sucking off Chinese businessmen day and night! Makes yer heart bleed, dun it?'

Slick's decking himself at this side-splitting observation buh me, I'm failing to see the funny side. Who they talking abou, exactly – the girls in the video or . . . ? Fuck, I knew this wadn right. I gohruh tell Becca.

I tiptoe back along the passage, opening doors as quietly as my shaking hands'll allow. The first room's empty buh as I poke my head into the next I yur this weird sound, sortuh like someone crying. Ih's dark except fuh the telly's flickering white light which provides the backdrop to a monstrous writhing shadow on the far wall, a nightmarish thing causing the squeals to increase in noise an urgency. Ih takes a second before I realise whas going on. The way tha creep looked at her before, I shoulduh known.

'Geh off her, yuh dirty bastard! Yuh sick fuck, leave her alone!' I scream, throwing myself on the wriggling bed heap, no more fear, no more nothing, just desperate to protect Becca like I swore I would.

The sheets fly back an the pair of um jump up, Becca so bare an stark an vulnerable ih makes me sick to my bones. She's noh scared though, she's angry an as she covers herself up wi the quilt she's going: 'Marvin, wha the fuck d'you think yuh doing? Who the fuck d'you think you are?' an ih's a question I probly gohruh ask myself an all, cos I certainly ain' wha I thought I was, the way she's giving herself up to some horrible sleazy creep right in front uh me.

'Sort your jealous little boyfriend out, will you? I haven't got time for this playground bullshit,' Dane growls at Becca through gritted teeth while scruffing me towards the door like I'm a pup in need uh house training. Now the meathead an Slick uv come to see whas going on buh I ignore the cunts an call out to Becca: 'Please Bec, we gohruh geh out uh yuh. He's dodgy. They're all fucking dodgy. I yurd um talking – they're gunuh take you up London an make you do things!'

'What things?' Dane says like butter wouldn melt buh I knows ih's true. 'What are you talking about, you sad little boy? You need to do some growing up, I think. Come on, it's time you weren't here.'

'Becca, come wi me, please!' I goes, my voice cracking up wi frustration.

'Go if you want,' Dane says to her, stepping out the way.

'No! Why you acting like this, Marv? I said I'd help you out an I did, buh if you cahn handle me being wi someone else then we'll have to go our separate ways. I goh a chance to geh out uh this hole an I'm noh having you dragging me back down. I'm going to London, with or without you.'

So thas ih? She turns on me as easy as tha after everything I've done. Bitch! Fucking slag, she is a slag, she was right tha time. I wanuh leh her know exactly wha I think of her buh the words geh caught in my throat as the meathead fold me up like a deckchair, like some useless piece uh junk. Then there's one last smack across the head an I'm out on the lonely street, ringing in my yurs an warm splashes on my cheeks.

Slut! Fucking tramp, I done my best for her, give her everything I had. Thought I meant summin buh ih turns out she couldn give two shits. She should be precious buh she's cheap, she makes herself cheap, lehrin all sorts uh dirty men use her body any way they wan. Well she's fuck all to me anymore. Nothing. I hate her. Honest to God, now – I hate her.

I stumble along the streets for who knows how long, pure cursing Becca an every other cunt thas ever done me wrong, finally crashing out in a phone box when all other options uv been abandoned. When I wake, daylight's creeping up over the blocks uh flats. I'm stiff an twisted an more knackered than when I conked out buh I'm calmer too, an as I stagger to my feet an find myself eye level wi the payphone I realise exactly wha I need to do.

The receiver's inches from my mouth when I freeze. This is the right thing, in ih? Course ih is. If I leh her disappear to London wi those sick fuckers anything could happen.

Buh if I make the call she'll never forgive me – ih'll be me an her finished fuh shewer.

So whas ih to be? Leh her go an hope fuh the best or turn her in an never speak again, never see her, have her hating me forever?

Down goes the phone. Think, Marv, think! I bang my head against the wall a couple uh times, as though thas gunuh somehow sort out the jumbled mess inside. If I dun't do summin soon ih'll be too late. Right, fuck ih, ih's the only way. Ih's the right thing to do. I pick up the receiver an gulp for air. No, I cahn. The phone goes back down an I'm abou to leave the phone box when I imagine her there, kept prisoner, like, Chinese businessmen doing all sorts to her, Slick an the meathead pissing umselves while ih's happening an an aching sickness forces my hand to snatch up the receiver an press nine three times.

*   *   *

Maybe they're noh coming. Been crouched in this fucking alley for ages, body shaking an fag craving. I shoulduh disappeared straight after hanging up the phone buh where else have I goh to go? Wha else have I goh left? The only thing with any meaning in my life is Becca – if I can just save her from those creeps, save her from herself then maybe my time on this planet will have actually been worthwhile. Ih's all abou saving Becca.

Or gehrin back at her?

Nah, nah, I been through this, fuh fuck's sake. I done the right thing.

Shit, there she goes now, stepping out wi tha sleazy Dane prick all over her like chicken pox. The way she moves is disturbing – slow an unsteady like the scummy fuckers uv give her summin to keep her quiet. Looks strange too, hair an make-up done up so different she might as well be another person. Ih's as if I dun know her no more. Just hope ih's noh too late. Meathead Tony's busy filling the boot wi cases when the police finally decide to show up. I was expecting some *Miami Vice* guns blazing stuff buh I almost dun notice the crawling panda car until ih's right on top of us. In a split-second my heart sinks, the reality of wha I've done truly hitting home. After everything we said, I've sold out my only friend.

Wi no blues an twos Becca's slow to clock the situation buh I can see ih all unfolding right in front uh me an I know I gohruh act now. There was a time when AK-47s an a couple uh grenades woulduh done the trick buh I left tha Marvin way back in Pengarw so there's nothing for ih buh to man up, stand tall an be counted. 'I'm sorry, Bec, I'm sorry!' I goes, breaking cover wi my arms held high. She just gawps, too stunned to move. I call to her again buh the coppers must see whas going on cos the siren blasts an they pull up hard in front uh Dane's car. I goh a moment to take in the mixture of hurt an confusion on her face cos she cahn quite believe wha I've done, an neither can I to be honest.

'No, no way,' she mumbles to herself buh ih's true alright, an I should know.

'Run!' I shout, grabbing her arm.

She drops her bags an goes for ih, jumping the car bonnet an bombing through the gardens so tha even I goh a job to keep up with her. We hit the back lanes, no fucking clue where we are, dodging an weaving like hares buh the greyhound coppers stick with us all the way. We come to a stop in this courtyard thing, a dead end wi steep grass banks an fences all around an now I reckon we're truly finished. Spurred on by distant police calls, Becca goes fuh the embankment buh slips back down, covered in mud an grass an shit. I pull her to her feet an the both of us fight our way to the top uh the hill only to be confronted by this fuck-off fence an the pigs closing in fast behind.

'I cahn geh over,' she says to me in a raggedy voice tha ain' hers.

Fuck, if only I can geh her out uh his, I'll make ih up to her, I swear.

One uh the coppers gehs halfway up the bank before falling, gifting us a few precious seconds to act. I dun waste a single one, grabbing Becca an hoisting her up against the fence. She disappears over the top an I follow close after using energy bought on the never-never. Shouldn uh bothered – all thas waiting for us on the other side is four lanes uh speeding traffic. This nightmare just gehs worse every minute. Becca's doubled over, coughing an holding her side.

'We gohruh keep going,' I says, buh ih's hopeless. She's broken an there's only one person to blame. Me. I've done this.

'Where, Marv?' she croaks. 'There's nowhere left to run.'

The policeman's hands clamp on to the top uh the fence like summin out of a horror film. Becca's right. There's no escape. I wanuh say summin to her, to make ih better buh words ain' gunuh cut ih no more. She's noh listening anyway, lost in a world of her own, face torn an twisted wi sheer desperation. Then she does ih.

'Becca, no!'

The screech uh tyres an the thud, ih's like someone's puh their hand inside my chest an squeezed my heart till ih stops beating. I dun wanuh open my eyes. The car horn blaring, the woman screaming, ih's all ringing in my yurs buh there's summin louder than any uh this, a roaring, rushing sound tha fills my brain an blocks everything else out. I take a step towards her, twisted up on the road like one uh Flash's chew toys. I've never felt so helpless, so alone despite the frenzied activity whirring all around me. She cahn be . . . please, this cahn be happening.

I'm trynuh force a sound buh I've forgotten how my lungs work. Summin clatters into me from behind an I hit the floor, air inside rushing out onto the warm tarmac. The walkie-talkie crackles in my yur an the cuffs click tight on my wrists buh I'm so numb ih barely registers. I roll over onto my back, looking up at the swirl uh grey faces an grey clouds, finally understanding wha ih is to have yuh world turned upside down.

Epilogue
Winter 2018

The man spits with fury as the nagging ringtone starts up again, mobile phone dancing impudently across the dashboard in front of him. He snatches it up and tosses it on to the back seat where it's lost amongst the pile of Christmas presents. There's no need to check. He knows it's her. He knows why she's calling. Told him to come over around eleven but it's half-past now and with every second that passes he's getting further and further away. Oh, he was there on time, alright. Parked just across the street, trying to build himself up for the big moment before eventually coming to his senses and turning the car right around. One last disappointment shouldn't surprise anyone really, and besides, this is for the best in the long run.

He plants his foot and the engine roars, providing a jolt of brutal relief as the power he's lacked for so much of his life surges through his body. The phone rings again and in the split-second his eyes are off the road some chancer looms up out of the cold morning mist, forcing him to swerve on to the hard shoulder. Prick. Another smart cunt thinking he can take liberties. He tails the other car, pounding the horn and showering the windscreen with spittle. By the time he pulls alongside, the other driver's shit it. Only a drippy-looking guy, a kid really, cowering in his seat staring straight ahead like his life depends on it. Clearly wants none of it, the fucking sap. Maybe think twice before crossing the man again.

The adrenaline fades as quickly as it came, replaced by that all too familiar draught of shame. The look on the boy's face, he'd seen it a million times on the faces of Karen and the kids. Anger flares again, at himself this time for the unwelcome reminder of how much he's hurt his family. Worse still is the fact that deep down he knows making it work simply isn't an option. It's not that he doesn't want to, it's that he's physically incapable of maintaining a real relationship with anyone. Over the years he'd proved that if nothing else. That's why he drove the wedge between them – better sooner than later. At least alone there was no chance of further heartbreak.

The dual carriageway dissolves into bare city streets, all frozen concrete and leafless, spiny branches. He shudders despite the heater's powerful blast. Through haste and distraction he'd left the flat in only a shirt and now he realises how fucking cold this winter morning actually is. Left turns, right turns, weaving aimlessly through his mind and the town in search of refuge. The warm glow of a petrol station offers a strange sort of comfort, a beacon out in this pea-soup sea and he glides his new-plate estate to a stop on the forecourt. A warm coffee could shake off this chill, even if it is brown service station sludge. He sits for a moment, staring at his reflection in the rear-view mirror, greying hair and world-weary eyes putting him way past his thirty-eight years. Still looks half-starved though – some things remain consistent. Never could put on weight.

In the queue for the till he picks up a local paper with vague notions of finding a hotel or B&B even though he must only be a mile or two from the city centre and his flat's no more than twenty miles up the motorway. He just needs to feel like a stranger – be someone else, somewhere else. Struggling back into the car he spills the coffee over the paper and the passenger seat, and for a moment the ever-present ball of rage threatens to ignite within him. This time he falters though, stunned into silence at finding himself face to face with someone he hasn't seen for years. It's her. He knows it instantly, although the grainy, coffee-stained mugshot should have made it difficult to tell. But that face, those eyes . . . he'd never forgotten. He wipes the paper down and focuses on the headline, his cantering heart breaking into a full gallop at the words that greet him.

SOUTH WALES WOMAN SOUGHT OVER
INTERNATIONAL FRAUD SCANDAL

Rebecca Lewis, 41, also known as Rebecca Johnson and Rachel Johnson is being sought by US authorities over several large-scale instances of mortgage fraud. Police attempted to apprehend her in the state of Massachusetts on the east coast of America last week but the suspect fled the scene and is now believed to have returned to the UK. Two other suspects are already in custody, including bank employee . . .

He drops the paper and raises a trembling hand to his forehead. Could it really be true? He grabs the paper again, reading and re-reading until the facts have gone in. Memories explode with shocking vividness, mines left dormant for so many years mere inches below the surface of his consciousness. Becca. She'd made it out of here just like she said, but her demons had only followed after her. Becca.

Suddenly a volley of horns rings out from the row of traffic backed up on the forecourt. Disgruntled drivers glare with ill intentions from behind their steering wheels but this time there's no flash of anger, no outrage at being disrespected. He simply waves a hand in apology and pulls off.

Becca.

How long has it been? They weren't allowed to speak to each other during the trial and when he got out of the YO unit everything from the past seemed to fade. Never went back to Pengarw, never really thought about anything from before – tried to become someone else and he'd almost succeeded, but the scars of his youth ran deeper than he ever liked to imagine. And now, as he closes his eyes he finds himself back there, clinging to Becca in the darkness of the squat, waiting for the world to come crashing down around them. And down it came. Probably wasn't all that far from here, come to think of it. Maybe he could . . . no, it was silly. Chasing ghosts that should be left to lie. And yet somehow . . .

Fuck it.

He pulls a u-turn and begins to scour the streets for familiar landmarks. But the city he knew is gone. Faceless yuppie flats have shot up everywhere like huge dandelions on the skyline. Not so long ago people with money wouldn't dream of going anywhere near a flat in a tower block but rename them apartments, put a skivvy behind the front desk and a lift that doesn't stink of piss and all of a sudden these mugs were paying through the nose to stay in their plasterboard boxes in the sky. Wankers. The buildings seem alien and the people seem alien, acknowledgments that only serve to accentuate his loneliness and spur him onwards, searching for a glimpse of a forgotten past.

Finally something catches his eye. One of the hoardings on a row of run-down shops hangs loose above the doorway and creeping out from underneath is a strangely familiar symbol. That naff Statue of Liberty on the takeaway . . . it can't be. Can it? It fucking is! He spies across the road. The squat must surely be long gone. It's been twenty-three years for Christ's sake. His worst fears appear confirmed when he finds only the rubble and machinery of a commercial-scale building site. Gone? Wait, some buildings are still standing – covered with scaffolding and netting but nevertheless there. The site's silent and empty on this listless Sunday morning so he parks the car and skips over to the fence, scanning from side to side and feeling like the lawless little tearaway he once was. He pulls at the metal sheeting, finds an opening and slides back into another time.

Long streams of condensation pass from his lips as he crunches his way across the gravel but he no longer feels cold. He feels alive. Gripped by intrigue he travels up through the ruins of the derelict building, aware of the dangers that lurk but refusing to let them constrain him. The place is a wreck, looking like it's housed every waster and dosser in Cardiff but it's a miracle it's still standing at all. When he reaches the top he carefully picks his way across the rotten floorboards, dodging litter and debris as he goes. The walls are covered in layer upon layer of graffiti, it's silly to even think it could be – it's there! Hidden amongst a fresco of scribbles, the faint remains of those scrappy blue bubble letters push through.

BECCA
4
MARVIN 9T5

Funny how something so insignificant can catapult you decades into the past to a time when things were so different. When he was so different. At least that's how he'd imagined it. But now as his mind races with the hows and whys he realises things haven't changed quite that much at all. He still wrestles with the same dilemmas, the same confusion he'd fought with back then, pushing people away, consistently making wrong moves and inflicting pain on the people he loves so that eventually they wanted nothing to do with him. Mam, Becca – it was only a matter of time before Karen followed suit. And who could blame them? Those few days in Cardiff might have been when it all really started. The consequences of his actions hadn't just wrecked the two most important relationships in his life, they'd also damaged him on some fundamental level, throwing him into a vicious cycle of negativity, destined to repeat the same mistakes forever.

A burst of cold sunshine rips through the slateless roof, dissipating spectral mists and banishing any harboured hopes of redemption this doomed spirit might hold. As he turns to leave something catches his eye, a glinting, glistening dot balanced precariously over the broken floorboard precipice. He crouches, heart skipping a beat, knowing instinctively what he's stumbled across. His mother's lucky American penny, the one he'd lost that desperate night so long ago. But it rolled into the blackness below, he's sure it did. There's no way it could have . . . wait – look at the date! 2018. Brand new! This isn't his coin . . . it's . . .

He wraps his fingers around the penny and closes his eyes, drawing in all the turmoil, all the hurt, all the guilt and anger and frustration he's bottled up for so many years. The sensation of another hand on his causes the man's eyes to flick open in disbelief, withdrawing from the tender touch like cotton thread in a flame. Before him stands a middle-aged eighteen-year-old, platinum blonde bob and designer jacket unable to conceal the crop-topped wild child within.

Allegations of hallucination would hold up but for a world-weary quality to the apparition which could truly only belong to a troubled human being fixed firmly in the here and now. It's really Becca. She's come back. Smiles and tears break simultaneously like sun showers across both their faces, ancient emotions as fresh and raw as the day they were conceived released like uncaged birds, leaving in their wake a new sense of clarity. The man knows it's no coincidence – this is destiny. Tightly he clasps the gaunt figure – Becca, Mam; through blurry eyes it could be either – tells her knows the trouble she's in, tells her he's here to help, will never let her down again. They'll stick together against a world that hates them, understand each other like one else ever could.

Becca shushes him, says they're not even the same people anymore but he insists they are, and these current circumstances prove it. They're both still lost, both searching for something. But hasn't he changed at all? Hasn't he got other people in his life? Friends? A family . . . ?

Family. The word triggers a mental deluge that pours from his mouth in an unstoppable torrent. Karen – maybe the only person he's ever been loved by despite his inability to return any affection, his dogged determination to remain unlovable. They'd been thrown together not long after his release, met at one of many halfway houses and bonded over troubled pasts and uncertain futures. Karen had emotional issues to rival his or Becca's any day of the week, products of another fucked up childhood but she'd always managed to deal with things so pragmatically. A loose friendship had developed and years later, following her divorce and his deepening isolation, they'd become a couple. When the kids were born she'd blossomed into motherhood while he tagged along in the background, a third wheel in his own family, festering resentment growing with each day that passed. They're better off without him anyway – what possible use could life's survivors have for a gigantic lead weight? He wants to be where he's needed, where he can make a difference – with Becca. He'll help her, hide her, fix her – whatever it takes to make things right for both of them.

She laughs softly, tells him he's still a divvy, still hasn't figured out the basics after all this time. There's only one person in the world that can save him, and it certainly isn't her – not his mother or wife either, for that matter. To be free you don't need anyone else's validation – God knows she'd learnt that the hard way. He just needs to set aside his fears like she set aside her anger and the rest will come in time.

They begin their journey back through the site in silence, the man chewing hard on her food for thought. Suddenly he stops. Hang on, if she doesn't need him, why did she come back? The answer's very simple – to say goodbye. Not just to him but to her, to Becca, to the person she was. From her expensive leather handbag she produces a new passport and driver's licence, together with a hefty wad of cash. Pretty soon Becca Lewis will no longer exist. But before she goes she wants to say thank you to the only person who ever loved her for her. And although she'd reacted to it the way she reacted to everything – with anger – deep down that unconditional kindness had stayed with her always. You see, she says, we don't need to find redemption in each other, but sometimes a helping hand proves invaluable when finding it within ourselves.

A lingering embrace seals an understanding words could never begin to express but before they walk away forever there's one last thing the man needs to do. If they're saying goodbye to Becca, then perhaps this is the right time to finally lay Marvin to rest too. Taking the coin from his pocket, he kisses the shiny metal surface and launches it back into the rubble-strewn structure with a satisfying jangle. Now they move forward, both steady on their chosen paths. She has a plane to catch but Lee's destination is a little closer to home, if only it's not too late. He needs to phone Karen. He needs to see the kids. There's someone he'd like to introduce them to.